Carnival of Secrets

D.F. Hart

The Vital Secrets Series

Wall of Secrets (prequel)[1]
Book of Secrets[2]
List of Secrets[3]
Web of Secrets[4]
Path of Secrets[5]
Carnival of Secrets[6]
House of Secrets[7] – Dec 2021
End of Secrets – June 2022
_Visit _2ofharts.com_[8] to sign up for my newsletter and get a special bonus supplement to the series!_

---

1. _https://dl.bookfunnel.com/6kzwo0cuij_

2. _https://books2read.com/BookofSecrets_

3. _https://books2read.com/ListofSecrets_

4. _https://books2read.com/WebofSecrets_

5. _https://books2read.com/PathofSecrets_

6. _https://books2read.com/CarnivalofSecrets_

7. _https://books2read.com/DHHouseofSecrets_

8. _https://www.2ofharts.com_

Follow me on:
[*BookBub*](#)[9]
[*Facebook*](#)[10]
[*Goodreads*](#)[11]

---

9. *https://www.bookbub.com/authors/d-f-hart*

10. *https://www.facebook.com/D.F.HartTx*

11. *https://www.goodreads.com/author/show/*
    18999540.D_F_Hart

COPYRIGHT

Custom Cover Design and Artwork commissioned for D.F. Hart
by:
Rocking Book Covers

Published 2021 by 2 Of Harts Publishing
Arlington, Texas

Acknowledgements

To my readers, who make the journey worthwhile. I appreciate every one of you.

D.F. Hart

CHAPTER ONE

It was the last night of work in Amarillo, Texas, and he was physically tired but mentally revved.

After he'd secured his area for the night, he retreated to his motorhome, shuffling along and muttering to himself to maintain his carefully constructed public persona. The ruse was highly successful - most of his co-workers gave him a wide berth, which was the way he preferred it.

Once the narrow door was closed and locked behind him, he drew himself up to his full height and straightened his shoulders, rolling them to dissipate the tension they'd built up from maintaining a defeated posture all night. With the change in position came an altered expression - no longer a slightly vacant stare, but clear, sharp eyes that missed nothing.

Not much more of this, and then I won't have to hide, he reassured his reflection in the tiny mirror perched over the equally tiny bathroom sink.

When the idea had first presented itself, he'd been intrigued. After all, enduring so many years without being able to openly flaunt his superior intellect had been physically painful. The same affectations that kept him off the authorities' radar had also stifled his creativity.

He threw a quick sandwich together then retrieved the thick reference book he'd stolen from the public library four towns over. Making himself as comfortable as he could on the dinette table's u-shaped bench seat, he opened the book to the section holding the slip of paper as a marker and continued his reading from the previous evening.

***

"Pretty!" Charlie Thomas exclaimed again from his car seat's perch in the back.

"Yes, honey, they were very pretty," Bella agreed as she buckled her seat belt for the ride home.

She and Nathan had taken Charlie to a Sunday afternoon Texas Rangers game, then enjoyed a spectacular fireworks show once the ninth inning was done.

Bella glanced back at their son, who was already rubbing his eyes.

"Betcha he's asleep before we even leave the parking lot," she whispered to her husband.

"I do believe you're right," he said, and grinned at her. "Especially with this line of cars waiting in front of us. But that just means he's gonna be easy to put down for the night. And when we get there, I'll carry him inside and get him situated, if you'll grab the wine and two glasses and meet me at the garden tub."

She reached over and took Nathan's hand.

"With or without bubbles?"

"Are you crazy? With, of course," he quipped, and raised her hand to his lips to kiss it.

***

"So, how much notice do you need to give Nathan about time off?"

Lizzie pondered it as she chewed.

"Not sure, really," she said once she'd swallowed the bite of pasta. "Did you find some good cruises?"

"That I did," Donny answered. "I think the one we'd like the best sails from Seattle on October first. And I was shocked to discover that there are spaces left on that one, so we need to get it booked quickly before they're all gone."

She smiled at her fiancé as she pulled out her cell phone.

"Well then. Sounds like I need to let him know as soon as possible. Might as well do it now. What are the dates again?"

"We'd need to fly to Seattle on September thirtieth sometime, and the cruise returns to Seattle on October sixth, then we'd fly home, so, eight days total," Donny confirmed.

She rapidly typed Nathan a text, then hit 'send.'

***

The first time the kid knocked on his door, he growled loudly but made no move to answer it.

"Come on, Pops, don't be such a hermit," came the plaintive whine, and he growled again and launched himself upward when a fist banging rattled the door a second time.

He willed himself to adopt his usual dim-witted scowl before he confronted the interloper.

"What?" he snarled as he yanked the door open just wide enough to poke his head out.

"I'm headed to a bar in town that's got a jukebox, pool tables, and lonely women. Wanna go?"

"No," he answered, and shut the door before his unwanted visitor could speak up again, then waited silently until at last he heard the kid's truck driving away.

Finally, he grumbled to himself as he locked the door and returned to his reading.

He picked up his highlighter and underlined the passage that he'd found right before he'd been rudely interrupted.

"Soluble in water," he muttered, and grinned. "That's brilliant. Absolutely brilliant. Time to get some and test it all out."

He stretched his arm across the narrow table to pull his laptop closer. He booted it up, opened an incognito browser window, and began to search for the items he desired.

Ten minutes later, he'd found a way to immediately acquire one of the items he needed - and was pleasantly surprised. He'd expected larger quantities to be harder to come by. But his search for the most important element in his scheme had him frowning at the screen.

"Licensed use only," he read aloud, and rolled his eyes. "I bet I can find a way around that."

Especially if we go far enough south. I can slip over the border where it's not regulated and get some that hasn't been altered...

He shelved that line of thought for the moment to lean back and contemplate the delivery method.

Huh. I'm going to have to test it both ways and see what works the best.

His mind immediately pivoted and conjured up his young, irritating co-worker's face, and his lips curled into an almost feral smile.

And I know just who to test it out on first.

*** *** ***

Nathan's phone buzzed just as he lifted a sleeping Charlie from his car seat and began to walk toward the front door. Once Charlie was tucked safely into bed, Nathan gently closed his child's bedroom door before reaching for the cell phone clipped to his belt.

He read Lizzie's text and grinned.

Just joined the team and already planning a vacation? Wow, Zimmerman. Didn't figure you for a slacker, he typed and sent, then waited a beat or two before he continued.

Just kidding. It shouldn't be an issue scheduling it out this far ahead of time. How many days off are we talking? he typed back, then waited.

Eight, came the swift response. *September thirtieth through October seventh. And nice one, boss. That was funny. Not.*

LOL. Sorry. Couldn't resist. Should be fine - unless we're working a case, that is. I'll email the unit secretary and let her know to make a note about it on the calendar, he responded.

Thanks. See you in the morning! was the final exchange he saw from Lizzie before he plugged his phone into the charger by the bed.

He turned and walked across the space and into the bathroom, where Bella was already pouring capfuls of bubble bath into the steaming water.

"I think three of these should do it," she told him as she screwed the cap back on the bottle and put it back underneath the sink.

***

"That was really good," Pete Jenkins said, and Trish and Joe Wallace both smiled.

"I'm serious! Joe, that brisket was awesome. And that potato casserole? The best."

"I can only take credit for the brisket," Joe chimed in. "My beautiful wife here is responsible for the excellent side dishes."

"Oh, you two. But he's right, Joe, that brisket was outstanding. Now, you guys want some coffee?" Trish offered. "And there's dessert, too. Apple pie."

"Yes, ma'am, if you don't mind. Thanks."

"I'll be right back, then," Trish said and walked into the kitchen.

"I'll be right there, babe," Joe told her, then leveled his gaze at their dinner guest.

"What's on your mind, Pete?"

"That obvious, huh?"

Joe chuckled. "Yes."

The young policeman blew out a breath.

"I think I'm ready to sit for the detective's exam. I mean, I *feel* like I am? But I wanted to get your thoughts on it."

Joe leaned forward and studied his former co-worker intently for a moment.

"I think you're ready, Pete. And I stand by what I've said previously. I think you'll make one hell of a good detective, because you've got qualities in you that no one can teach you."

"Such as?"

"Empathy. That ability to truly relate to the victim's family members. That's not something you learn in any book anywhere. People either have it or they don't. You have it. I saw it myself when we were at crime scenes together. That plus your other skills? It's not even a question in my mind you'd be a great detective, son."

Pete smiled. "Thanks, Joe."

"No problem," Joe said, then stood to go help Trish bring in coffee and slices of pie to the table.

"When is the exam scheduled?" he called out over his shoulder.

"Next Wednesday. Any idea how long it takes to find out something after I take the exam?" Pete called back.

Joe and Trish reappeared with coffee and dessert.

"Let's see now. I want to say it took around three months from the time I applied until I got a final decision," Joe shared as he and Trish settled in at the table again. "Keep in mind that was 1989 and there was a lot less technology around than there is now. *Everything* was on paper back then. I would think it'd be faster these days."

"But that's still a good timeline to work with, Pete," Trish added as she handed him a slice of pie. "Use three months as your baseline, and if things move more quickly than that, great."

Pete nodded his agreement as he stirred sugar into his coffee.

"Now. No more shop talk," Trish announced with a twinkle. "So, Pete. You still seeing Shannon?"

"Yes, ma'am."

"How's that going?"

Pete flushed scarlet.

***

"I don't get it. If he's such a weirdo, tell me again why you even invit-ed him?" Blake asked Toby later as they racked the billiard balls for another game.

"Because he's good for a laugh," Toby replied with an evil grin. "You should hear him. He walks around talking to himself all the time. I never know what weird shit he's gonna say or do. It's funny."

"He sounds creepy as hell," Jason interjected.

"He is," Toby agreed. "But I'm gonna make *three times* what I'd make hauling hay with you two losers. I think I can handle working with a freak for the summer for that kind of coin. Besides, hot chicks with very little clothing on should be plentiful. Why be stuck in some hayfield when I can be getting laid?"

"Can't argue that. Cheers," Blake said, and they held up their bot-tles.

"Don't supposed you can get us on, huh?" Jason asked.

"Nope. They've got a full crew now according to the foreman. You snooze, you lose."

"Lucky bastard," Blake muttered. "When do you leave?"

"Six a.m. We're supposed to be in Lubbock and ready to rock to-morrow night."

Toby finished off his beer, then said, ""Your turn to break, Jason. Loser buys the next round."

***

"So, have you asked Nathan to walk you down the aisle yet?" Rick asked as they cleared the table after dinner.

"No, I haven't. Not yet," Faith admitted. "I wanted to wait until he closed that last case of his. It just didn't seem right to ask him about it when he was so focused on trying to catch that guy."

***

The next morning Nathan was settling in at his office and had just fired up his desktop unit when his cell phone rang.

"Thomas."

"Hey, baby brother," Faith said warmly. "You have just a minute to talk?"

"For you? Anytime. What's up?"

"I need to ask you something. And it's okay if you don't want to."

"What is it?"

"Well, I was hoping you'd agree to walk me down the aisle at the wedding."

A long beat of silence.

"Nathan? You there?"

He cleared his throat.

"It would be an absolute honor to walk with you the day you and Rick get married, Faith."

***

With the setup in Lubbock in full swing there wasn't much chance to stand around and talk, even if he'd wanted to.

And that's just fine with me. Every single person here gets on my last damn nerve on a regular basis. Especially that Toby kid. He is such a pain in the ass.

But he won't be for much longer, he thought to himself, and grinned eerily.

He muttered to himself as he loosened the straps and began to unload and set up his area pretty much on autopilot. His hands busied themselves while his mind retraced what he'd Googled about the town and surrounding area.

That one place sounded promising, but I'd have to go overnight to get what I need.

Unless I can forge a license?

He mulled it over for only seconds.

Screw that. Too much hassle and it'll leave a paper trail. I'll just get what I need the usual way, and it's better to wait and get it in Mexico where there's a greater chance of getting the pure stuff.

As he moved around to the other side of the flatbed trailer, he glanced to his right and saw the bane of his existence.

Out of all the newbies, the boss just had to saddle me with the dumbest one. Jackass...

"Hey Pops! Need some help?" Toby called out as he approached.

He glared at the kid but said nothing.

No. But you will. Very soon.

***

"Morning, boss. What's up?" Lizzie said immediately when she stepped into Nathan's office.

"Morning."

"Nathan, are you all right?"

He grinned. "I'm great. Faith just asked me to walk her down the aisle."

Lizzie's hand flew to her heart. "That's so sweet!"

"It meant a lot, that she asked."

"Well of course she would! You kidding? You're her brother."

"I know, but still. I'm surprised she didn't ask someone older."

"It's not about the age, Nathan. It's about the amount of respect and love she has for you. Speaking of wedding stuff, the reason I asked for those dates off is that Donny and I are planning on an Alaskan cruise - and we're gonna get married on the boat."

"Congrats! And you'll have to tell me about the cruise when you guys come back. I've been thinking about surprising Bella with one soon, maybe for our anniversary next year. She puts up with a lot because of my career. Flying out at the drop of a hat, late dinners, canceled plans, the works. I figured a cruise would be a great 'thank-you', don't you think?"

"She *does* have the patience of Job," Lizzie agreed. "Donny does, too. We really lucked out with our better halves, Nathan. Not everybody would be so understanding. Takes a special person to be married to someone in the military or law enforcement."

"You're right there. You and I both got extremely lucky."

***

A rap on the doorframe broke into their conversation.

"Hey, Lizzie. Morning, boss," Ben said. "I just followed up on a voicemail from a deputy with the Wise County Sheriff's department. They've got three cases they think are related, and they're asking us to build a profile. Can we round table about it?"

"Are they sending the case files over?"

"They should be here any minute. He said they were sent via overnight courier for early delivery."

"Sure," Nathan answered. "Review the files and get your presentation ready. We'll meet in the conference room at ten-thirty."

***

"Move your asses and let's get this done! We need to be ready to go by six o'clock sharp!" came a booming voice from his left, and he swiveled his head slowly toward Jake, the site foreman.

Hm. There's another one I could test it on if needed, he realized.

"You. Kid," Jake sputtered. "Toby, right? Don't just stand there taking up space. Help get this unloaded."

Motion in his periphery had him narrowing his eyes at the greenhorn that was now scrambling to obey Jake's orders - and pulling on a strap that could wreck the entire setup.

"Back off," he muttered at Toby through clenched teeth as Jake walked away. "You're gonna screw it up."

Oh, yeah. Yeah, I think they both *need to go at some point.*

He silently counted to three in his head before he turned his full attention to Toby.

"Just watch me and learn."

"Sure thing - *Pops*," the kid shot back with a sardonic smile.

He gritted his teeth and willed himself to not break character.

Change of plans. I need to get some as soon as possible, he thought as he focused on peering at Toby. *My trial runs cannot possibly start soon enough.*

***

At ten-thirty on the dot Nathan walked into the conference room. Ben was writing details of each of the three Wise County cases on the whiteboard.

Nathan sat and steepled his fingers. "Lay it on me."

Ben took a breath and plunged into his summary.

"All three victims were Hispanic males in their early twenties, and all three died of a single gunshot wound to the left temple."

"Caliber?"

Ben flipped back through his notes. "Same size in all three cases. A twenty-two round."

"From how far away?"

"The coroner noted pronounced stippling around each of the wounds but nothing indicating direct contact like a muzzle imprint. His best estimate was that each shot was fired from a distance of no more than six to eight inches."

Ben paused only long enough to take a small sip of water.

"All three were found outside city limits, all three were nude, and investigators at each scene noted that they likely weren't killed where they were found," Ben revealed. "Site pictures and the coroner's reports back up those assertions."

"Interesting. Go on. What's the time lapse between the cases?"

"The first two were four weeks apart, and the third one was two weeks after that. First guy was found north of Chico on May fifteenth, second guy on June twelfth down by Lake Bridgeport, and the third one on July third just south of Boyd."

"Whoever's doing it is confining their activity to Wise County, it seems. Makes sense, since the victims are likely being lured - or forcibly taken - to the same location each time to be killed. My gut says the killer is a resident in the area. Still, it would be prudent to check the database for any like cases elsewhere."

"I agree, and that was my next step. How wide should I search, to start?" Ben asked.

"Neighboring counties, to begin with, and you can widen it further if needed. Now, did the coroner's reports indicate any similarities in length of time between death and the discovery of the bodies?"

"They did, actually. He estimated that each man had been dead roughly forty-eight hours prior to discovery."

"Friday night party, Sunday remorse, maybe?" Nathan murmured.

"What?"

"Nothing, just thinking out loud. Have the victims been identified?"

"All three listed as John Does so far."

Annie appeared in the conference room's open doorway.

"Ben," she said quietly, "Deputy Greisen's holding for you on line four."

Ben exchanged a knowing look with his boss as he reached for the phone in the center of the conference table. He picked up the call and listened, then asked three questions, scribbling on his notepad as he did so.

"Thanks. I'll be out there as soon as I can," Ben said, and hung up.

"Another one," Nathan guessed, and Ben nodded.

"They just found a fourth body seven miles west of Greenwood. Greisen's on scene now, and he says it definitely fits the pattern."

"Get going, and take Annie with you," Nathan directed. "You guys know the drill. Walk this latest scene first, then check out the first three. Take pictures and notes. And get a copy of whatever is available on the latest victim to bring back with you. Send Lizzie in here on your way out. I'll have her set up the database search, and I will start the profile on their suspect."

"Yes, sir," Ben said, and went to tell Annie about their assignment.

A few minutes later Lizzie entered the conference room.

"What's up, boss?"

Nathan pointed to the whiteboard, then the files spread out on the table.

"Build a search, one county each direction surrounding Wise County, to start," he told her. "We need to know as soon as possible if there's any open unsolved cases that match these."

"I'm on it."

***

Lizzie stood in Nathan's doorway just before three p.m.

"I set the search for all counties whose borders are adjacent. Nothing turned up at all for Montague, Cooke, Denton, Tarrant, Parker or Jack counties."

"Good to know, thanks."

"You want me to expand the parameters?"

"Not at the moment, since my gut says the killer is keeping to Wise County for a reason."

"I'll be at my desk if you need me," Lizzie said before she left, and Nathan nodded, then turned back to his profile.

His desk phone rang.

"Thomas."

"Hey, boss," Ben said. "We're almost done with the Greenwood scene, and we're heading out to Chico next. It's the furthest westward, and we'll work our way back east."

"You may lose daylight before you're able to walk them all," Nathan reminded him.

"No worries, boss," Ben replied. "Deputy Greisen has a great big spotlight on his SUV that we can work with."

"Nice! Keep me posted."

CHAPTER TWO

When Lizzie's cell phone rang on her drive home she frowned, not recognizing the number that was displaying on her SUV's hands-free console.

She pressed the button on her steering wheel.

"Agent Zimmerman," she said as she picked up the call.

"Zim! Hey there. It's Jones. How are ya?"

She was surprised to hear from her fellow Academy graduate.

"Hey, yourself. I'm doing well. How are things with you?"

"Well, I'm thinking about making a change, and I wanted to run it by you. I'm considering asking for a transfer down to Dallas, Zim. We'd be working out of the same field office! Wouldn't that be great?"

"Really? When would you be coming down?"

"If it's approved, I would think it'd happen within the next few weeks."

They talked a few more minutes, then Jones said, "Well, it's good to talk to you, Zim, and I'll keep you in the loop."

"Can't wait," she said. "Catch you later."

As she hung up, she frowned again, remembering the conversation she'd had about the kid with one of her instructors.

I just can't get a feel for how he'd do under fire in a real-life situation. He might stand up just like he's been trained to do, and he might fall completely apart. There's really no way to know, Lizzie had observed when asked directly about Jones' skill set, and her instructor had voiced the same opinion.

Now there was a good possibility that the kid she had reservations about was going to join the Dallas team, and Lizzie wasn't sure how to handle things.

Should I share my concerns with Nathan ahead of time, or keep them to myself? I don't want the team here to form a subconscious bias against Jones, but at the same time if I don't say anything and some-thing happens...

Not to mention he's only been at his current assignment for a couple of months. Why the sudden change?

The whole situation just didn't feel right, and she was still mulling it over thirty minutes later as she pulled into her driveway and walked into the house.

Huh. I'll run it by Donny and get his opinion. He always has good insights.

"Hi babe," Donny called out from the home office, and she fol-lowed the sound of his voice.

"Hey there," she answered as she closed the distance between them and started to lean in for a kiss. But she stopped when she no-ticed the tension in his frame.

"You okay?"

Her fiancé looked up at her from his chair, and the raw grief shimmering in his hazel eyes hit her squarely in the heart.

"Not at all. Phil Tucker passed away late last night. I got the call from his wife Terri about a half hour ago."

"Oh, Donny. I'm so sorry, honey."

She immediately wrapped her arms around his shoulders as Donny laid his forehead on her chest and put his arms around her waist. She stroked his hair, trying her best to give comfort as he clung to her and shared his pain in a voice hoarse with sorrow.

"Out of everybody I knew when I was a professional athlete, he's the only one that stood by me, Lizzie. The only one I brought for-ward from my old life, and his faith in me never wavered at all, even when I hit my lowest point. Phil wasn't just my agent. He was one of the best friends I've ever had in my life."

"I know, baby. I know."

"Terri asked me to speak at the service and be a pallbearer. The funeral's on Thursday morning."

"The service arrangements are made already?"

"Terri is devastated, of course, but she made it a point to thank me for encouraging them to think ahead. I stressed the importance of pre-planning to them both when they had me set up their policies."

He leaned back in his chair and wiped his face with his sleeve.

"I need to book a flight to Los Angeles for Wednesday morning. I want to get there a day early in case Terri needs help with anything."

Lizzie leaned down and kissed him tenderly on the lips, then softly said, "How about I order us some Chinese food and mix us a couple of drinks, and you can tell me more about him. Share some memories. Celebrate his life. Whatever you want to do, babe. I love you, and I'm here for you."

He nodded and exhaled shakily.

"I love you too, Lizzie."

"And I'll come with you to California, if you need me to. Just say the word."

"I know, babe."

Donny stood and ran his hands through his hair.

"I'm feeling the need for a hot shower. Will you join me? We can order the food when we get out."

She reached forward and took his hands in hers.

"I think that's a great idea."

***

"Okay, here's what I don't get," Annie began as they followed Deputy Greisen from Chico down to the Lake Bridgeport location.

"What's that?"

"According to everything we've learned so far, none of the victims showed any signs of a struggle. No defensive wounds or marks at all, right?"

"Right."

"Don't you think that's strange? I mean, I don't think anyone would just stand still and *let* someone shoot them, right? I know I sure as hell wouldn't. I'd put up a fight, at least."

"I agree. And yes, that's strange. Unless they were drunk or otherwise incapacitated in some way."

"Or distracted. But it would have to be a pretty damn big distraction to not notice that someone standing so close to you has a gun pointed your direction," Annie pointed out.

Ben's eyebrow raised as he thought about it.

***

Nathan paused his typing and glanced back through a section of the coroner's report on the man found north of Chico.

"Wait, *what*?"

He cross-checked the other two files and found more of the same notations.

"Interesting. That alters my approach, for sure," he murmured, and began to backspace his cursor. He amended his additional impressions, then saved the file before he shut down his desktop unit for the day.

As he moved to the elevator, he called Ben's cell phone.

"Hey guys, what's the status?"

"We're almost to Lake Bridgeport, where the second man was found."

"Let's gather in the conference room at nine a.m. and go over your intel from the scenes."

"Sure thing, boss. See you in the morning."

Nathan's next call was to Bella.

"I'm headed home. Need me to pick up anything?"

***

It was just after two in the morning when he crept out of his motorhome and climbed into his truck, then winced at the roar of the motor echoing through the still night air.

Can't be helped. Get going.

He eased his battered Ford forward through the night, pleasantly surprised that the beast's rumbling hadn't seemed to awaken anyone else in the group. Once he got to the main road, he glanced at his cell phone's screen to confirm his route, then turned left.

He let his truck coast to a stop two blocks from his destination ten minutes later. A glance ahead of him, then in his rear-view mirror, confirmed his hunch.

Just as I suspected. This side of town pretty much rolls up Main Street after dark.

He turned off the ignition key and settled in to wait.

Once he'd satisfied himself that he wasn't likely to be intercepted, he pulled his baseball cap down low, stepped down out of the cab and gently closed the driver's side door behind him.

Glancing skyward, he noticed the moon partially obscured by cloud cover.

Nice, he thought. *Just enough light to see my way.*

He strolled casually, his long legs covering the distance with little effort. As he walked, he recalled what he'd read about the chemical compound that he'd come to liberate from its licensed owner.

The smell should be masked well enough once I'm done mixing things together, he noted. *And the emetic should be neutralized too. I just need this last piece and I can get started.*

And then, Toby my boy, then you and I are gonna have some fun.

He turned the corner and traveled along the pitifully easy to breach chain link fencing until he was at the southeastern edge of the lot. The panels were tall, eight feet high, but strangely not fortified in any manner that he could readily see.

Still, better safe than sorry, he decided as he moved the bandanna around his neck up to mask the lower half of his face. He carefully scrutinized the length of chain link to confirm his assumptions as he pulled on his gloves.

Not electrified, and no razors. That's a bonus.

But the sarcastic common-sense side of his brain piped up loud and clear.

Electrified? Razor wire? Seriously? What were you expecting, exactly, guards in towers? It's a mom-and-pop place, not Area 51. Now focus.

As he chuckled at himself for a brief moment, he also thought about simply scaling the fence.

Not as young as I used to be, though. And the posts don't seem all that sturdy, either. Climbing it will shake the whole fence and make a hell of a lot of noise. Easier to go through it rather than over it.

He slipped the wire cutters out of his pocket and went to work, carving an inverted L-shaped entry point. Within ninety seconds, he was through the flimsy barrier and headed toward the back of the squat gray brick building.

Another twenty minutes elapsed as he bypassed the business's antiquated alarm system, then turned on his tiny flashlight and began to search for their supply of the compound that was so crucial to his plans.

He rubbed his hands together gleefully when he realized the company that he'd chosen to steal from actually possessed *both* forms in their inventory - the premixed ready-to-use blue liquid, and the less commonly available white crystalline solid.

From the fine layer of dust on the tops of the two containers, he could tell that the solid form wasn't the favored choice in the facility's day-to-day operations.

He immediately reached past the liquid to pick up a six-ounce canister of the crystallized version. He rotated the package in his hands, read the front label by flashlight, and smiled wolfishly into the dark.

Whoever bought this opted to cross the border, too.

He slowly turned the package until he found the section with technical data, then did some quick calculations in his head since he had zero intentions of using the compound as designed.

This should do nicely.

He reached forward and grabbed the second canister, tucked one in each of his jacket's oversized inside pockets, then made his way back out of the building.

Once he restored the interior security system, he hustled back through the fence, where he worked the section that he'd cut away and lifted up back down into place. Several small lengths of fine wire snipped from the slender spool he'd brought with him was enough to stitch together the L-shape he'd previously made. Unless someone walked the fence and looked closely, he was confident that the sabotage and subsequent repair job would remain undiscovered.

He resisted the urge to whistle as he walked away to return to where he'd parked his ride. He arrived back at the Ford without having seen a soul, but he still waited a few moments before he fired up the truck and drove away.

By two-forty-five he was settled once again in his home on wheels. His ill-gotten gain was locked securely in the fireproof safe that he'd installed in what was now the makeshift lab at the rear of his living space. Then he stretched his frame out on the over-cab bunk and smiled as he drifted off to sleep.

***

Lizzie and Donny were both out of bed for the day by four a.m. after a futile attempt at sleep.

"I'm going for a run," Donny decided, and moved to the closet to pull out some clothes. "Want to go?"

"And then, breakfast. With coffee. *Lots* of coffee," she answered as she headed into the bathroom to pull her hair up into a ponytail. "Waffle House?"

Donny grinned briefly. "Deal."

***

When Lizzie got to work, she logged into her terminal, then made her way to Nathan's office.

"Morning," he said, then frowned when he glanced up at her. "What's wrong?"

"Very little sleep," she confessed. "Rough night. Donny got word that Phil passed away, and he's pretty torn up about it."

"Understandably," Nathan replied. "I recall Donny mentioning Phil when I had Donny in protective custody up in D.C. He spoke very highly of the man."

He narrowed his eyes and looked at her more carefully.

"But that's not all, is it?"

She shuffled on her feet.

"What else is on your mind?"

Ben appearing behind her derailed the line of questioning.

"Morning guys," he said, oblivious. "Still on for nine?"

"Yep," Nathan confirmed. "And I noticed some things in the coroner's reports that we need to cover in depth, as well."

"You got it, boss," Ben sketched a salute and walked away.

Nathan refocused his attention on Lizzie.

"Lizzie," he said gently. "Talk to me. What's going on?"

She took a deep breath and closed his office door.

Nathan's eyebrows raised.

"Must be serious."

"It is."

She sat in the visitor's chair across the desk from him, and began to fill him in.

"There's this kid named Jones I went through the Academy with. Fresh out of college, no experience, had delusions of grandeur and a massive attitude problem. He wasn't taking it seriously. I finally lost my temper with him and that seemed to get through to him."

"Why do I feel a 'but' coming on?"

"But I just.... he's one of those that you just don't know if he'll be dependable in live fire situations. He's a good kid, don't get me wrong, and he does have some skills, especially when it comes to research and analysis. I just..."

Nathan leaned forward. "Lizzie, be honest with me here. You just, what?"

"I just don't know if I'd want to have to depend on him to keep a team member safe, Nathan. If I had my choice of who to go through a door with, Jones would *not* be someone I would pick."

Nathan was silent for a moment.

"That speaks volumes, Liz."

"I know. Here's the thing. I could be completely wrong about the kid. He could turn out to be the strongest link in the chain."

"But your gut says otherwise."

She sighed.

"Yes. My gut says that's unlikely. I don't want to damage his chances of making a career for himself as an agent, which is why I hesitated to say anything at all. But at the same time-"

"At the same time," Nathan chimed in, "if you kept quiet and then he got somebody hurt..."

"*Exactly*. And he called me yesterday on the way home to tell me he's asking to transfer down here to Dallas. If it goes through, he could be down here as soon as next week. And honestly, my next thought was, *why*? He's only been in the Chicago office about three months. Doesn't a transfer this soon seem a little strange to you?"

"It's unusual, but not unheard of. I can look into it discreetly and see what I can find out about the situation. I presume he's not coming specifically to *my* team, or I would already know about this. It could be they just needed additional staff down here. It may even be as simple as a clash of personalities," Nathan pointed out.

"You think?"

"It's a possibility. Not everyone gets along as well as this group here, and in that situation usually the least tenured guy involved would get reassigned. Or, it may be that Chicago branch has identified a serious issue, and they're passing him off to another location because of it. But I have to say I don't believe that to be the case, Lizzie. If someone's that big a liability, they'd be gone outright, not just bounced around. Not really any way to know for sure without doing some digging."

"I just don't want anyone here to form a bias, Nathan. Because like I said, I could be completely wrong about him."

"I wonder what his instructors thought."

"Well," she said on a sigh," I can tell you that at least one of them had the same reservations about him that I do."

"How do you know that?"

"The man flat out asked me my opinion on Jones. He said he really wasn't supposed to talk to one cadet about another, but since I'd spent so many years on the job, he was interested to know my take on it."

Nathan leaned back in his chair.

"That's not *technically* against the rules that I'm aware of, but it's definitely not typical, either. You know that, right?"

Lizzie nodded.

"So at least one of his instructors picked up the same vibe," Nathan frowned. "But it wasn't strong enough to recommend terming him from the program. Interesting."

"And I kind of feel responsible for that," Lizzie added. "My running interference helped him get through."

"How so?"

"He was struggling badly with some of the combat sims. I took him under my wing, gave him some pointers, and he got through them. So, he *is* teachable - under simulation conditions. But real-time, with real bad guys and live ammo? I just don't know."

"Let me see what I can find out about the transfer, and we'll go from there. And what you've told me will stay between us. All right?"

"All right."

Nathan checked his watch.

"I've got about forty minutes before Ben and I meet in the conference room, and I need to firm up some things in my preliminary profile before then. Why don't we reconnect about this on Friday afternoon? I should have more intel by then."

"Sounds good."

Lizzie stood and started to leave. She had her hand on the door-knob when Nathan said, "Hey."

"Yes?"

"You did the right thing, telling me about this. I know you feel bad, thinking you've torpedoed the kid. But this is the kind of stuff I need to know about an agent that we might have to send out on a warrant team."

"I know. Doesn't make it suck any less."

"No, it doesn't."

Lizzie straightened her shoulders, opened the door, and walked away.

***

He woke refreshed and stretched luxuriously before he climbed down from his bunk. A quick shower was followed up with making himself a light breakfast.

Once his food was plated, he sat at his dinette table, arranging his papers so that he could figure out the desired ratios as he shoveled scrambled eggs into his mouth.

It occurred to him that he needed to add something to make his formula's presence more subtle. A quick check through his stolen book provided the simple and obvious answer, and he got to his feet to rummage through the tiny pantry, then growled in frustration.

Dammit. It figures.

The trial run of his grand experiment would have to hold until he could make a trip to the grocery store.

He checked the time, then grabbed the keys to his truck.

***

Ben met Nathan in the conference room and asked, "Can Annie join us? She had some pretty good insights."

"Sure."

When all three of them were seated, Nathan looked at Ben.

"What are your thoughts so far?"

Ben gestured to Annie to take point.

"I couldn't help but wonder why none of them had defensive wounds. I would think that most people would have put up a fight, or at least attempted to get away from someone being that close to them with a gun," she said. "So, I was wondering if maybe they were incapacitated in some way, maybe drunk, or drugged."

"Nothing at all showed in toxicology," Nathan answered. "I had that same thought myself, so I checked."

"And then I thought perhaps they were just really distracted," Annie continued. "But I mean, come on. How distracted do you have to be to not notice something like *that*?"

"I found something in the coroner's supplemental notes on the first two cases that might actually help answer that one."

Ben leaned forward. "What?"

"The coroner noted traces of residue across each man's lower torso in those cases," Nathan stated. "It resembled soap, but the coroner's notes don't indicate if anyone was able to identify the brand."

"Just lower torso, nowhere else? That's weird," Annie said, slightly confused.

"Huh," Ben exclaimed, then, "*Oh*. I get it."

Nathan nodded.

"What?" Annie looked at them both.

"Like whoever killed them was maybe trying to wash away any evidence of sexual activity, Annie," Ben told her gently, and watched her flush scarlet.

"Well," she finally said, "I suppose sex could be a pretty damn big distraction."

An awkward silence fell among them as Annie took a long drink of water.

Nathan moved to another topic.

"So. Site walks. Anything in particular stand out?"

"Well, the Greenwood, Chico, and Lake Bridgeport dump sites had a lot in common. Each was on a gravel road that terminated onto private property about a half-mile past where the bodies were found. None of them had any sort of 'dead end' or 'no through street' signage that was readily visible. The road just ended at a cattle guard at each location. And whoever placed the bodies had to travel for a while down the gravel road to reach each site. Annie calculated the distances."

Annie nodded and picked up the story.

"Yep. From the time we turned off the paved farm-to-market road onto the gravel road until we arrived at each site, we traveled..." - she flipped through her notes- "four point two miles in Greenwood, just under eight miles in Chico, and almost six in Lake Bridgeport."

"Pretty far off the beaten path."

"Absolutely," Ben confirmed. "No way someone who wasn't already very familiar with the area would know about these three roads. Even if they happened to stumble across the first one, what are the odds of getting lucky *two more times* with backroads with the same configuration?"

"Interesting," Nathan murmured. "And it immediately brings up a huge question - if those three dump sites were so remote, then *how were the bodies discovered so quickly*?"

"Greisen said that the Wise County 911 switchboard received anonymous tips about the bodies in Chico, Lake Bridgeport and Greenwood."

"What about the other scene? The one close to Boyd?" Nathan asked, after a long, thoughtful pause.

"Not nearly as isolated," Annie revealed. "By a long shot. That body was seen by a passing motorist, and he stayed onsite and talked to the police when they arrived."

"Any indication at all that perhaps that site might have been an impulsive choice, rather than a deliberate selection?"

"What do you mean?"

"Let's take them in order for a moment," Nathan suggested. "Pull up a map of the county and let's plot them in order."

A few minutes later Ben had an area map of Wise County projected onto the white pull-down screen that Annie had lowered into place.

"Okay, first victim was found here, in a very isolated place," Nathan indicated with a laser pointer. "Then there are two more sites - here, and here. One is like the first, but the other, by comparison, is a high-traffic area, right?"

"Right," Ben confirmed. "A drainage ditch that runs along the south side of the main road through town."

"Then the killer reverts back to an isolated spot to place the fourth body up near Greenwood. The question is, *why*? Why change that part of their process with the third victim?"

He started to speak further but the phone trilling in the center of the conference table broke his stride.

"Yes," Nathan said into the handset, then listened for a moment. "Let him know I will call him back within five minutes, please."

He stood, then looked at Ben and Annie.

"I need to go. Start thinking about the questions we've formulated so far."

As he walked toward the door, Nathan continued, "And as you work to find those answers, also keep in mind that the body found in Boyd *didn't* have that residue on it."

"It didn't?"

Nathan paused in the doorway and looked at them over his shoulder.

"No, it didn't. It's also off pace from the four-week spacing - and we need to ask 'why' on those two points, as well. I have a feeling the answers are all interconnected. We'll reconvene at two p.m."

"On it, boss."

***

"Thomas," Nathan said once he was seated behind his desk and pushed the flashing button.

"Hey, Nathan," Steve, his boss, answered. "I saw your email about the newbie coming down to Dallas. Got a few minutes to talk?'

"Hang on, let me close my door."

That accomplished, Nathan told him, "All right. What's going on there?"

"Well, information isn't exactly readily available. On the surface it seems to be a straight up transfer. But from what I've found so far, two huge red flags have popped up."

"Like what? Who initiated it?"

A pause.

"The branch Director up there is the one that put it through channels."

"Really?" Nathan was incredulous. "He submitted the transfer personally? That's... unusual."

"Indeed," Steve agreed. "Normal transfer paperwork gets filed with HQ by the division secretary. It feels to me like someone does *not* want this kid staying in Chicago."

"Huh." Nathan's mind whirled. "That could mean anything."

"Yep. The other thing is, everything that I could see indicates he's moving to the Bureau's *Tampa* branch, not Dallas. Which is why I plan to dig deeper. Something's not right about this, Nathan. Not at all. I'll be in touch."

CHAPTER THREE

Once Nathan was gone, Annie looked at Ben.

"I've got more legible handwriting than you do," she announced. "*You* read the files aloud, *I'll* make the notes on the whiteboard."

"Maybe we'd better have a working lunch. I can order a pizza. You want the usual?"

"Yep."

As Ben placed their order, Annie grabbed a dry-erase marker. On one side of the whiteboard, she wrote out the questions surrounding the four Wise County murder cases, then stepped back and reviewed them.

1. Why the change in dump site on case #3?

2. Why were two of the bodies partially washed?

3. Why didn't victim #3 have residue on his skin?

4. Why doesn't victim #3's case match up with the four-week interval?

Then she stepped over to the other side and made four columns, one for each murder victim.

Annie glanced over at Ben, who sat at the table with the first victim's full case file spread out in front of him.

"You ready?"

He nodded, picked up a page and began to read aloud.

"Okay, first guy. Five feet seven inches tall, one hundred fifty pounds. Single gunshot wound in the left temple, twenty-two caliber, fired from roughly seven inches away."

Annie made her notes, then nodded at Ben to continue.

"Found out near Chico on Sunday May fifteenth, and the coroner placed time of death sometime Friday evening, between six and ten p.m."

Annie duly recorded the data and added *'Residue found in lower torso area. Soap?'* to the area of the board dedicated to the first case.

They repeated the exercise with the second and third case files and had just begun to discuss the results when the unit secretary called and let them know their pizza had arrived.

"Perfect timing. I'll go get it," Ben told her. "And then we can review what we've got while we eat."

***

The moment he got back to his motorhome he locked himself in and proceeded to the rear compartment where his lab equipment waited. He made sure that everything he needed was lined up on the worktable underneath the filtered exhaust hood.

Safety first, he thought smarmily as he donned rubber gloves and a clear face shield. He double-checked his calculations, nodded, and very carefully measured out exactly one-half teaspoon of the grainy white substance into a glass beaker before reaching for the second item called for in his formula.

Once the two solids were gently stirred together with a glass rod, he poured out the first of the two liquid ingredients involved in his scheme, and very slowly a quarter-cup of it joined the crystalline at the bottom of the beaker. When the final addition was made, he patiently stirred again with the glass rod until at last all solid matter had been dissolved.

I can't wait to see the look on Toby's face, he acknowledged with sadistic glee as he poured his fatal cocktail into an empty but thoroughly washed Fireball whiskey bottle and screwed the lid on tightly.

The final step he took was to make a small tick mark on the upper left corner of the label with a blue marker. Then he carried the bottle to the fridge and set it inside right next to his other, unopened bottle of the potent liquor.

"That should be nice and cold by tonight," he murmured, and smiled.

He glanced at the clock.

Perfect timing. My shift's about to start.

Before he stepped down out of the motorhome, he made sure that the standard-frame exterior door separating his lab from the rest of his living space was securely locked. He shoved that key down into his front pants pocket, then made his way to the door leading outside and took a moment to assume his eccentric persona before he shuffled out and locked the outer door behind him.

***

Lizzie smiled when she saw Donny's number come up on her cell phone screen.

"Hey, babe. What's up?"

"I have to get to L.A. as soon as possible. I'm about to head to the airport now."

The thick steel ribbon of tension in his voice was almost palpable.

"What's wrong?"

"Phil's business partner is a total prick, that's what's wrong. I missed a call from Terri earlier. She left me a voicemail, but she was crying so hard I couldn't understand half of it. She needs my help."

"Oh," Lizzie said quietly. "That's a shame. She's already going through so much right now."

"Yeah. Anyway, I just wanted to let you know I'm flying out today instead of tomorrow like I'd planned. I'll be home Sunday."

"Oh," she said again, and thought, *the funeral's on Thursday, so... Don't ask, Liz. I'm sure it's fine.*

But her cop radar was tingling.

"I gotta go, Lizzie. I love you. I'll call you when I land."

"Okay. Love you too, Donny."

She hung up the phone, set it down on her desk, and frowned.

***

"You know what?" Annie said as she reached for another slice. "I'm wondering if the third guy ties in with the others at all."

"Why not?"

"Well, there's some pretty big variances here. He wasn't washed, for starters. And he wasn't dumped in the boonies like the other three. And if you remove him from this timeline? Look. The other three are spaced out *precisely* four weeks apart."

She paused, then tapped the side of the board where she'd written the questions.

"Check it out. Three of these directly relate to this third victim," Annie pointed out, and Ben nodded his agreement.

"I think maybe we could have a copycat on our hands for that third guy," he suggested. "It's a theory that makes sense. At the very least it would explain the lack of residue and the timeframe not being consistent, don't you think?"

"That's precisely what I think. A copycat wouldn't *know* to wash the body, because the residue wouldn't be public knowledge at all. Only the killer, and law enforcement working the cases, would know about it. General comments about the type of injury and a rough description of where the bodies were found might make the local newspaper, but not fine details like trace evidence."

"Okay," Ben exclaimed. "So, let's dig and see if anything else about victim number three veers outside of the parameters."

"He's a match for height and weight. All four men are about the same size," Annie reminded him.

Ben flipped pages and compared notes between the three cases.

"But he's the only one with tattoos, Annie. Come take a look at this."

She joined him at the table and peered over his shoulder.

"Gang tat?"

"Possibly. I have a buddy on Fort Worth PD Gang Division. Let me make a call and run this by him."

"When did Greisen say the fourth file might be ready, again?" she asked.

"If I recall correctly, he said that the coroner's report would be complete by Thursday and that he'd send it all over once he had that piece," Ben replied. "We should have it before the weekend gets here."

"I'm going to reach out to Deputy Greisen and get a better feel for when the Greenwood victim's case file might be ready," Annie offered, and Ben nodded as he pulled the cell phone from his holder at his waist to call his friend and former platoonmate Brody.

***

Nathan stopped by Lizzie's desk just after eleven-thirty and said, "Want to grab lunch? It's a bit early but I figured we could talk some more. I have some news."

She shrugged. "Sure."

"You all right?"

"Home stuff. It's fine. Let's go."

Once they were settled into their usual booth at the café the team frequented, Nathan quietly filled her in.

"I sent Steve an email asking general questions about Agent Jones coming down to the Dallas team. What he found out so far was unusual enough that he plans to dig further."

"And that was?"

"One of upper management submitted the request personally. I don't just mean he signed off on it. I mean he sent those files himself. That's atypical. Usually, the division secretary processes all transfer orders through to HQ."

Lizzie's left eyebrow raised as she sipped her tea.

"So, what does that mean?"

Nathan shook his head.

"I'm honestly not sure. It could be a multitude of things. Steve's been around a long time, and it seemed strange to him too, so he's doing what he does best, which is investigate. But that's not the strangest part. There's something else."

"Go on."

"Steve says the kid's transfer papers are for Tampa, not Dallas. He's digging further."

Lizzie's eyes went wide in surprise.

"How long until you hear back from him?'

"No clue. In the meantime, we'll act like it's any other transfer when Jones gets here. I haven't told anyone else what you and I talked about, and I won't unless it becomes necessary."

"I know, but I appreciate you saying that."

***

At two p.m. Nathan returned to the conference room to get an update from his team members.

He glanced at the whiteboard first and nodded his approval before taking a seat.

"Looks like you two have been busy. Read me in."

"We think murder number three may have been the work of a copycat, boss. Three major points are out of line with the other cases," Ben stated. "The lack of residue, the dump location, and the timeframe. Annie and I think that someone read about the other two cases in the paper and decided that it would be a good cover for them to get away with murder themselves."

He paused, then said, "And we realized something else. We also noticed that victim number three was the only man that had tattoos. I thought some of them might be gang-related, so, I reached out to a contact I have with the gang unit in the Fort Worth police department."

Nathan leaned forward. "Were you able to get any information?"

"Yes. He confirmed that three of our victim's tattoos are signature marks of a well-known Mexican cartel. And even more telling - he says the number of incidents involving gang members that are affiliated with the cartel have more than *tripled* in Fort Worth in the last six weeks."

"Sounds like a battle for real estate, or clientele, maybe," Nathan thought aloud. "We will work that information into the final profiling report we send back to Deputy Greisen - including recommending that they expand the identity search for the third man to include international databases. Anything else?"

***

Lizzie sighed to herself as she walked into a quiet and empty house. Although Donny had called as promised when he arrived in California, he shared no further details about the situation that had so drastically altered his travel plans.

Yeah, something's weird there, for sure, and I don't know why he's not sharing whatever is going on with me.

But I don't like it.

Her cell phone rang as she was rummaging through the refrigerator for sandwich ingredients.

"Hey Joe! What's up?"

"Well, I haven't talked to you in a while, so I thought I'd check in. Would you and your man like to join us for dinner tonight? It'd be great to see you."

"Donny's in Los Angeles until Sunday, but I'm game. What time?"

"Six-thirty."

"Sounds good. Do I need to bring anything?"

"Hang on, let me ask," Joe replied, and she bit back a chuckle as she heard him cheerily call out, "Hey, honey!" followed by him and Trish talking in the background.

They're so good together. I'm so happy he's found someone again.

"Nope, Trish says just bring yourself."

"All right. See you then."

She hung up and glanced at the clock on the microwave.

Five-forty-two. Just enough time for a quick shower, she decided, and hurriedly put away the lunchmeat and cheese before she hustled down the hall.

***

Nathan swooped up Charlie, who as usual had run to meet his father at the front door.

"Hey, buddy. How was your day?"

"Great!" the toddler replied.

"Where's Mom?"

Charlie extended his hand and pointed toward the back of the house.

"Wanna go see what she's up to?"

"Let's go!" the child replied with his typical bubbly attitude.

"Hey, you," Nathan said as they walked into the home office.

"Hi!" Bella said as she paused her typing to greet her husband with a kiss. "Give me two minutes, I'm just about done here. I got an email about a change in our class schedule this week that I need to respond to."

"Sure. Wanna order pizza?"

"Works for me," Bella answered with a grin.

"Yay, pizza!" Charlie exclaimed loudly.

"Sounds like we have his vote."

"You think?"

Nathan chuckled. "I'll call it in."

He turned and left the room, Charlie still tucked in his arms, and Bella smiled to herself as she heard Nathan ask their son, "So, what happened at day care today?"

***

The last night of operations in Lubbock slowly wound to a close at eleven, and his impatience grew by the minute. At long last, he was able to shut down his station, arranging things so that loading up the following morning would be seamless.

Especially since I'm about to be short one helper...

The sensation of being watched caused him to swivel his head, and he realized Toby was standing off to his left side.

"This is it for here, right? We move to the next town?" the kid asked.

"Yeah. We'll be on the road by eight in the morning."

"So, what do we do in the meantime?"

It was all he could do to keep a predatory gleam out of his eyes as he gazed at Toby and said, "You like drinking games?"

Toby grinned at him, oblivious to his impending fate.

"Yeah, Pops. I like drinking games. Let's see what you've got."

This kid thinks he can drink me under the table, he realized, and barely managed to stifle a smirk. *We'll just see about that.*

"Come on, then," he said instead.

They walked side by side back toward the far end of the lot where the workers' vehicles and RVs were grouped together.

"So, what's the next town we're going to?" Toby asked.

"San Angelo, I think."

"Oh. All right. That's not too bad."

He shrugged noncommittally and continued to shuffle forward toward his motorhome.

"Nice rig, by the way. I bet it's got lots of space inside," Toby observed.

He grunted in response and fished the motorhome's exterior key out of his pocket.

"After you," he announced as he opened the door.

They started with a half-empty bottle of tequila and a friendly game of quarters. To his credit, Toby held his own for the first three rounds.

An hour later Toby was three sheets to the wind, and his host was almost giddy with delight, although he took great pains not to break character.

When the tequila ran out, he grabbed the unopened bottle of Fireball, and after the first round of shots with it he could tell by the look on Toby's face that the kid had never tried it before.

"M-m-man," Toby sputtered and wheezed, his eyes wide with surprise. "That stuff burns going down! I see why they call it Fireball."

He allowed himself a small chuckle. "You get used to it. It's your turn."

Four shots later Toby was seriously intoxicated but demanded they keep playing.

After another ten minutes, the Fireball bottle was empty, and Toby pouted like a small child.

"Aw, *man*," he whined.

To which his host replied, "No worries. I've got more," and held up the doctored bottle. "Shall we keep going?"

Toby nodded, clapping his hands together in drunken glee.

He observed Toby with intense interest as the kid lost the next two rounds, and each time slammed down another forty-four-milliliter shot of brilliantly concocted liquid death. Toby could barely maneuver the shot glass to his own lips, much less notice that the man pouring out the booze had not poured himself a shot at all from the new bottle.

By the time Toby swallowed the second shot and set down the tiny glass with a very wobbly hand, he'd already turned pale.

"I don't feel so hot," the kid moaned, and tried to slide out of the dinette's u-shaped seat to stand up. But the toxins combined with hard liquor and an empty stomach conspired against him, and instead of standing upright, Toby crumpled to the floor.

"Time for you to go, then," the man he'd insisted on calling 'Pops' said aloud as he watched and waited.

Now, how should I do this?

He thought for a moment, nodding to himself in approval as he capped the bottle and put it away, then pulled on surgical gloves.

He crouched down and felt for Toby's pulse.

Thready, and getting weaker by the second. Good. Not much longer.

He hoisted the kid up to a standing position as easily as a sack of potatoes, then carried him outside and laid him in the passenger seat of his truck.

"Seat belt, young man. Seat belt," he whispered, and giggled as he strapped Toby in tightly.

***

Lizzie rolled to her left, stared at the vacant pillow beside hers, and sighed again.

"I am *never* going to get to sleep," she lamented as she threw the covers back in frustration and went to the living room to see if surfing channels could hypnotize her into restfulness.

Forty-five minutes later, Lizzie was still flipping back and forth between a documentary on sea lions and a classic Audrey Hepburn film when her cell phone rang.

Her heart skipped a beat when she noticed who was calling.

Donny.

"Hey there," she said softly.

"I didn't wake you, did I?"

"Nope. Can't sleep. How are things there?"

"Not what they seemed to be at all. I'll explain when I see you, but I just wanted to let you know I'm flying home right after the funeral on Thursday."

"You sure?"

"Positive."

The edge in his tone filled her head with a million questions, but she refrained from asking them.

"I love you," she said simply.

"I love you, too," he replied. "Don't ever think otherwise, Lizzie."

Lizzie closed her eyes as the razor-sharp bite in his voice melted away to warm tenderness that enveloped her like a blanket.

"Now, if I know you as well as I think I do, you're flipping TV channels, right? Let me guess. Some sort of nature something-or-other and an old black-and-white."

"How would you know that?"

Donny laughed.

"Because that's what *I'm* doing, and I know we watch a lot of the same stuff. So, what are you watching?"

"Sea lions and Audrey Hepburn. You?"

"Something about the volcanic eruption that took out Pompeii, and *Young Frankenstein*."

"*Young Frankenstein*? I love that movie! What channel?"

***

He drove south past the city limits sign, searching for the ideal spot to stop at almost one a.m. that wouldn't attract too much attention.

A half-hour later, in the middle of nowhere and under a moonless night sky, he eased his Ford to the side of the road, killed the headlights, and waited for five minutes. No one passed by.

Perfect. Now's the time.

He got out, moved around the front of the vehicle to the passenger side, and opened the door that Toby was slumped against. Another quick check of the carotid had the mastermind smiling in triumph.

The kid's body fell toward him as he leaned in and undid the seat belt, then tugged hard, one arm under each of Toby's shoulders. Gravity assisted the descent from the passenger seat to the gravel shoulder, and he adjusted his stance, placing Toby between himself and the steep decline that loomed in the darkness.

A well-executed shove rolled Toby's now lifeless body down the sharp slope to land face-down in a drainage canal below.

He closed the passenger door and got back behind the wheel, pausing only to catch his breath before he put the old Ford into gear and made a U-turn.

As he drove back toward town, he reviewed his first experiment's results in his head.

Let's see... he drank eighty-eight milliliters total, about three ounces, and was dead within an hour. I made it too strong, or the dosage was too aggressive, or both. That much is obvious.

Ah, well. In every first round of testing there's some room for improvement. I can dilute the liquid form further, and I should be able to achieve the same end results with much more subtlety....

I wonder what saturation level would be required for an aerosol to be effective. If I can get that figured out, that would be even more *ideal. Less product over more area. Think of the range...*

No way to know unless I test it out.

He whistled happily all the way back to his motorhome and spent another hour running new calculations before he yawned, stretched, and moved to his bunk to tumble into dreamless, satisfied sleep.

CHAPTER FOUR

Nathan, Annie, and Ben met up again in the conference room at eight a.m. for a final run-through of the data. Wise County had expedited both the coroner's report and case file for the fourth victim, and the first order of business was to log those details on to the whiteboard next to the others.

"Looking at all this," Nathan said when Annie finished updating the board, "my gut says two things. One, that the third murder was *definitely* committed by someone else attempting to hide what they've done by mimicking these other cases, and two, that the suspect in the other three homicides is most likely a female."

"A female? What makes you say that?"

"The residue. Washing a body in that manner just strikes me as something a female would think of, not a male. It speaks to a cover up, yes, but also perhaps to guilt in some fashion. If their lab can determine the brand of soap used, they might be able to narrow down their search more quickly."

"But the size of these guys.... none of them were that tall or overly bulky, but still, one hundred fifty pounds, on average? That's a lot of mass to move around, Nathan."

"Yep. Which is why your suspect is either not your average-sized woman, or she has an accomplice, maybe not for the murders themselves, but definitely to dump the bodies."

"Husband-wife team, maybe? Or boyfriend-girlfriend? Maybe the woman likes side action, and something about it triggers her to kill, and then her partner helps her cover it up?" Annie asked for clarification.

"That's my theory."

"A Hispanic woman? Serials tend to hunt within their own ethnic group," Ben pointed out.

"She'll be either Hispanic or Caucasian, probably mid to late forties, and an otherwise upstanding resident citizen of her town. My money is on her residing somewhere in or near Decatur, as that is the one big town out there that hasn't been the site of a find yet. She'll have property large enough to have a fair amount of privacy, and I bet if Wise County extends its search and adds more details, they will find that none of the victims are residents of Wise County. I think their suspect is crossing county lines to find her targets and taking them home with her. As far as the remote locations where the bodies were discovered, I think they'll find their suspect and/or her accomplice own or work in a profession that requires extensive knowledge of the entire county's road systems."

He handed Ben a folder.

"Here's a printed copy of my analysis on the female suspect they need to focus on for three of the murders. Review it, write up yours and Annie's copycat theory for the Boyd victim, then send them both over to Deputy Greisen. Let him know we're available to assist further if the need arises."

"Will do, boss."

"'I'll be in my office if you have any questions," Nathan confirmed, and left the conference room.

***

When the breakdown and move prep got started in earnest at first light Wednesday morning, Toby's absence wasn't noticed immediately.

But by nine o'clock it was obvious, and the site foreman was furious.

"Anyone seen Toby?" Jake bellowed yet again.

No one had.

No one that would admit to it, anyway.

It damn near broke his cover persona wide open when Jake stormed through a third time, ruddy faced and neck veins bulging from temper. He had to bite hard on the inside of his cheek to keep from laughing in the man's face.

"You see him before I do you tell him he is *fired!* I don't have time to babysit his punk ass. He's out of here!"

"Yes, sir," he managed to say in a neutral tone.

He held it together until Jake walked away, then pulled out his handkerchief and held it to his face so he could giggle softly with at least some small amount of privacy.

After a few minutes he'd composed himself sufficiently to complete the required last-minute checks, then signaled to the big-rig driver that would haul his work equipment to San Angelo that all was clear for him to roll out.

He shuffled his way back to his motorhome, drove the Ford's front tires up onto the tow dolly, then made sure his truck was secured for the trip before he climbed up into his motorhome and got behind the wheel to fall in line behind the others.

***

"Zimmerman," Lizzie said when her desk phone rang.

"Hey, it's Jones again. How are you?"

"I'm doing well."

"Good. Hey, there's something I wanted to talk to you about."

"Sure," she replied, and tried her best to keep the uneasiness out of her voice. "Whatcha got?"

"Well, it's about...," he began, then hesitated.

"Jones?"

"I can't talk right now. I'll have to call you later," he said abruptly, and hung up.

Dumbfounded, Lizzie held the receiver away from her ear for a moment before she placed it back in its cradle.

What the hell was that about?

***

Fort Worth police officer Pete Jenkins arrived at the testing site almost an hour early. He opted to fight back against a severe case of nerves as he waited out the extra time by sitting in his car listening to the radio.

At a quarter to ten he left his vehicle and proceeded inside to the front desk. After he signed in, the gray-haired woman behind the counter handed him a set of papers.

"Through there, then to the left," she instructed. "Give your paperwork to the man standing just inside the door. He'll tell you what to do next."

"Yes, ma'am," he replied quietly, and her face took on a more compassionate look.

She leaned forward and smiled at him. "You'll do just fine, son. Just take your time."

He smiled back and made his way down the hall with a bit more confidence than he'd had when he got out of his car.

Five minutes later he was sitting at the desk he'd been assigned, taking a deep breath and mentally preparing. Whether or not he achieved his dream of becoming a Fort Worth detective was hugely dependent on the next ninety minutes of his life.

***

He'd been surprised to realize that they weren't heading to San Angelo as expected.

Once the caravan stopped, he'd gone to the foreman's tiny trailer that served as a traveling command center for the group, where his suspicions were confirmed. Rather than make their annual loop from Lubbock to San Angelo then heading northeast up through the Dallas-Fort Worth Metroplex, the owner's nephew, who had cajoled his way into senior management, had revamped the rest of the summer and fall schedule at pretty much the last minute.

"He called me *right after* we left Lubbock. Can you believe that? I had to scramble to turn half the guys around and get them heading this direction instead. So now," Jake complained bitterly, "I get to babysit all you guys from here to Fort Stockton to freaking El Paso, *then* haul ass back east and hit San Angelo."

"And you know what else he did? He *doubled up* the number of stops in North Texas, but he shortened the stay at each one! We only get two days in each place now when it used to be four. So now, we're going to have *twice* the setup and teardown costs. Idiot. We won't even get a chance to break even at each stop before we'll have to pack up and move - and I just know he's gonna bitch at *me* about the fact that his dumbass plan is losing money. Not to mention, I only have about half of the oversize hauling permits we need, I can't keep temp labor worth a damn...".

Jake started to vent further but a violent sneezing fit interrupted.

"And I got these freakin allergies to deal with on top of everything else," the foreman grumbled.

That's it! That's *how I can test smaller doses and a longer exposure time....*

"I need to run to the store before my shift later anyway, boss. Happy to pick you up some nasal spray."

"Thanks, I'd appreciate that. I'm not gonna be able to get away long enough or I'd go get it myself."

If you weren't such a micro-managing prick, you'd find you have plenty of time to run your own errands, the foreman's captive audience thought sarcastically but did not say in reply.

With his next words Jake proved him right.

"Now get going and get your shit set up. I don't want to have to come stand over *your* shoulder, too."

"Yes, sir."

He almost skipped on his way out the door to go set up his area for the first of two nights of operations in Midland, Texas.

Need to get moving. I've got nasal spray to buy - and tamper with.

***

"Okay, read this and tell me what you think," Ben suggested, and pressed 'enter' to forward her the file.

From her desk across the aisle, Annie reviewed the copycat summary he'd built, and nodded.

"Looks good. You covered it all pretty well."

"Okay, then," he answered. "Just let me tell Nathan we're ready for his electronic report, and I'll get these sent over to Greisen."

He picked up his desk phone's receiver and dialed Nathan's extension.

"Ready to go, boss, just need the electronic version of your profile."

"On its way."

A few minutes later, Ben skimmed the email he'd built one last time before he sent it and the corresponding attachments to the Wise County Sheriff's deputy.

"And, done," he announced. "What's next?"

***

As soon as his area was set up and ready to go, he quickly retreated to his Ford and made the drive to the nearest grocery store. He entered through the automatic sliding doors, then turned left, scanning the signs hung along each aisle to find his way.

He located the pharmacy section at the far end of the building, then spent a few moments until he found the cold and allergy medications.

He studied the choices carefully. To anyone looking he might have been considering quantity or price. But what he was really interested in was the packaging.

It needs to be plastic, but not so rigid that a needle mark shows up easily…. Ah! There we go. That's even better, no needles required at all.

He picked up three packages of the nasal spray he'd selected and headed toward the front of the store.

"Got the summer sniffles, hon?" the chatty checkout clerk asked as he handed them to her to scan and bag.

"Something fierce," he replied.

"Well, this should fix you right up," she said cheerily.

"Yes, ma'am. I think this will work very well."

He took his change, nodded once at her, and left.

Once he'd returned to the privacy of his lab, he uncapped the three one-ounce bottles he'd bought from the nosy clerk. Before he emptied their contents straight into his bathroom sink, he measured the average volume of medicine dispensed with everyday use by spraying them into a calibrated measuring spoon.

He made notes of the results, ran some calculations, then mixed another, much smaller batch of his formula, this time using a variation of the liquid ingredient that would render a more medicinal smell to the finished product.

Using an eyedropper, he slowly and carefully refilled each empty bottle with his lethal concoction before replacing the screw-on lids tightly.

"Okay," he said under his breath. "Let the second round of testing begin."

He tucked the three bottles back into their boxes, bagged them up, locked his lab door, then left his motorhome to return to the site foreman's trailer.

***

"*What?*" he heard Jake snarl when he knocked on the door.

"I've got your medicine," he replied as he stepped inside and held out the bag.

"Thank God you're back, man. I haven't gone more than three minutes without sneezing since you left," Jake proclaimed as he snatched the bag away and immediately ripped into the first box.

He pulled out the bottle, shoved the tip into his left nostril, and squeezed.

"Man, that burns a little," Jake said with a grimace.

"You might have let it go too long, sir," came the answer. "If you're not better by the end of that third one you might have a sinus infection."

Jake waved him off. "I'm sure it'll be fine. I'll just make sure I use this stuff three times a day. That should knock these damn allergies out."

He kept a straight face as Jake repeated the dose in his right nostril.

"Gah," Jake mumbled. "That stings."

"Like I said, sir..."

"I know what you said. Get back to work."

"Yes, sir."

He turned and left, waiting until he'd closed the trailer door behind him before unleashing an evil grin.

Gonna be a good day today.

***

Nathan checked his watch after wrapping up the last unanswered email from the prior day.

"Ten-forty-nine.... Hmm. Not too late for one more cup of coffee," he decided, and walked to the breakroom.

He beat Lizzie to the coffeepot by mere seconds.

"I've been meaning to ask where you got that thing," Lizzie said, pointing to the oversized mug in his hand as she waited her turn for a refill.

"No idea. Bella got it for me last Christmas," he chuckled. "But I've been meaning to ask her so we can get some this size for the house."

Moments later, armed with a fresh cup of coffee, he gestured to the machine.

"All yours," he said with a grin.

"You saved me some, right?"

"Sure," he replied.

Lizzie smiled and turned her attention to refueling her own caffeine fix.

***

He bit back a smile when Jake came around at noon with a deep scowl on his face.

"Yes, sir?" he asked politely.

"Is that nose spray supposed to keep burning like this?" Jake demanded.

"Why? What do you mean?"

"Just what I said. I used it earlier. You saw me. And it stung like hell when I used it, and it's still burning some."

"Well, sir, like I said. Could be you let it go too long and now you have a sinus infection."

Jake frowned so hard that his forehead formed deep creases.

"How would somebody like *you* know that?"

He deliberately cowered a bit as cover, and replied, "Well, sir, my mama always had bad allergies, and she always said that sometimes it took a while to feel better."

"I suppose you're right," Jake finally grumbled.

"You really ought to give it a chance to work, sir. It may take all three bottles to knock that stuff out."

Jake huffed in frustration.

"Fine," he conceded, and stomped away.

He lifted his head to watch his boss's retreat.

Somebody like me? his mind raged as he clenched his fists tightly. *How dare you! Compared to me you have the mental capacity of a fire hydrant...*

He stuffed down his reaction and took a few deep breaths to calm himself, still very much aware that he was out in the open where co-workers could see him. Once his temper subsided and his head cleared, he was able to view it from a more dispassionate standpoint.

Hmmm. Will be interesting to document this little trip I'm taking him on. Curious to know just how long it takes to wipe him out completely.

In the meantime, I'm really, really going to enjoy watching his decline. And at the very end, I'll tell him it was me *that got the best of him. Won't that blow his mind?*

The thought made him chipper enough that he began to hum a little tune as he went about his work - and thought about other ways he might use his formula.

***

Lizzie had just finished sending an email when the cell phone on her hip vibrated.

When she opened her texting app, her eyebrows raised. The new text had been sent to her phone from a number that she did not recognize.

She chewed her bottom lip, then shrugged and opened the message.

Zim - call me tonight please, at this number. I need to talk to you - Jones.

She answered immediately.

You okay? And what's with the new #?

I will be once I get to Dallas. Burner phone. Long story. I'll tell you tonight.

Her brow furrowed with tension.

Roger that, she typed back.

She mulled it over for a few minutes, then stood and moved in the direction of Nathan's office.

***

"A sprayer," he blurted out loud, then glanced around quickly to make sure he hadn't been overheard.

Watch yourself. Don't draw attention.

He nodded once as an acknowledgement to the rebuke in his head.

Yeah. I don't have to pressurize the mixture after all. A hand-held sprayer should work just fine, based on my tests with Jake's nasal spray bottles. The only question is, how many of them should I use?

Why not all *of them?* came the answer in the back of his mind. *Think about it. It's gonna be too obvious if you only use the one assigned to* your *station, now, isn't it? You want to be thorough, not caught, right? Besides, don't you want a big, grand experiment? Why limit the scope of your vision to just your area?*

"Right," he decided under his breath.

The more the better. Every single sprayer we have.

He tallied up the number in his head.

Twenty-six two-gallon units that Jake keeps locked up when they aren't being used...

I'll need to make more formula - and get those keys.

***

"Hey, you have a minute?"

"Sure. What's up?" Nathan asked.

"I'm not certain," Lizzie admitted. "Jones called me earlier and said he needed to talk to me, then got off the phone abruptly. And just now, he texted me from a new number, and asked me to call him tonight. I asked if he was okay, and he said he would be when he gets down here."

"Interesting."

"I know, right? I wonder what the hell's going on. Any more word from Steve about this?"

"Nope. But I'll touch base about it here in a bit and let you know."

"One more thing," Lizzie said as she leaned forward and lowered her voice. "The new number that he used to text me. I asked him about it. He said it's a burner phone, Nathan. I don't think his being transferred is about getting rid of him, I think it's about *protecting* him. And that would explain the misdirection on the paperwork."

She sighed heavily.

"I have a very strong, very bad feeling the rookie has landed himself in deep shit somehow."

Nathan's face was grave as he processed what she'd just told him.

"Get as much information from him as you can when you talk to him tonight, Lizzie," he finally answered. "And we'll go from there."

***

Bella stretched and sighed, rolling her shoulders to try to get rid of the kinks that had formed in them from being hunched over her keyboard working on another paper for her degree program.

Three o'clock. Almost time to go get Charlie, she realized.

She stood, stretched once more, and made her way to the kitchen to check on the pot roast that she'd placed in the crock pot at seven a.m. before dropping Charlie off at the day care.

That smells so good! I'm so glad Faith shared her recipe with me. Tired of making the same old things. Wonder what our munchkin will think of it?

She rolled her eyes, then grinned.

He didn't start off being a picky eater but man, here lately if it's not chicken nuggets, macaroni and cheese, or pizza, Charlie's fussy about it. Hopefully it's just a phase.

***

It was late afternoon when a City Maintenance employee radioed in about one lone vehicle still parked where operations staff had been assigned for the duration of the company's brief stay in Lubbock.

A routine check of the Department of Motor Vehicles database revealed that the 2017 GMC was registered to a twenty-one-year-old named Toby Bryton, a native of Amarillo, Texas. Other than his vehicle, which was duly towed to the Lubbock Police Department's impound yard, no trace of Toby was found in the vicinity.

***

After Lizzie closed her front door behind her and kicked her shoes off, she reached for her cell phone and navigated through to her texting app.

"Okay, let's see what's going on," she muttered, and pressed the call button out beside the burner phone number displayed on her screen.

Jones answered on the third ring.

"Listen, I can't talk long," he began, and Lizzie was alarmed to hear he sounded out of breath.

"Jones, what the hell's going on? Why all the mystery?"

"I gotta lay low for a while, Zim. I'm flying down there tonight. I'll be landing at Meacham Airport at eleven p.m. Can you pick me up? I'll explain everything when I see you, I promise."

"Meacham, not DFW International?"

"Charter flight, Zim."

Okay... that doesn't sound ominous at all...

"Yes, I can pick you up. Do I need to come armed?"

A mirthless chuckle.

"If you like. Once I get out of Chicago things should be safer, hopefully. I'll see you tonight. And hey, one more thing."

"What's that?"

"I appreciate your help, Zim. I didn't know who else I can trust."

He hung up, and Lizzie took a deep breath, her mind racing as she replayed their brief conversation.

"Don't have much choice," she decided, and pulled her shoes back on before she grabbed her keys and headed back out to her SUV.

***

Nathan, Bella, and Charlie had just sat down to eat when the door-bell rang.

"I'll get it," Nathan offered, and moved toward the living room.

"Hi," he said, surprised to see Lizzie standing there when he opened the front door. "Is everything all right?"

"I don't think so," she confirmed, "and I didn't feel comfortable calling about it."

"Come on in. We're just sitting down to dinner. Want to join us?"

"I don't want to intrude..."

"Oh, whatever. You know you're always welcome here, Lizzie. And Bella and Charlie will both be happy to see you."

Lizzie shrugged, then smiled. "Okay, sure, thanks."

"So, what's going on?" Nathan asked as they walked side-by-side toward the kitchen.

"Talked to Jones. It was a very brief but rather alarming visit," she summarized. "I can tell you more after dinner."

Nathan nodded, then called out, "Hey babe! Lizzie's here."

CHAPTER FIVE

"Lizzie! How are you?" Bella met her at the doorway to give her a hug. "And you've got perfect timing. I just got everything to the table. Nathan, grab her a plate."

"Already on it," he called out as he closed the cupboard door and walked back across the kitchen to the four-seat table.

"Hi, Charlie," Lizzie cooed, and the toddler responded with a squeal, holding out his arms for her to pick him up from the high-chair.

"Not so fast, buddy, we're about to eat," Bella gently told her son, and he pouted.

"Izzy!"

"Yes, I know, but we need to have dinner first," his mother countered, a bit more firmly.

"'Kay," Charlie replied, still pouting.

Lizzie smiled at him and his pout was promptly replaced with a toothy grin.

***

Another wave of loud, disrespectful, obnoxious 'patrons' had him growling low in his throat.

Some children have never been disciplined a day in their selfish little lives, and it shows, he thought in disgust. *Need to be taught a lesson. Too bad my setup's not complete yet, or I'd start right this minute.*

To mollify his growing agitation with his surroundings, he focused on his calculations, stringing them through his brain like warm misty ribbons of comfort.

Let's see... fifty-two gallons... I can make that much ahead of time, but where to store it until I can get my hands on the sprayers?

He let that question simmer as he maneuvered the controls to entertain the current set of self-absorbed, arrogant brats that had invaded his work area.

As usual, when that wave left, they did so noisily, and he already knew there was zero hope of even a moment's peace and quiet before the next demanding horde descended.

Patience, he told himself as he felt the usual full-blown headache coming on. *You need just a little more patience, and then you will set it all right again.*

***

"Well, that settles it. Anytime I want to try to feed him something new, I'll make sure you're here," Bella announced to Lizzie with a wry smile thirty minutes later.

As Bella had anticipated, Charlie had at first been upset that dinner didn't consist of one of his three favorite foods. Bella had been braced for another struggle to get her child to eat.

But he'd taken one look at Lizzie enjoying her food and begun to mimic her movements. To his parents' amazement and delight, their son ate every bite that had been placed on his highchair's tray.

Lizzie was equal parts amused and confused.

"I have no idea what I did to help, but you're welcome," she answered, and chuckled as a tiny voice echoed "*welcome!*" before Charlie squealed with laughter.

"You're a miracle worker, seriously," Nathan chimed in. "If it's not pizza, chicken nuggets, or mac and cheese, he fights us on eating it."

"When did that start?"

"A few months ago," Bella confided. "And it's been a challenge. We worry he's not eating enough."

"I'm sure it will pass," Lizzie told her.

"Here's hoping," Nathan answered. "He's a terror when he's mad."

"Well, he comes by that honestly - from both sides, poor thing," Bella quipped as she wiped down a squirming Charlie's hands and face.

The moment he was freed from his chair he made a beeline for Lizzie and clambered up into her lap.

"Izzy," he said solemnly, gazing into her eyes for a moment before he threw his arms around her neck, turned his head, and laid his cheek against her chest.

"Hi there, buddy. I missed seeing you, too," she murmured to him as she patted his back.

I so love this child, she thought, and the fierce rush of protectiveness she felt made her a little misty-eyed.

***

When he had a chance to take a break, he made it a point to saunter over to the pull-behind box trailer that housed the sprayers featured in his scheme.

He looked around to make sure that no one was paying him any mind, then crouched and shined his penlight.

"Simple padlock," he murmured, and scoffed.

Stupid, really. Anyone who wanted in here badly enough would only need a set of bolt cutters...

Speaking of which...

He mentally rummaged through the inventory of tools in his possession.

Perfect. Good backup option if I can't get the keys.

He turned off his tiny light and shoved it back into his pocket before he shuffled off to grab a quick bite to eat.

***

The three adults made small talk for a bit while Lizzie held Charlie. After a while Bella glanced at the clock.

"Okay, kiddo, it's bath time," she announced.

Charlie's head popping up from its resting place like a meerkat scouting the terrain made Lizzie giggle.

"Bath? 'Bye, Izzy!" he managed as he kissed her cheek then wriggled down out of her grasp and followed his mother down the hallway and out of sight.

"That kid is an absolute delight. And I have no idea what his fascination with me is, but I love it," Lizzie told Nathan.

"He's very fond of you," Nathan agreed. "Would you like some coffee?"

"Like you have to ask me twice," she retorted with a friendly grin. "I think between the two of us we keep whoever stocks the office breakroom working overtime to make sure we don't run out."

"Ain't that the truth!" Nathan laughed. "Coming right up."

***

Once they'd settled in with two mugs, Nathan prodded, "So. Tell me about your talk with Jones."

Lizzie told him exactly what had been said, concluding with, "And I'm supposed to pick him up at eleven tonight."

"Want backup? I'm happy to ride along," Nathan immediately offered.

"You sure? That's kind of late."

The combination of a raised eyebrow with the look on Nathan's face spoke volumes.

"Not in our line of work it's not. Besides, what he said was a little troubling. I'd really rather you not go alone. And we're *both* going to have our weapons with us. Better safe than sorry."

"Okay," she conceded. "It's not even eight o'clock yet. I'm going to head home for a bit, but I will swing back by around ten-thirty and pick you up. Sound fair?"

"Works for me."

She stood and moved to the sink to rinse out her coffee mug before putting it in the dishwasher.

"Tell Bella thanks for dinner. It was really good."

"Will do," he replied as he walked her to the door. "See you in a little while."

***

Lizzie had been home only minutes when Donny called.

"How are things there?" he asked.

Should I tell him what's going on later tonight? I don't want to worry him...

"About the same, I guess," she said deliberately. "How about there?"

"I'm ready to be home," was his immediate answer.

Wow, Lizzie thought. *I can feel the tension from here.*

"You all right?"

A sigh.

"I'm just... I'm ready to get tomorrow done and get the hell out of here."

"Anything I can do to help?"

"No, babe. Just have to get through tomorrow."

They talked a few minutes more before Donny said, "I'm going to go downstairs and hit the hotel gym."

"I'm confused. I thought you were staying at Phil's house?"

"Yeah... that would be *no,*" she heard him say, and her eyebrows raised at the extra edge his tone had acquired.

Lizzie pursed her lips.

O...kay... something tells me he'll have a very interesting story to share when he gets home.

"All right. What time does your flight land?"

"A little before five o'clock. Should be home by six, hopefully."

"I love you, and I will see you when I get home from work, then."

"Love you too. I'll call before I get on the plane, okay?"

Once the call was disconnected Lizzie moved to the living room, staring at the television but not absorbing the program she'd selected. Her mind was busy going over two unusual conversations that she'd experienced in the course of under two hours.

***

At ten p.m. she gave up on the TV and turned it off. She checked that her service weapon was loaded and ready, then placed it in the holster on her hip and grabbed her keys.

"Okay then," she said aloud to no one, and locked her front door securely before strolling to her SUV to make the return trip to Nathan's place.

Because of Jones' cryptic comments, what should have been a routine pickup was sparking her cop instincts - hard. As Lizzie drove, she found herself creeping into what she always referred to as 'ready mode'; that silent grounding of feeling and clarity of thought that she'd experienced on every single warrant team she'd been on in her career.

She just prayed that the hyper-awareness she was fine-tuning with each passing moment would turn out to be unnecessary.

Lizzie pulled into Nathan Thomas' driveway at ten-twenty-seven. A brief knock on his front door was all it took. Within two minutes they were sitting in her SUV and strapping on their seat belts.

"You ready for this?" Nathan asked her, and Lizzie could hear the clipped syllables that let her know he was in 'ready mode', as well.

"I wish we had more intel," she admitted. "But yeah, I'm as ready as I can be, with so little to go on."

"Let's go pick him up and see what he can tell us."

By ten-fifty, they'd reached the tiny municipal airstrip in north Fort Worth named Meacham Airport. Lizzie shoved the SUV's transmission into park, and they settled in to wait outside the main hangar.

***

"One more hour," he muttered as he glared at more patrons drifting his way. "One. And then I can get to work."

But first, I want to go see Jake, see how he's feeling. He must've taken at least three full doses by now.

The thought brought a vile curve to his thin lips.

***

Nathan's cell phone ringing abruptly made them both jump a little.

"Thomas," he answered, and listened while whoever was on the other end spoke rapidly.

She glanced over at her boss to find him looking at her with a grim expression.

"On it," Nathan finally said. "I'll keep you informed."

"What's up?" she asked the moment he got off the phone.

"That was Steve. Your buddy Jones, along with two other new agents, was in the wrong place at the wrong time about a week ago. Long story short, they got on the wrong side of the most powerful cartel in the country," he told her. "He's not being transferred down here as an active agent, Lizzie. We're supposed to *hide* him."

In her gut, Lizzie knew the answer she was about to hear, but she felt compelled to ask the question anyway.

"What about the other two agents?"

Nathan somberly shook his head.

***

Lizzie was the first to spot him coming out the front entrance, and she stepped out of the SUV and waved to get his attention before she climbed back behind the wheel.

Jones saw her and jogged over rapidly, wrenching open the back door and tossing his duffel bag inside before climbing in and quickly closing the door.

He stopped short when he noticed Nathan sitting in the front passenger seat.

"Who's this?" he said warily as he stared Nathan down.

"Nathan Thomas, my boss. No worries, Jones, he's cool. Nathan, this is Jones, my Academy classmate."

Jones relaxed and put on his seat belt.

"Nice to meet you, Agent Thomas."

"You too, Agent Jones."

Once Lizzie got the SUV underway again Nathan looked over his left shoulder at Jones and said, "Things are a bit cloak-and-dagger here. Care to read us in?"

"When we get wherever we're going, sir, if that's all right."

Lizzie glanced at Nathan. "Where are we heading?"

"My house, for now," Nathan directed. "And we'll form a battle plan and go from there."

***

Bella came into the kitchen long enough to say hello to the new arrival, then retreated to the master bedroom. The three agents settled into Nathan's home office once they'd each grabbed a cup of coffee.

"You look exhausted," Lizzie observed.

"I am," Jones admitted with a wan smile. "Haven't slept much the last three days or so."

Nathan took a sip of coffee and set his mug down.

"Read us in," he said simply.

Jones took a deep breath.

"Well, about a week ago, me and Joey and Kevin... I mean, Agent Abes and Agent Michaelson – decided to hang out together after work. There's a nightclub in downtown Chicago that hasn't been open long, and we thought we'd go check it out."

"We got there a little after seven, and the place was already packed. There were so many people you could barely weave through the crowd to get to the bar, you know? Just, wall to wall," he revealed, and his face took on a haunted look.

He paused to take a drink.

"So anyway, we were standing at the bar trying to order, and suddenly all hell broke loose behind us. Before I even knew what was happening Abes had one guy on the ground, and Michaelson had his backup weapon pointed at two more, and suddenly a big space had opened all around us."

"I pulled my backup piece and spun around and saw this fourth guy coming up behind Abes with a knife. I had a clear shot, so I sighted in and took it. I hit the guy dead center of the chest and down he went."

"By that time people were hauling ass out of there in a panic. Cops and EMTs arrived a few minutes later. The three guys that Abes and Michaelson had detained were arrested, and they called the coroner for the one I shot."

He paused again and ran his hands over his face.

"What we found out later was that this club was ground zero for a huge turf war going on between two drug cartels. Evidently some big outfit based down in Mexico has gotten really aggressive about expanding its reach in the U.S. They've been seizing territory left and right, and the club was just inside the border where the older more established cartel's territory starts. Those four guys were with the Mexican cartel - and it turns out the guy I shot just happened to be Izan Cortinas - the cartel boss's *youngest son*."

Lizzie and Nathan exchanged pointed looks.

"On Saturday afternoon, Abes was on his way to a friend's house and was killed during an attempted carjacking. And yesterday morning, when Michaelson never showed up for his overnight shift and no one had heard from him, another agent went to check on him and found him murdered in his apartment. They're still calling that one a 'botched home invasion', for now," Jones snarled.

"Why do you think they didn't try for you as well?" Lizzie asked.

"They very well may have," he admitted, "but fortunately, I haven't been at my place in almost a week. The unit above mine had a water line break Thursday afternoon, and it ruined my apartment. I've been staying at a motel while they replace everything. Never in a million years thought I'd ever be happy about water damage."

"Tonight's actually the first time I've set foot outside the Chicago branch office since before Michaelson was found dead," he added. "I thought I was being followed on my drive in to work on Monday, and the branch Director decided to play it safe and have me just stay in the office."

"Okay, so when you called me Monday afternoon and told me you were transferring down here... what was *that* about?" Lizzie asked him.

"I had every intention of asking for a transfer down here, Lizzie. My mom's family all live in East Texas, and she just moved back down there. I just hadn't filed the official request yet. But when the Director found out about Michaelson, he read me in, then he filed the Tampa transfer papers for me instead and started working on getting me out of the area. He called in a favor from a private-sector friend of his and arranged my flight down here so I could leave and there'd be no official record with the Bureau."

"The FBI has its own aircraft, you know," Nathan pointed out. "I can understand not flying commercially, but why take a *private* plane?"

Jones sighed.

"Because the Director is concerned that someone with access to the branch's mainframe is on the take. Not able to get to me directly, but able to intercept and pass on data - such as Michaelson's address, or my flight information. That's why that fake transfer has Tampa all over it."

"*Wow*. That's... that's not good," Nathan said on a heavy exhale.

"Tell me about it," Jones muttered.

He looked from Lizzie to Nathan, then back again.

"So, what do I do now?"

"For starters, you can stay at my place," Lizzie told him. "I've got a spare bedroom that you're welcome to use as long as you need. You should be safe there."

"And we'll form a backup plan over the next day or two, just in case," Nathan added. "It's much better to have options and not need them than the other way around."

***

Once they'd left Nathan's house, Jones asked, "Can we swing through a drive-through or something? I'm starving."

"Ever had a Whataburger?" Lizzie answered.

"Not in ages," Jones said with a grin. "But that sounds perfect."

"Good. There's one on the way."

Twenty minutes later they pulled into Lizzie's driveway. Lizzie grabbed the food while Jones retrieved his duffel bag, and they walked into the house.

"Guest bedroom is the second door on the left," Lizzie indicated by pointing across the living room toward the narrow hall. "Make yourself at home while I grab a couple of plates."

***

He rapped loudly on Jake's trailer door and heard the man moaning.

Look worried, not pleased, he reminded himself, and slowly opened the door and peeked into the dimly lit trailer, revolted by the stench that assaulted his senses.

"Boss? You all right?"

"No," Jake managed in a hoarse whisper from the loveseat. "Throat really hurts."

"Did you take some more?"

"Yes. Not helping, though. I think ... the infection's .... worse. Getting ... hard to breathe," he rasped.

After just one tiny little bottle? Impressive, his assailant thought but did not vocalize.

Instead, he purposely widened his eyes in an attempt to project concerned surprise.

"Do you need me to take you to the emergency room, sir?"

Jake waved him off.

"Seriously, sir," he pressed. "If you're starting to have trouble breathing you need to get checked out."

"Help me... sit up...," Jake pleaded, holding out his hand.

Although he really didn't care to get any closer to whatever was causing that terrible smell, he entered the trailer, walked over to the man, and helped raise his victim to a sitting position, then placed pillows behind him.

"Better?"

Jake nodded. "Gonna try... to sleep... not better by morning... we'll go...okay?"

"Okay, sure. I'll be back to check on you first thing in the morning," he said, forcing the sincerity he didn't feel into his voice as he spoke.

"Night," Jake managed, and his malevolent visitor exited quickly and quietly and barely kept himself from skipping back to his motorhome like a little kid.

"Now then," he exclaimed cheerfully, "I can get started."

He'd already decided that Mason jars would be fitting vessels for stockpiling formula - after all, the beaker he'd mixed the chemicals in was made of glass, and it had withstood the concoction's corrosive properties just fine.

He paused only long enough to eat a sandwich, then suited up in his protective gear, turned the fan motor on over the vented hood, and went to work in earnest.

CHAPTER SIX

Lizzie quietly locked the front door behind her and moved to her SUV for the drive in to work.

She and Jones had stayed up until almost one a.m. before finally calling it a night. As they'd parted company in the living room, she'd told him, "I'll be going in to the office in the morning. You should be fine here, but if you need me for any reason, just text or call, all right?"

"Sure thing," he'd responded. "And thanks again for the help. I just hope all this gets resolved soon. I want my life back."

"I bet."

She'd spent another restless night tossing and turning without Donny by her side before finally getting up for good around five-thirty a.m. After a round of coffee and a hot shower she'd dressed, then paused outside the guest bedroom door. Light snoring confirmed her houseguest was sleeping peacefully, and she smiled before heading down the hallway to grab her gun, purse, and keys.

The commute was uneventful, and by six-thirty she was seated at her desk and logging into her computer.

***

He stretched his frame to its fullest extent and yawned, then clambered down out of his bunk and made a beeline for the ancient four-cup coffeepot on his extremely narrow kitchen countertop.

Late night, but totally worth it, he assured himself as he dumped the old grounds into the trash and replaced them with a fresh scoop.

Once the machine had started up, he glanced at the clock. Six-forty-three a.m.

I'll have breakfast first, then go check on Jake. Not like he's going anywhere.

The thought made him giggle, and the sound echoed eerily through the small living space.

He pivoted and moved four steps forward and one to the right to enter the cramped shower stall/toilet combination.

Sell your formula to the right people, you can pay cash for one of those monster motorhomes that actually has a decent sized shower, his brain supplied without warning.

He tilted his head, considering the possibilities as he rinsed off then dried himself and got dressed.

Sell my formula. Never thought about it. Hm. The idea has merit - except for the chance of being caught...

I've had to suppress my brilliance long enough as it is. The last thing I need is to wind up in a jail cell somewhere, the rational side of him pointed out.

True, retorted the greedy side, *but you're much too smart for that. You're still free, right? How many years has it been now? Besides, think of how well you can disappear with a wad of cash! Don't you get tired of taking a shower in a space that you can barely even turn around in?*

"Good point," he said aloud.

A chime from behind and to the left of him let him know his coffee was ready, so he tabled the internal debate for the moment as he moved back across the space to grab his favorite mug.

Four system-reviving sips later, he reluctantly set the mug down and got started on preparing his bacon and eggs.

***

"Morning. You're here early," a voice behind her said just after seven a.m.

"Yeah. Didn't sleep much. How was the rest of your night?"

"Not bad," Nathan answered with a grin. "But I figured I'd come in to the office and get some things done before everyone else shows up."

He moved to sit at the desk opposite hers.

"So," he began, "any ideas on what to do with Jones if the situation heats up?"

"I had a few possibilities that came to mind," Lizzie told him. "For starters, a couple of my dad's friends have deer leases about three hours south of here. They even have little cabins onsite. Push comes to shove I could make some calls and try to line something out. My other thought was that maybe Joe could help figure something out, too."

"I wonder if that place up in Kentucky would be available at all," Nathan thought out loud. "Problem is, with Max gone I really don't have a good point of contact to look into that possibility without having to go through official channels - and the fewer people that know what's going on, the better."

"Agreed. I meant to ask you last night, but I didn't get a chance to speak with you one-on-one," Lizzie said. "What did you think about what Jones told us?"

"That he's in a great deal of danger. I also am starting to wonder if that cartel is the same one that's stirring up so much trouble locally."

Lizzie frowned.

"What are you talking about?"

"Those Wise County cases that Ben and Annie worked on? The third victim wasn't killed by the same person as the others. Ben asked about some tattoos that victim number three had, and his point of contact with Fort Worth PD's Gang unit relayed that a cartel out of Mexico has been stirring up a lot of violence in the area recently."

"Matter of fact, now that I think about it," Nathan continued, beginning to frown as well, "I'm wondering if this isn't all interconnected somehow."

"How, exactly?" she asked. "Jones was in *Chicago*, not to mention it was a complete fluke that he and Abes and Michaelson were in the wrong place at the wrong time, Nathan. The odds would have to be astronomical that that is somehow directly related to a body dump in Boyd, Texas."

"I know it sounds farfetched. Still," Nathan's jaw tightened, "my gut feeling is that this is all gonna dovetail together - and it won't be pretty when it does."

There it is... Lizzie sighed internally even as her left eyebrow raised at the resignation in her boss's voice.

Just what I was afraid of... because Nathan Thomas' gut is never wrong.

"Anyway," he continued after a long silence, "keep thinking about a plan B for hiding Jones. And after that, let's hope we won't have to use it."

***

Once he'd plated his food, he poured himself a second cup of coffee, then sat at his dinette table.

He'd just about finished his meal when he heard a noise, faint at first, then growing stronger. Curious, he walked to the exterior door, opened it, and stood on the first step down so he could hear more clearly.

Sirens.

Hmm. Guess somebody else figured out that good ol' Jake's not doing so well lately.

He went back inside long enough to put on his shoes, then locked up his motorhome and went to investigate.

He arrived at Jake's camper just before an ambulance came into view. A very worried-looking co-worker named Ralph approached him.

"I knew he wasn't feeling well yesterday so I thought I'd check on him, and he won't wake up," Ralph babbled, clearly upset. "So, I dialed 911."

The two stepped out of the path of the EMTs approaching with a gurney.

This could be a problem. If Ralph knows Jake was having severe allergies... I need to get ahead of this.

"What do you mean, not feeling well? Did you talk to him?" he asked casually.

"Well, no," Ralph replied. "But when I saw him yesterday afternoon, it was obvious he didn't feel good."

Whew. Dodged one there, I guess. And it sounds like Jake's unconscious, so they won't get any information out of him either. I can get in there and take the other two doctored bottles and no one will ever know.

He clapped the much younger man on the shoulder.

"Somebody should follow the ambulance to the hospital," he intoned. "Can you handle that part? I'll stay here, keep the place running and try to get a hold of the big boss."

Ralph nodded enthusiastically as he pulled out his cell phone.

"What's your number so I can keep you updated?"

They traded numbers then turned to watch as a very pale, barely breathing Jake was wheeled past them on the gurney. His caregivers hustled him into the back of the rig as quickly as they could.

Once the ambulance's back doors were shut, the driver looked their direction.

"Your friend's not in good shape at all. We need to get moving. Follow us there," he directed, and Ralph gave him the thumbs-up sign.

"I'll let you know something as soon as I can," Ralph told the innocent-looking man he'd been speaking with, then turned and sprinted for his car.

He watched with carefully disguised amusement as the ambulance driver who'd climbed behind the wheel immediately turned on the lights and sirens, and as Ralph's Toyota pulled out right behind the emergency vehicle.

That went even better than I'd hoped for. Ralph finding him means zero suspicion of me...

Once they'd disappeared from view, he turned his attention to Jake's trailer.

Now then. Need to find those bottles.

And his keys.

He looked around once, then opened the door and walked inside - and immediately wrinkled his nose in disgust.

"This place stinks to high heaven," he observed aloud as his eyes watered. "And in daylight, I can see why."

Empty takeout containers covered every available flat surface in the eighteen-foot-long trailer - including one entire bench seat of the dinette table. The mildewed reek of old food combined with the acrid stench of several ashtrays crammed with ancient cigarette butts made his stomach roll.

Make this quick, he told himself.

Without any sort of bandanna to breathe through, he had to improvise. He raised his left arm and shoved his face into the crook of his elbow, then looked around quickly, trying to locate one set of keys and two tiny spray bottles in an ocean of debris.

Five minutes in, he caught a huge break and found the nasal sprays. He tucked them into his jeans pocket.

Now the keys. Lord knows where they are in this mess, he thought miserably.

A crumpled pile of clothing on the floor grabbed his attention, and he rummaged through pockets until at last he found what he sought.

It seemed to take forever to wade back through the space and get outside where he could finally take a deep - and clean - breath again.

That was so gross. I can't believe he lives like that, he thought as he walked back to his own motorhome. *Never would have guessed. His little mobile office is pristine.*

He promptly dismissed the unpleasant experience and focused instead on the next steps of his master plan.

Let's see... Yep. Should be able to have all twenty-six sprayers loaded and ready before we set up in the next town.

Speaking of which...

He diverted his route toward the locked box trailer that housed the equipment.

The sixth key he tried slid into the lock effortlessly, and he grinned as he swung the door open and picked up the first two units.

Empty. But not for long.

He closed the door, locked it, and returned to his motorhome to begin filling canisters.

***

He'd gotten four of them done and was swapping out for two more when his cell phone rang. He paused and pulled it out of his pocket.

Ralph. This ought to be entertaining.

"How are things there? How's Jake?" he asked, infusing as much fake concern into his tone as he possibly could.

"They had to put tubes down his throat to help him breathe," Ralph shared. "And they're running a bunch of tests. They don't know what's wrong with him."

And unless they know what to look for, they never will, he thought with smug satisfaction.

Ralph's next words drew his attention back to the conversation.

"They're saying we might want to call his family. Do you know any of that contact information?"

"I don't," he replied, "but I can look around in his office and I still need to call the big boss anyway. Maybe they will have it at the home office."

"You haven't called him yet? Why not?"

Oh, Ralph. Don't test me, son. You have no idea who you're messing with.

"I didn't call yet because I was waiting on an update," he explained slowly and patiently, as he would to a very small child. "Now that you've updated me, I will have more information to share. I'll call as soon as you and I are done, okay?"

"Okay," came the petulant answer. "Sorry, I'm just... this is stressful."

Not to me, it isn't.

"Everything's going to be all right, Ralph," he soothed instead of shouting in victory. "You'll see. They'll find out what is wrong with Jake and make him all better."

Cannot believe I just managed to say that out loud without cracking up.

A few more comforting words got Ralph off the call, and he grimaced as he locked up the box trailer.

"Let's go get this over with," he muttered as he strode the thirty feet to the tiny mobile office.

After playing pick-a-key again he finally found the right one and stepped up and into the space.

A quick check of the lone file cabinet and the three desk drawers yielded nothing useful, and he sighed as he dialed the number for the corporate office.

Three rings later he identified himself and said, "We have a problem down here that you need to know about, sir."

As he explained the situation, the awful feeling that he was about to be stuck with the big boss live and in person grew exponentially. As a result, it was a huge wave of relief to hear the man's brisk and businesslike response.

"We'll let his family know. I'm going to send Clint Asters down. He'll run things for the rest of the circuit."

"Yes, sir. When will he be here?"

"In the morning sometime. Think you guys can handle things for one day?"

More than you know, you pompous ass...

"Yes, sir."

He hung up the phone and laughed out loud.

"Not until tomorrow? That's *perfect*. I'll have all the sprayers switched over by then," he gloated.

He left the office, making sure to lock the door tightly, and returned to preparing the other twenty-two canisters for his biggest experiment yet.

***

While Lizzie was figuring out what she wanted to eat at lunchtime in Texas, her fiancé Donny Atherton was exiting his rental car and walking forward slowly toward the church entrance in Los Angeles, mentally preparing to say a final goodbye to Phil Tucker.

One of the best men I've ever known.

He sighed.

I'm also expected to sit beside Terri, I think. The trick will be to do it and leave as much space as possible between us without making it obvious, he thought to himself with resignation.

Damn her and Alfonse. Damn them both to hell.

He closed his eyes for just a moment and took a deep breath to center himself.

Okay. Let's do this.

It wasn't until he was inside the chapel that he realized the pallbearers were sitting together in the two front left pews, and the family would be placed in the right front section.

Thank you, Lord.

He walked to the front and paused next to Phil's casket.

"Thanks for everything, Phil," he whispered, tears coming to his eyes. "But especially for being my friend."

Then he quietly took his seat in the left front row and waited for the service to begin.

His phone vibrated gently, and he touched the screen to read the message he'd received.

I love you, honey. - Lizzie.

***

Donny's hands trembled slightly when the pastor gestured to him to approach the elevated platform. It wasn't until he was standing behind Phil's cherrywood casket that he saw the chapel had been filled to overflowing with people paying their last respects.

He cleared his throat and spoke.

"When I got the call that we'd lost Phil, I was completely shocked, as I can imagine you all were," he began, and the crowd seemed to nod their agreement in unison.

"Phil and I met when I was sixteen years old," he revealed. "It was on the ski slopes in Colorado. We talked for a while, and I could tell right away that he was someone who truly cared about the athletes he worked with. To Phil Tucker, we were never commodities, but flesh and blood people, and everything he did to help us along in our careers was with one eye also keeping a tight focus on life *after* sports for us, as well."

Murmurs of assent rippled through the room.

"For me personally, Phil became more than an agent. He was also my mentor, and a true friend. He never stopped believing in me and watching out for me, even when I'd given up on myself, and for that, I will be forever grateful."

He blinked back tears as he retook his seat.

After a pause, the pastor called for a hymn, then said the final prayer.

Once the mourners in attendance had paid their respects to Phil and to the family, Donny and the other seven pallbearers maneuvered the casket out to the waiting hearse, then climbed into the second limousine for the short drive to Phil's final resting spot.

Twenty minutes later the eight men fulfilled the last of their duties, carrying the casket to the rectangular metal platform and setting it down gently, then retreating to one end of the small, open-sided canopy where three short rows of chairs held Phil's grieving family.

The pastor said a few more unscripted words, read a Bible verse, then led one final prayer for Phil, and it was done.

Donny purposely kept his distance and let others interact with Terri first. When the crowd had thinned considerably and only a few remained, he walked over to her.

As he embraced her to put on a good show for the pastor's benefit, he softly whispered in her right ear.

"Lose my number, and don't ever contact me again."

Donny stepped back abruptly from a visibly shocked widow, took two steps to the left to shake a visibly confused pastor's hand, and strode away to the limousine for the return trip to the church without once looking back.

The moment he reached his rental car in the church's parking lot he called Lizzie.

"I'm heading to the airport now," Donny told her when she answered his call.

"You all right?"

"I will be once I see you," he answered honestly.

"Be safe. I'll see you at home."

***

He got another call from Ralph a little after three p.m.

"He's gone," the young man said simply in a wobbly voice full of shock and grief.

YES...

"What do you mean, gone?" he asked, imitating Ralph's timbre to try to convey the same feelings he was hearing through the line.

"They pronounced Jake dead about fifteen minutes ago."

"That's.... unexpected."

Only because I would have sworn it would take a little bit longer than that...

Quit gloating and focus! You're going to blow your cover!

He cleared his throat.

"Did his family make it there in time, at least?"

"Yeah," Ralph said on a shaky exhale. "Yeah. They got here right around noon."

"Well," he told his clueless co-worker, "at least they got to say goodbye."

Unlike Toby's family, who I am sure still have no idea...

He swallowed hard to choke back the tittering laugh building in his chest.

"So," Ralph sniffled, "I'm on my way back. Did you talk to the owner?"

"I did. He's sending someone down to take over starting tomorrow."

"That's good, I guess," Ralph sighed. "Hey thanks for taking care of that part."

"Not a problem. See you when you get back."

He hung up the phone and stared at it for a moment.

Let's just hope Ralph stays unaware of what really happened. He's a good kid, but if he causes any trouble, I have no problem at all moving him to the front of the line.

***

An emotionally drained Donny Atherton turned the key in the front door's lock just before six p.m.

He'd no sooner walked through and closed the door behind him when from down the hallway he heard a strong male voice call out, "Hey, Zim! Glad you're home. I'm thinking pizza for dinner, my treat."

The owner of the voice came into view, and Donny saw red when he noticed a young, built, handsome man standing in Donny and Lizzie's living room like he owned the place.

"*Who the hell are you,*" he ground out through clenched teeth, "*and why the hell are you in my house?*"

***

Lizzie smiled when she pulled into the driveway at two minutes past six and saw Donny's truck.

He's home.

A wave of happiness overtook her, and she quickly jumped out of the SUV and walked briskly toward her front door.

She'd almost reached the top step when she heard a loud thud, then a curse.

When she opened her front door and rushed inside, what she found stopped her in her tracks. Donny and Jones were engaged in an all-out brawl in the middle of her living room.

"What the hell is your problem, man? I'm a *guest* here," Jones yelled right before a crushing right cross from Donny knocked him back to the floor.

"That. Is. *ENOUGH*!" Lizzie yelled at the top of her lungs, and both men froze in place at the iciness of her tone.

Donny turned and looked at her, and she gasped at the furious jealousy on his face.

"*Who is this?*" he thundered.

CHAPTER SEVEN

Oh, hell no, baby, I know you did not *just take that tone with me...*

"Donny, calm down. This is Agent Jones," Lizzie retorted, hands on her hips, "and I'm helping hide him from some major shit that went down up in Chicago."

"Agent Jones..." Donny blinked rapidly. "The kid from the Academy?"

"Yeah," she said, moving past him to help Jones to his feet.

"Come on, both of you. Let's get to the kitchen so we can get an ice pack on that eye of his, and I can fill you in on what's been going on around here," she snarled, and shot Donny a look that very plainly said *we are so having a conversation about this later.*

***

The mid-week night shift was the usual mix of sheer boredom interspersed with waves of frenzied activity.

But nothing could dampen his spirits.

He'd gotten all twenty-six sprayers loaded and ready - and passed out every single one of them to the crew for use in their disinfecting routine.

The excitement of finally seeing a grand-scale version of his experiment about to begin had him almost dancing in place at his workstation.

There's really only one unknown in all this. If it's sprayed, then settles, is it still toxic? How would I even test that?

He strained to recall what he'd read about the specific properties of the main substance in his formula. The sound of someone clearing their throat interrupted his thoughts.

"*Excuse me*," the blond woman with the 'I'd-like-to-speak-to-your-manager' expression on her face snarled. "Is there a reason why you're just standing there daydreaming instead of collecting tickets and letting my Timmy play?"

"Just a moment, ma'am," he said as politely as he could rather than slapping her the way he wanted to. "I just need to disinfect first before I open this up. Can't have the little tykes getting sick now, can we?"

"Oh," she said haughtily. "Well, I suppose that's fine, as long as you don't take too long."

He smiled at her, picked up the canister that he knew he'd loaded with a more potent mixture, and thoroughly saturated every single square inch of his area that dragon lady's precious Timmy might come into contact with. As he did, he made sure to position himself so that he was always upwind of his activity.

The fact that Timmy and his mother happened to be standing downwind of the sprayer's contents was just an unexpected bonus.

And now, he thought, *let's use your attitude against you.*

"Okay, so, we need to let that sit for ten minutes, then he can play," he informed her.

"My child is not waiting ten minutes! He wants to play *now*. Don't you, sweetie?"

What. A. Bitch.

Any sympathy he might have had for the kid being stuck with such an overbearing parent dissipated the moment he saw that the same self-satisfied smirk the mother wore was mirrored on Timmy's pale round face.

"Ma'am, it's really best if we -"

"No, *now*."

He held her gaze only long enough to let her think she'd won, then dropped his eyes and feebly said, "Of course, ma'am, my apologies. Go right ahead, young man."

"Mommy, come play with me!" Timmy demanded, pulling hard on her hand.

"I'm sorry, it's for..." he began but trailed off at the twin death glares he received.

Perfect.

He sighed, projecting defeat, and moved out of the way so they could both enter the now extremely dangerous attraction.

And now, we wait, he thought smugly as Mrs. Walking Terror and her obnoxious offspring waded right into the middle of the killing field that he hoped like hell he'd just created.

***

"And *that's* why he's staying here for a while," Lizzie concluded. "And I have no idea at all why you thought I'd *ever* cheat on you. None, Donny. You know me way better than that by now - or at least you *should.*"

"If I can interject here for just a moment," Jones mumbled behind the bag of frozen peas held against the right side of his face, "I don't even think of Zim like that. *At all.* She's like a badass older sister to me."

Embarrassed, Donny hung his head for a moment.

"Why didn't you call and tell me about all this, so that I'd be prepared when I got here?" he asked softly.

Lizzie sighed.

"Because I could tell whatever was happening out in L.A. wasn't good, and I didn't want to add to your stress, honey."

"That's fair. And you're right. L.A. was... something else, for sure," he admitted, then extended his hand across the table toward Jones.

"I'm sorry I punched you," he offered.

Jones shook his hand.

"I'm sorry, too. You had every right to know who I am and what I'm doing here, and I shouldn't have been a smartass about it."

"So, are you two good, or am I gonna have to put you in separate corners?" Lizzie queried.

The two men looked at each other.

"We're good," they answered in unison.

"Good," she said firmly. "Now. *You*," she pointed at Donny - "order the pizza, and *you*" - she pointed at Jones - "are paying for it. I am headed to the shower."

And Lizzie Zimmerman stood up and walked out of the room, leaving two grown men sitting, rebuked, at her kitchen table.

"Nice right cross, by the way. Solid," Jones mentioned when he was sure Lizzie was out of earshot, and Donny grinned as he rubbed his left side where the kid had gotten a good hit in.

"Got a pretty mean swing yourself. Well," he continued as he stood, "guess I'd better order dinner, then go see just how far in the doghouse I am."

Jones chuckled, then moaned a little.

"Don't make me laugh, dude. It hurts my face."

***

"*Unbelievable*," Lizzie muttered under her breath as she paced the bathroom, waiting for the shower's water stream to heat up - and her temper to cool down a bit.

A soft knock at the door had her closing her eyes.

"Yes?" she said, a little sharply.

"May I come in?"

She sighed.

"Knock yourself out. But I'm still getting in the shower," she told her fiancé as he walked in and closed the door behind him.

"I'm sorry, Liz. Truly. I'm a complete ass. You've never, ever given me a reason not to trust you."

"You're right. I haven't. So, what the hell was all *that* about? What happened in California that would cause you to just disregard *every single thing you know* about me - especially how I feel about cheaters?"

Since she had a feeling the answer would not be a short and simple one, Lizzie turned off the water, then folded her arms across her chest, raised her left eyebrow, and waited.

"Well, I don't know if I ever told you this, but Phil and Terri's relationship? That's the kind of marriage I always wanted to have. They were always laughing together, supporting one another, and you could just look at them and tell they were happy."

Lizzie frowned. "Why do I feel a 'but' coming on?"

"But," Donny continued, "I landed in L.A. and called Terri's cell and it went straight to voicemail. So, I got my rental car and headed to the house - Phil and I gave each other spare keys years ago."

He leaned against the bathroom counter.

"I got to Phil's house and let myself in, and when I walked into the living room, I found Terri going at it with Alfonse."

"Who's Alfonse?"

"Phil's business partner," Donny said bitterly. "And evidently, Terri's been sleeping with him for several months at least. I called her out on it, and she just shrugged and said Phil had gotten boring."

"And *then*," Donny's eyes took on a fiery rage, "she had the nerve to ask me if I'd rather take cash, or if I wanted to join in as payment to keep quiet about it. The man that meant the world to me *wasn't even in the ground yet*, and his wife was hitting on me."

"*Wow*," Lizzie said, and thought to herself *she better hope she never comes across my path.*

"Yeah. You know that I'm not typically a violent person. But it took everything I had, and I mean *everything,* not to slap her senseless and then kick his ass. I turned around and left and found a hotel to stay in, and right after the funeral this morning I told her to stay the hell away from me and never contact me again."

He paused when Lizzie's brow furrowed in confusion.

"Wait a minute. When you called me and said you had to fly out early, that Phil's partner was causing trouble - what was all that about?"

"I have no idea," Donny said. "Once I walked in on them, asking that was the last thing on my mind. Whatever he said or did that upset her, she certainly got over it and was fine being around him, based on what I caught them doing."

"Why would you need to keep quiet about it? If Phil were alive, I could understand her trying to bribe you, but..."

"She knows just as well as I do about the adultery clause that he put in all his paperwork - including his will. Once I left his house, I called his lawyer, and he confirmed for me that Phil had already gathered solid evidence of her and Alfonso's affair and was gearing up to kick her ass out of the house. If he hadn't been killed in that car accident, he'd have filed for divorce. But as it is, she's disinherited. Everything Phil owns will get redistributed to whoever he named as his secondary beneficiaries. "

Lizzie's cop brain whirled at that last bit.

"You think they had a hand in that accident?"

"I asked that question. And no. It was quite literally an accident. Phil's car was broadsided on the driver's side by a man who had just suffered a fatal heart attack."

"Man," Lizzie murmured in sympathy. "And then after all that, you come home and there's some strange guy in our house. Okay. I understand now why you reacted the way you did. I'm still not happy that it seemed like you didn't trust me, but if our roles were reversed, I might have jumped to the same conclusion."

She moved forward and wrapped her arms around him.

"I'm glad you're home. I missed you, and I haven't slept worth a damn since you left."

"I haven't either," he chuckled, resting his cheek on her head. "Want some company in the shower?"

"That would be yes," Lizzie said, and squeezed him.

"*Ow*!"

"What?"

"Your buddy Jones landed a couple good ones. Got me right in the ribs. They're a little tender."

"Serves you right for being a distrustful jerk," she teased, then kissed him before she moved over to the shower to turn the water on again.

***

Pete Jenkins had finished his shift, clocked out, and was driving home when his cell phone chirped.

Once he pulled into his apartment complex's lot and parked, he opened and scanned the email he'd just received.

Grinning wildly, he immediately called Joe Wallace.

"I did it, Joe!" he exclaimed. "I passed my detective's exam."

"Like there was any doubt at all," came the reply. "Good work, kid. Knew you could do it."

***

When Lizzie and Donny rejoined their houseguest, he had just carried the pizzas to the table and was rummaging through the kitchen cabinets.

"What are you looking for?"

"Plates."

"Third from the left," Lizzie called out, and Jones moved his search over as she'd instructed.

"So. You two are good, right? I'd feel really awful if my being here caused a problem in your relationship," Jones began as he grabbed three plates and returned to the table.

Donny nodded his head as he took three glasses out of the cabinet next to the refrigerator and filled them with ice and tea.

"No worries. We got it sorted out. Everything's fine, and you're welcome to stay as long as you need," he told the younger man as he handed him a glass.

Jones blew out a relieved sigh.

"Thanks. I just wish like hell I knew how long it's going to take before I can get back to my life, you know?"

Donny and Lizzie took their seats at the table and smiled at each other.

"Actually," she said, "believe it or not, Donny and I both know *exactly* how that feels. Just wait until you hear what happened to us."

"We would have never even met had it not been for one particular case Lizzie and I were both involved in," Donny confirmed with a wink at his fiancée. "But I'll let her fill you in on most of it - she tells it better than I do."

***

It was almost an hour before his unwanted guests finally exited his area, exhausted and with t-shirts and shorts still slightly damp from frolicking in the chemical soup he'd sprayed everywhere.

"See? That wasn't so difficult, was it?" she snapped at him, then turned to her spoiled brat.

"Come on, sweetie, let's go get you a hot dog."

"I want a snow cone and cotton candy, too, Mom."

"Well, honey, I don't know, that's a lot of sugar, and-"

"I said I want a snow cone and cotton candy!" Timmy yelled at the top of his lungs, stamping his feet with each syllable.

"Of course, pumpkin. Whatever you want."

When they'd disappeared from sight, he casually moved his right hand toward his left wrist and pressed a button to halt the stopwatch feature on his digital timepiece.

No way to accurately measure their weights or exactly how much was absorbed... hm.... I'll have to go with best estimates.

***

"And here you two are," Jones observed when Lizzie had finished telling the story of how her and Donny met. "That has got to be one of the most unique ways to meet somebody that I've ever even *heard* of."

"Definitely not common, for sure," Donny agreed, and he and Lizzie laughed. "And I think we both might have been too afraid to try for something more if we hadn't had to go into protective custody together. That kind of ... escalated things."

"Do you think you still would have gotten together?"

Donny and Lizzie gazed at one another.

"Eventually," Donny answered. "I mean, I would have *eventually* told her how I was feeling about her. But being sequestered like that kind of took it up a notch. It became a 'do it now because anything could happen' moment."

"I absolutely agree," Lizzie chimed in. "I knew I cared about him in a more-than-friends way, but I was too scared to say anything about it, thinking I'd mess up the friendship that we'd built. Then you find out a lunatic is on the loose and you're both in danger, and, well, that tends to remove a few of those obstacles and shift priorities - or at least it did for us."

"Huh," Jones replied, and lapsed into silence for a bit.

"So, there may be some good that comes out of all this?" he finally asked.

"You never know," Lizzie told him with a shrug. "It depends on your outlook, quite frankly. You can look at this situation and say, *'man, this sucks, my life is on hold'*, or you can say *'I have a rare chance right now to stop, look around, breathe, and re-evaluate some things'*. Sometimes, it really *is* a matter of your perception."

***

The next forty-five minutes were uneventful. It wasn't until he took his break and was walking toward the employee lot that he came upon the two of them again.

Little Timmy was standing by the back bumper of a shiny white Lexus heaving his guts, with his mother patting his shoulder and saying, "Now, sweetie, I tried to tell you all that sugar wasn't a good idea."

Not looking all that hot yourself there, Mom. But then again, you're larger than he is so it may take more time for you...

Unable to resist, he sang out, "Have a great night!" and waved merrily at them as he passed.

When he got to his motorhome, he made a quick sandwich and grabbed his book to look up something while he ate. He flipped to the bookmarked page and ran his right index finger down the middle until he found the passage he was looking for.

"That's what I thought," he murmured, and started to close the book again when another paragraph got his attention.

As he read it his eyes went wide.

So standard emergency procedures will kick in and do the rest of the work for me, he realized.

Man, I feel like I just won the freaking lottery...

He finished off his sandwich, put the book back on its narrow shelf, and locked up his motorhome to get back to work with a new spring in his step.

"Thanks," he told Ralph, who had come over to cover his area so he could take his dinner break.

"No problem. You okay?"

"Fine. Why?"

Ralph shrugged. "Just checking on you."

"Are *you* okay?"

"Not really," Ralph admitted. "Thinking about Jake. Poor bastard. I really hope they're able to figure out what the hell happened to him."

Oh yeah? Well, I don't, he thought smarmily.

***

Around eleven p.m., while the man responsible for it all was closing down his station for the night, an overbearing blond woman hovered by little Timmy's bedside in the emergency room. She'd decided to seek help for him when he'd been unable to stop vomiting. By the time she'd pulled into the hospital's parking lot he was pale, limp, and unresponsive.

She sat on the left side of his gurney and refused to move, making those tending to him work around her, and she watched and waited as doctors and nurses tried to figure out what had made her only child so ill.

"What's wrong with my son? Why aren't you helping him? Could it be food poisoning?" Timmy's mother railed. "Or some sort of stomach bug? Honestly, it can't be *that* difficult to figure out."

A lab tech walked into the room, approached the on-call pediatrician leading Timmy's treatment, and said, "Doctor, a word, please?"

Without a word to Timmy's mother the physician stepped out into the hallway and the lab tech followed him.

"What is it?"

"We've got some preliminary results back. Timmy has nicotine in his system, among other things. We're still trying to identify the rest."

"Call the police and Child Protective Services," came the soft reply that belied the rage clearly evident on the pediatrician's face. "Get them up here as quickly and as quietly as possible."

"Yes, sir."

The moment he stepped back into the room Timmy's mother hurled another verbal assault his direction.

"Well? Why are you just *standing* there?" she challenged.

The doctor's eyes locked with hers.

"We're running tests," was all he would tell her.

Moments later, an alarm sounded, followed immediately by a shrieking symphony of others.

"Pulse and respirations are both dropping!" one nurse called out, and the pediatrician looked over his shoulder at the monitors.

To Timmy's helicopter parent he said, "I need you to wait outside for just a moment, please."

"I'm not leaving my child," she snapped. "And you can't *make* me."

"Fine, but stay the hell out of the way," was the snarled reply, and the man in charge of Timmy's care called out to his lead nurse.

"Nancy, get that oxygen mask off of him and get him intubated. *Now.*"

***

The last thing he did before retreating to his motorhome for the night was collect all the other sprayers that had been distributed to his co-workers.

To his delight, he noted that most of them were almost completely empty.

Good. Hopefully I got a really nice mixture of test subjects.

He carefully rinsed each one with a mixture specifically designed to neutralize all traces of his formula before he refilled each canister with its usual non-toxic disinfectant. That accomplished, he set them all back into the storage trailer and locked the door.

***

By two a.m. seven other patients ranging in age from seventeen to forty-nine appeared in the emergency room of Midland's hospital. While all had symptoms similar to Timmy's, none of them were as ill as the six-year-old.

At three-twenty-one a.m., once all measures had been exhausted, his devastated pediatrician looked at the wall clock and soberly pronounced Timmy's time of death.

Timmy's mother, who had become increasingly pale and agitated, collapsed before she could be questioned by police and case workers. She was quickly carried into the triage space adjacent to her son's so that she could be examined and treated.

Timmy's physician walked out of his young patient's triage bay dabbing at his eyes with his handkerchief. Upon hearing of the others that were being treated for symptoms eerily similar to Timmy's, he immediately said, "Run a test on each of them for nicotine."

When every result came back the same - obvious nicotine levels plus other, unidentified substances - he grabbed for the cell phone at his waist, dialed, and waited.

"This is Doctor Andrew Maunrey," he announced when his call to the local Department of Health's emergency line was answered, "and I believe we have a problem down here in Midland."

***

By seven a.m. Timmy's mother would also have to be hooked up to a ventilator to help her breathe. Before lunchtime, she too would be pronounced dead.

CHAPTER EIGHT

"Tell me again when your summer session is done?" Nathan asked as he sat down to breakfast with his wife and son.

"Three more weeks."

"And when does the next one start?"

"None of the classes I need were offered in the second summer session, so, I won't start again until September fifth."

"Is that so?"

Bella's eyes narrowed.

"What do you have up your sleeve, Agent Thomas?'

"What? Can't a guy make conversation with the love of his life? Not everything I do has an ulterior motive, you know."

Now she grinned at him.

"Nice try. What are you up to?"

"Fine. I was attempting to gauge when might be a good time to whisk you away for a romantic weekend. I was *trying* to make it a surprise."

"Oh. Then by all means, continue planning, and I promise to act surprised," she told him, and batted her eyelashes.

He laughed and leaned in for a kiss.

"I so love you. Okay, I'm headed out. See you tonight?"

"See you tonight," she replied. "And I love you too."

"Hey, little man," he told Charlie as he bent over and kissed his son on the forehead. "Have a great day today, okay?"

"Kay! 'Bye, Daddy!"

***

Clint Asters arrived onsite at seven a.m. and immediately gathered everyone together for an impromptu meeting.

"I am sure that most of you have heard about Jake by now," he began. "For those who haven't, here's the situation. He became ill sometime over the last couple of days and was found unconscious yesterday morning. He was immediately transported by ambulance to the local hospital, but unfortunately all attempts to revive him were unsuccessful, and he passed away yesterday afternoon."

"Now, I've been sent down here to oversee the rest of this year's circuit. But before we begin tearing down and loading up to get on the road, I'd like us all to observe a minute of silence for our friend and co-worker. He was a good man, and he will be missed."

Every head in the group bowed respectfully in response.

But only one was holding back a smirk the entire time.

After a minute had passed, Clint said, "Okay, gang. You know the drill. Wheels up in four hours. Let's get this thing moving."

But as the workers began to disperse, a line of eight cars - including three Midland Police Department units and a Department of Health van - came into view.

A tall, robust man with a glint in his eye and a squared jaw exited the passenger seat of the first vehicle and strode forward.

"Need to talk to whoever's in charge here," he commanded.

Asters stepped forward.

"That would be me. Hello, I'm Clint Asters. What seems to be the issue?"

"May I speak to you privately for a moment, Mr. Asters?" the visitor leading the group said.

"Of course. Right this way," Clint gestured, and they walked together toward what was once Jake's mobile command center.

Fifteen minutes later, Clint made another announcement to the crew he'd just inherited.

"All right, guys. Everybody stands down until further notice. Stop all activity. Our guests here need to do an in-depth inspection, and I expect each and every one of you to cooperate fully with them at all times. Whatever assistance they ask for, we're going to provide. And we cannot proceed with breakdown and loading up until their visit is complete."

***

Bella dropped Charlie off at the daycare at eight-thirty-two a.m. and made her way toward the University of Texas at Arlington's campus.

Although her first class of the day didn't start until ten, she'd gotten into a routine of stopping in at the student center coffee shop. Each morning she enjoyed a small latte along with a window of quiet time to clear her head and focus on the upcoming day's schedule.

And today, I really need that quiet time, she admitted to herself. *Not just to focus on school, but to try and figure out when to tell Nathan we're having another baby. The test I took this morning turned blue even more quickly than when I got pregnant with Charlie! But that explains the constant nausea for the last week.*

I wonder how far along I am... Huh. Probably ought to set up a doctor's appointment and confirm it all before I say anything to him about it.

She contemplated calling Stacy and confiding in her, then remembered that it wasn't even seven a.m. yet in California.

And she is so not a morning person either, Bella remembered with a giggle. *I'll wait and call her after class when she's good and awake.*

***

Man, I'm really glad I covered my tracks with those canisters, he thought to himself as he watched Department of Health workers swarm over the site.

But he noticed that their focus was extremely narrow, and his heart soared.

They're only taking samples from each food and beverage station. It hasn't even occurred to them to consider anything else!

Yes, his common-sense side agreed, *but it's only a matter of time before they do. Don't assume anything. When they don't find anything wrong with the consumables, they'll figure out that they need to widen the search. At that point, just switch your process back to ingestion. It's not like you can't access the food and drink stations. And you've already seen firsthand how effective swallowing it can be.*

***

As usual, morning traffic was unnecessarily bogged down at the corner of Cooper and Pioneer Parkway, one of the bigger and busier intersections near campus.

"They really need to change the timing of these lights," Bella muttered. "Only three cars get the protected left signal before it turns red again? *Seriously?*"

It took five cycles through the four-way stoplight sequence before she was at the front of the line in the outside lane of the double left-turn setup. As she waited, she sang along and tapped on her steering wheel in time to Shinedown's "Sound of Madness" playing on her radio.

When the light finally displayed the long-awaited green arrow again, Bella smiled and started forward into the intersection to make her left-hand turn, as did the car next to her on her left.

But a long, piercing wail of locked brakes and screeching tires sounded suddenly from somewhere to her right, and time seemed to slow to a crawl, then stop completely as Bella Thomas' world went pitch black.

***

It was almost nine-thirty when Lizzie realized her coffee mug was empty. She grabbed it and made a beeline for the breakroom, knowing she had to hustle to have a shot of getting in line ahead of Nathan for a caffeine fix.

"Ha! Got here first, for once," Lizzie crowed as she poured the last of the coffeepot's contents into her mug just as Nathan walked into the breakroom. "But don't worry, I'm making more. I'd hate for that massive cup of yours to stay empty - that would just be sad."

"I agree - and thank you. So, how's Jones doing?"

"Fine, except for the shiner Donny gave him."

"What?"

"You heard me."

"Yeah, and I want details," Nathan stressed, pointing at the thin trickle of coffee just beginning to move from the machine's tank to the glass pot. "It's not like we don't have time while we're waiting on that to finish working its magic."

Lizzie shared an abbreviated version of the events that led to Jones sitting at her kitchen table with frozen vegetables pressed to his face. By the time she was finished, so was the freshly brewed pot of coffee.

"But it's all straightened out now, right?" he asked her as he added creamer to his mug, then poured himself some java.

"Yeah, they made up," Lizzie grinned. "I'm glad, too, because I was about to knock their heads together."

She picked up her mug and started to leave the breakroom. Behind her she heard Nathan's cell phone ring, and him answer it.

"Thomas."

A few beats later, Lizzie heard Nathan exclaim, "I'm sorry. *What* did you just say?", and his shocked tone of disbelief caused her to whip around to look at him.

He locked eyes with Lizzie, and she watched as the color drained out of his face, then as his Christmas gift tumbled out of his hand

and shattered on the breakroom's tile floor, sending ceramic shards and scalding hot coffee everywhere.

"When?" he whispered, his voice breaking. After a few moments he murmured, "I'm on my way."

As he hung up the call, Lizzie could see he was trying his best to hold it together.

"Nathan. What's wrong?"

His eyes filled with tears.

"Bella's been in an accident. They've taken her to Harris Hospital. By helicopter," he managed.

Lizzie's mind churned.

They only transport critically injured patients by chopper... Oh, no. Please, God, no...

"I'll drive you," she said immediately. "Let me tell Ben and Annie where we're going and grab my keys. I'll be right back, Nathan, okay?"

Nathan nodded numbly as Lizzie turned and sprinted down the hall to the bullpen.

"Guys, Bella got hurt and I'm driving Nathan over to Harris to check on her," Lizzie announced as she hastily moved to her desk and grabbed her purse and keys. "Can you call Steve and let him know?"

"Sure," Annie said.

"How bad?" Ben asked.

Lizzie paused for a second.

"They used Care Flight for transport," she replied, her tone grim, and Ben and Annie both gasped.

"Oh, shit," was all Ben could get out as Annie's face crumpled into tears.

"Yeah. I've got my cell. I'll keep you updated as we find out more."

***

Within five minutes they were in Lizzie's SUV driving at breakneck speed away from downtown Dallas toward Harris Methodist Hospital, some thirty-three miles to the west.

As they drove Lizzie said, "We need to call Faith," and used her Bluetooth button on her steering wheel to do just that.

"Hey bestie!" Faith's voice rang out perkily through the SUV's speakers. "I can't talk long; I have a meeting at ten. What's up?"

"I've got Nathan with me," Lizzie answered.

"Faith," Nathan croaked in anguish. "Faith...Bella's hurt."

***

Rick Connor was looking over the day's projected shipment arrivals when Faith called him.

Bella... wreck was all Rick could make out between her loud sobs.

"You stay put, Faith. I'm coming to get you," he told her, and called out to Micah, "Watch the store!" as he raced outside.

He drove as quickly as he safely could over to her office about ten minutes away, and saw her standing in her company's parking lot waiting for him the moment he pulled in.

He got out of his truck and went to her side.

"Come on, Faith," Rick said gently as his fiancée clung to him and cried. "Let's get to the hospital and see what's going on, okay?"

He felt her nod against his chest and maneuvered her to the passenger seat.

***

By the time Lizzie and Nathan arrived at the emergency entrance to Harris Hospital, Jandy and Stacy had also been notified. Out in California, a hysterical Stacy swore she'd make the earliest possible flight to Dallas. Jandy, calmer only on the surface, had insisted on picking up Charlie from daycare.

"You need to focus on Bella right now, honey. Don't worry about Charlie. I've got that part taken care of, all right? And I'll call Sarah, too. Keep me posted, little brother. I love you," she'd told Nathan tenderly, but Lizzie could hear the raw emotion threatening to come undone behind the soothing words.

Lizzie pulled right up to the emergency room's patient drop-off zone in front of the double sliding doors so that Nathan could get inside as quickly as possible. He'd unfastened his seat belt and opened the passenger door before she'd even brought the vehicle to a complete stop.

"Go. I'll be right there," she urged, and he leapt out and ran in.

She circled around and parked in the first available space she saw, then jogged toward the entrance to catch up to him.

"Lizzie!" a voice called out, and she whirled around to see Rick and Faith walking briskly her direction. She paused and waited for them, and the trio entered as a unit.

They veered his direction when they saw Nathan at the intake desk, talking earnestly with hospital staff and a City of Arlington policeman. Nathan glanced over and saw them, stopped mid-sentence, and closed the distance to wrap his big sister up in a hug.

"She's hurt pretty bad, Faith," he managed, his voice shaky with emotion. "They took her into surgery as soon as she got here."

"I can go with you to the waiting area," the officer prompted, "and bring you all up to speed on what happened this morning."

Nathan stepped back from Faith, wiped his eyes, nodded, and motioned to the group to head toward the elevators.

The ride to the second floor was tense and silent. It wasn't until they were all seated in the surgery waiting lounge that Nathan gestured to the policeman.

"Go ahead."

"The short version is that Mrs. Thomas' SUV was broadsided by a driver who ran a red light this morning at the corner of Cooper and

Pioneer. The impact pushed her SUV into the car next to her," the officer informed them. "The driver at fault will be taken into custody once emergency personnel at Arlington Memorial clear him."

"Taken into custody?"

"Yes. We suspect he was either distracted or impaired in some way."

"He was *drunk*? At nine o'clock in the morning?" Rick's voice, usually the one in the group that was the most level and calm, was scathing, overflowing with anger.

"Toxicology will confirm," the officer replied.

The radio on his belt chirped once, and he said, "Excuse me a moment," and stepped away to respond to his dispatcher.

***

"What did the emergency room staff say about Bella?" Faith asked her brother as they waited for the officer to return.

"They didn't get much of a chance to update me. They said that she was brought in by helicopter, that her condition is critical, and that the chopper team called ahead to let the hospital know that she needed to be taken straight into surgery. But as far as specifics...," Nathan's voice trailed off as he hung his head and fought to keep his composure.

Faith slipped her hand into his and squeezed.

After a long moment of silence, Lizzie spoke.

"I'll be right back," she told Nathan. "I'm going to make a couple of calls."

"Call Steve for me, please," Nathan requested.

"Already done. I asked Ben and Annie to let home office know what's going on."

As Lizzie started to walk away, Nathan's cell phone pinged with incoming messages. He opened his texting app and scanned them.

"Charlie's with Jandy, she just picked him up and she's taking him to my house. And Stacy and Steve are both on their way here," he revealed to the group. "Stacy's plane lands at twelve-fifty and Steve's lands right around one o'clock."

"I can handle getting them here from the airport," Rick offered.

"No need for Steve. Annie just said they have him covered."

"What's Stacy's flight information?"

Nathan pulled up her message and forwarded it to Rick.

"There you go."

***

Lizzie stepped out into the hallway and dialed Donny's number.

"Hey, babe," he said.

"Hi," she replied, finally allowing the emotion she'd tamped down for Nathan's benefit to surface. "I really need you here right now."

"What's wrong? Where are you?"

"Bella's been critically injured in a wreck. They brought her to Harris Hospital via Care Flight and took her straight into surgery."

"Oh, man. How's Nathan holding up?"

"He's not," she sniffled. "And I am trying to be strong for him but seeing him like this is crushing me, Donny. He's usually so... so..."

"I get it," Donny said softly. "He's usually the rock."

"Yeah," she whispered, wiping away tears. "Anyway, I need to get back in there, but I just needed to hear your voice for a minute."

"I'm on my way, honey. I'll have Jones drop me off and take my truck back to the house. Tell Nathan I'm thinking of him and Bella both. Okay? And I'll be there shortly. I love you, Lizzie."

"I will. I love you too."

She hung up the phone and walked the short distance to the ladies' room to compose herself before she returned to support her boss and her best friend through one of the worst days of their lives.

***

By the time Lizzie rejoined the group the policeman had more news to tell them.

"The at-fault driver's tox screen came back clean," he shared. "When he was questioned at the hospital, he admitted to being in the middle of a text conversation while driving."

"I hope they throw the book at that guy," Rick growled.

"The chances of that just increased exponentially," the officer responded, "because the passenger of the car that Mrs. Thomas' SUV was pushed into was pronounced dead about fifteen minutes ago."

Nathan closed his eyes and shook his head in disbelief, clutching Faith's hand for support.

"I'll give you guys some privacy for a while, but I'll be back by later to check in," the officer said, shook Nathan's hand, and walked away.

"What now?" Faith whispered.

"Now, we wait," Nathan answered despondently.

***

Twenty minutes later Lizzie stood and walked forward to greet Donny. He held her tightly for a moment, then returned with her to where Nathan was sitting.

"Got here as soon as I could, man," he said, leaning over to give Nathan and then Faith heartfelt hugs.

By two p.m. the group's number had increased even more; Rick returned with Stacy, followed in short order by Steve, Ben, and Annie.

Stacy rushed to Nathan and pulled him into a hug.

"Any word?" she whispered, fresh tears glimmering in her eyes.

"No updates yet," he confirmed once they'd stepped apart again.

"I know you're probably not hungry, man, but you need to try to eat something," Steve told him, and Nathan nodded, then ran his hands over his face and back through his hair.

"I think there's a sandwich shop downstairs," Rick pointed out. "I'll go grab some food and bring it back."

"I'll come with you," Faith said as she took Rick's hand in hers. "I need something to keep me occupied. Text me if they come with an update before we get back?"

"I promise," Nathan replied solemnly, and Faith kissed his cheek before she left with Rick to head to the elevators.

"Want some coffee?" Lizzie offered. "There's a beverage station just down the hall."

"That'd be good, thanks," Nathan answered, and tried his best to smile but couldn't quite manage it.

"I'll be right back, then," Lizzie told him, and glanced at the rest of the group. "Would any of you like some?"

The rest of them shook their heads, and as she and Donny walked away hand-in-hand toward the coffeepot, Nathan began to tell Stacy, Steve, Ben, and Annie what had happened to Bella on her way to class.

***

It was almost three-thirty before the foreman once again summoned his workers together at the Midland site.

"Our visitors got what they needed, and they have just left," he announced. "Now, I was under the impression that we'd still be able to keep to our schedule and leave for El Paso today. But it turns out we're required to stay right here until they get some lab results back."

"So, are we gonna operate tonight, at least?" a man from the back of the group called out.

"No. At this time, we are officially barred from active operations, as well," Asters revealed. "We're closed, guys. Shut down until the Department of Health tells us otherwise. Now, we *are* allowed to break everything down and load it all up. I did get permission for us to at least do that much. But after that, we're just going to have to wait until they say it's all right for us to leave."

He gazed at the workers staring back at him.

"Any other questions?"

When no one spoke up, he nodded.

"All right then. You guys know what to do. Go ahead and get this place packed up. I'll be in the mobile office updating the owner."

***

Just before four p.m. a tall, slender, silver-haired man in scrubs entered the waiting area.

"Thomas family?"

"Over here," Nathan answered, his voice hoarse.

"I'm Dr. Mesa," the man said as he took the seat directly across from Nathan in the row of chairs facing the group. "I'm the lead orthopedic surgeon here at Harris, and I wanted to give you all an update on Bella's condition. I'm sorry you've had to wait this long, but I wanted to have the full picture before I came out to speak to you."

Nathan could only nod.

"This is going to be hard to hear, but I can't in good conscience sugarcoat this, much as I'd like to," Dr. Mesa began gently. "Bella's SUV was caught between two very severe points of impact, and she suffered a hell of a lot of damage as a result. We had to go in and find and stop some internal bleeding as well as put plates and pins in her pelvis and left leg. She also suffered a head injury."

Nathan swallowed hard.

"Is she going to be all right?"

CHAPTER NINE

Dr. Mesa sighed.

"She's stabilized for now, but still in very serious condition, Mr. Thomas. At this point, we wait, and watch, and hope for the best. We've done all we can for now. The neurologist, Dr. Adamal, thought it best to keep her in a medically induced coma for the next twenty-four to forty-eight hours, to give her body a chance to combat the swelling on her brain. As the swelling recedes, we'll lighten the medication to gradually bring her back to awareness, then run some more tests and see if and where there's any damage."

"Doctor Adamal's the best. She's in good hands, Nathan," Lizzie stated.

"I agree completely," Mesa replied.

When Nathan glanced at her with a curious expression, Lizzie explained.

"He was Dad's neurologist when my father had his stroke."

"That's good to know, thanks."

Nathan turned his attention back to Dr. Mesa.

"When can I see her?"

"We're finishing up the surgery now, and she'll be moved to the Neuro Critical Care Unit immediately. You can see her once we have her situated up there. Another forty minutes to an hour, give or take."

The surgeon paused, then leaned forward, and his already kind brown eyes took on even more empathy as he looked directly at Nathan.

"Mr. Thomas, there's one more thing you need to know about, and there's no easy way to say it. When we got her into surgery, we discovered that the injuries to her pelvis caused her to miscarry. The best estimate was that she was about five weeks along. There's a good possibility that Bella wasn't even aware of the pregnancy yet."

Nathan's face went stark white as he stammered, "My... my wife was *pregnant*?"

"I'm afraid so. I'm very sorry, Mr. Thomas. There was nothing we could do."

A moaning sob escaped a devastated Nathan as he put his hands to his face, leaned forward, and fell apart.

Dr. Mesa stood and walked toward him to rest a hand on his shoulder in a show of comfort.

"I'll send someone to get you when it's time to go see her, all right?" Mesa said softly. "And I'm so very sorry for your loss."

"Thank you for the update, Dr. Mesa," Faith said on her brother's behalf as her tears also streamed freely.

The surgeon nodded sympathetically and left the waiting room.

***

Faith rested her hand on her brother's back, patting him gently. No one spoke while Nathan composed himself.

Finally, he lifted his head.

"Steve, what do I need to do to take a leave of absence?" was his first question once he was sitting upright again.

"Don't worry about that, I've got you covered," Steve assured him. "I can run the team down here for a while if needed."

"Whatever you need us to do, boss, just let us know," Ben chimed in, and Annie nodded her agreement.

"I just - I need to check on Charlie, and I need to figure out if they're even going to let me stay here with her or not," Nathan explained, his weariness evident in both his tone and expression.

"Why don't we do this," Faith began. "Once they've let you go see her, why don't Rick and I take you and Stacy back to your house. You can line some things out over the next couple of days once you know more about Bella's condition. But in the meantime, you need rest, and no, I don't think staying up here will be an option with her in a critical care wing."

Nathan nodded, scrubbing his face again with his hands.

"My car's at work," he managed.

"We'll get it to your house," Lizzie interjected, and looked at Donny, who immediately nodded his agreement. "Matter of fact, we can do that now, if you'd like."

"I appreciate it."

Lizzie held out her hand. "Keys."

"They must be on my desk," he replied after checking his pockets produced no results.

"It's all good. We're on it," she assured him.

Meanwhile, Ben turned to Steve.

"Got a place to stay? I have a spare bedroom at my apartment. You're welcome to it."

"Thanks, I'll take you up on that."

The four FBI agents and Donny stood to take their leave.

"We're as close as the phone, Nathan," Annie told him gently, and closed the distance to give him a small hug. Lizzie followed suit, and Steve, Donny and Ben clapped him on the shoulder before the group headed to the elevator.

***

"We'll meet in the conference room tomorrow morning at eight o'clock sharp to go over anything we need to handle while he's out," Steve told the agents on the ride down to the ground floor.

"Yes, sir," they answered as a unit.

When the elevator doors opened, the five walked to Ben's car in the main hospital lot and climbed in. He drove around to the emergency room lot to drop Lizzie and Donny at Lizzie's SUV. Annie gave them a small, somber wave as she, Steve, and Ben drove away.

***

Once they were alone, the strong façade she'd maintained in front of Nathan and Faith gave way, and Lizzie let loose. She stepped into Donny's arms, laid her cheek on his chest, and began to cry. He said nothing, simply held her and stroked her hair as her body shuddered with each sob.

After a while she raised her head and moved her trembling right hand to her face to wipe her tears.

"Guess we'd better get moving, huh," she managed in a raw whisper.

"Probably. You want me to drive to your office? Might do you some good to just relax for a bit."

Lizzie nodded.

Donny saw her to the passenger seat, then climbed behind the wheel to make the thirty-three-mile drive back to the FBI's downtown Dallas location.

***

It was another half-hour before a nurse in surgical scrubs approached Nathan.

"Mr. Thomas? If you'd like to come with me, please."

"Go on," Faith said as soon as he glanced her way. "We'll wait right here for you."

He stood and said, "Call Jandy for me. Tell her what we know so far, and that I'll be home in a little while."

"Will do," Faith assured him. "Now go."

He followed the nurse out of the waiting room.

***

As they walked down the hall to the elevator, Nathan asked, "Do you happen to know what the visiting hours are for the Neuro Critical Care wing?"

"Fifteen minutes three times a day, at nine a.m., one p.m., and four p.m.," his guide replied. "You're getting to come in right now because she's just arrived in the unit. But otherwise, the guidelines are pretty strict."

"I guess there's no chance of being able to stay with her, then."

"I'm so sorry, I'm afraid not. Not until she's moved to a regular room, Mr. Thomas. But hopefully, that will happen very quickly."

The elevator whisked them to the fifth floor, and the nurse guided him to the unit's main station.

"For Bella Thomas, please," she said, and her counterpart at the terminal responded, "Room twelve."

"Right this way, Mr. Thomas. It's just ahead on the right."

They stopped just outside the door.

"I'll be right out here, and I'll take you back to the waiting room once it's time," she told him. "And I know it's hard, but please try not to worry. Your wife's in extremely good hands here."

Nathan struggled to find his voice, finally managing a rough "thank you" before he closed his eyes, took a deep breath to steady himself, and entered Bella's room.

But no amount of preparation he'd done was enough when he closed the door behind him and opened his eyes.

Her hair, always a gorgeous ebony, lay in stark contrast to both the crisp white sheets and her deathly pale complexion. Her lower left leg was free of the sheets that draped the rest of her but was so heavily bandaged that only the ends of her toes were visible.

The gentle monotonous rasp of the ventilator breathing for her sounded huge in the small still space, and the pressure of each artificially obtained breath caused her chest to rise and fall jerkily under the sheet.

As he stepped closer, he gasped without even realizing it. Across the left side of her face, from her temple to her chin, were several lacerations that had been deftly stitched up, leaving ugly bruising slashes across her delicate skin.

Nathan gently took her battered left hand in his.

"Bella. I'm here, honey. I'm right here," he began, then trailed off.

Just doesn't look right without her wedding rings on, was all he could think as a torrent of fresh tears engulfed him, and he sank to his knees by her bedside, still holding her hand, and fervently prayed for a miracle.

***

When the soft knock on the door came ten minutes later, Nathan got to his feet, then leaned over and kissed Bella's forehead tenderly.

"I love you, and I will be here with you every single moment I can, honey," he whispered.

He kissed the hand he still held before carefully setting it down at her side again, then turned and headed toward the door, wiping his tears as he went.

As he stepped out into the hallway again, he asked, "Where are her wedding rings?"

"We've got her belongings in a bag at the nurse's station," he was told. "I can get those for you on the way out."

"Yes, please," he answered as they walked back in the direction they'd come from.

Once she comes home to me and Charlie, I'm going to put her rings back on her finger where they belong, Nathan thought with determination.

He would not allow himself to even speculate about any other outcome.

***

When they arrived at the office building Donny said, "I'll wait, to make sure you can find his keys. Then I can follow you to Nathan's house."

"Works for me. See you in a bit, this shouldn't take long," Lizzie told him, and leaned over and gave him a kiss before she got out of the vehicle.

She got upstairs and immediately proceeded to Nathan's office. His keys were right where she thought they'd be - in the top right drawer of his desk.

When she shut the drawer, it jostled the desk just enough that his computer's dual monitors popped to life, and she glanced at them.

Good. He's got his system set up so that it requires his password after a certain point, she acknowledged, then froze as she saw the mouse's little arrow icon zipping around Nathan's right-hand screen of its own accord.

Without taking her eyes off the screens, she pulled her cell phone from its holster and used voice commands to place a call to Steve.

"Hey. We have an issue," Lizzie said as soon as her boss's boss picked up the call. "I'm in Nathan's office, and it sure as hell looks like someone's managed to remote in to his computer."

"I'm on my way," Steve told her.

"Roger that, I'll keep watching this."

Her next call was to Donny.

"Something's going on. I won't be downstairs for a bit."

Without waiting for confirmation, she hung up the phone, opened her camera feature, pointed it at Nathan's screens, and hit 'record'.

***

The short drive to Nathan's house was overpowered with a strained silence, each of the four wrestling with their own worrisome thoughts.

Stacy and Nathan walked side-by-side to the front door. Rick retrieved Stacy's small suitcase from the bed of the truck before he clasped Faith's hand and followed.

"Daddy!" Charlie squealed the moment the door opened and ran, giggling, to greet Nathan.

Nathan swooped him up immediately, gathering him into a tight hug.

"Hey, buddy," was all he got out before the tears threatened to start again.

"Hey, kiddo," Jandy said quietly from the doorway. "How are you holding up?"

"Oh, Jandy," Nathan answered on a sob.

She stepped forward and wrapped her arms around her little brother and nephew.

"Daddy, no cry," came a muffled command from between them.

After a moment Jandy stepped back, dabbing at her eyes.

"I know you're probably not hungry, but dinner's just about ready anyway," she said, her inner matron coming to the surface. "Come on."

***

By the time Steve arrived he'd already made contact with Mitch, the IT super guru up at FBI headquarters.

"Mitch is running interference," he told Lizzie. "He's also back-tracking to see where it's coming from."

"Good," she said. "And I've been recording this. So far, everything the hacker's tried to do has been unsuccessful."

They watched the screens as the intruder encountered roadblock after roadblock, before a message flashed that announced the unauthorized access had been terminated.

"He either gave up, or Mitch booted him," Steve said with a grin that quickly faded. "I just hope whoever our mystery guest was hung around long enough for Mitch to get a solid lead on where he is."

"Why would someone be hacking into Nathan's computer? We don't even have any active cases right now," Lizzie pointed out.

"No," Steve said thoughtfully. "But aren't both of you involved with whatever's going on with Jones?"

Lizzie's eyes went wide.

"What?"

"Steve," she gasped, "*he's staying at my house right now.*"

"Who knows about that?" he demanded.

"Me, Nathan, Donny, and now you. That's it - that I'm aware of."

She moved quickly out to her desk to check Steve's hunch and lo and behold, their unwanted visitor was attempting to access items on *her* hard drive, as well.

Steve immediately got Mitch back on the phone, who confirmed he'd already spotted - and was already dealing with - the second breach.

"Two different IP's, though," Mitch said in the brusque staccato fashion that he commonly slipped into when he was actively working on something. "Cross-correlating now. I'll let you know."

He hung up before Steve could reply.

Steve looked at Lizzie.

"We still need to take Nathan his car. And we *definitely* need to think about another place to hide Jones now, as well."

"I'll have Donny drive Nathan's car over to him," she decided. "And you and I can handle Jones. How did you get up here?"

"Ben dropped me off. I told him I'd take an Uber back to the apartment when I was done here."

"Right," she said. "Let's get moving."

When they got downstairs, she drove Nathan's car out of the employee garage and around to the front of the building where Donny was waiting.

"Change of plans, babe. Something's come up that Steve and I need to handle," she said as they met in the middle between the two vehicles. "Can you drive Nathan's car to his place?"

"Sure. Be safe, Liz. Call me later?'

"I will. One thing, honey."

"What's that?"

"Don't go home. Stay at Nathan's or go to Rick's until you hear from me."

Donny frowned.

"Something's going on concerning Jones, right?"

"Something like that. I'll fill you in later."

They traded keys, and she grabbed a fistful of his shirt and pulled him down for a big kiss.

"For luck," she said with a wink, then turned to Steve, who had just walked over with two bulletproof vests.

Lizzie quickly put hers on then said, "Ready when you are, boss."

***

He had his entire area dismantled and ready to load up in about two hours - which left him plenty of time to plot out his next moves.

He got back to his motorhome just in time to watch the local station's six o'clock newscast. At first, he just had it playing in the background, not paying much attention, while he tried to decide whether to cook something, or splurge and have a pizza delivered.

Then the station mentioned something about a breaking news story, and he smiled when the reporter mentioned several cases with mysterious symptoms surfacing at the local hospital's emergency room.

His smile morphed into a full-on belly laugh when the reporter mentioned two deaths resulting from the mysterious ailment - a woman in her mid-thirties, and her six-year-old son, whose identities were being withheld pending notification to next of kin.

I'll bet that was that dragon lady bitch and her horrible brat... what was his name... Jimmy? Tommy... Timmy. *That was it.*

I wonder just how long it will take them to realize there's nothing wrong with the food and drinks here? he asked himself during the commercial break. *I would think they'd rule that in or out as soon as possible. Is it too much to hope they'd let it go at that and start looking elsewhere besides here for answers?*

And what would be the best way to approach this going forward? The sprayed version works, no question, but it's even better in liquid form, obviously...

I've got it! The syrups. But not just the syrups. The icemakers, too. That way it doesn't matter what flavor someone gets - they'll still be exposed.

But the mixture has to be just right for the ice machines. Otherwise, it will be very obvious that it's been tampered with.

The good news is, I've probably got at least forty-eight hours to play around with it and get it optimized.

He began to whistle as he decided to indulge himself and order a pizza.

***

The sense of foreboding that suddenly filled Donny as he'd watched Lizzie and Steve drive away stayed with him all the way to Nathan's house.

He pulled Nathan's car up next to Rick's truck, then got out and knocked on the front door.

"Hey," Faith said, moving aside to let him in. "Where's Lizzie?"

"Some work-related thing came up, and she and Steve went to handle it," he replied with a shrug as they walked into the living room together.

"Hey, man," he said to Nathan as he held out the keys. "Brought your car. Here you go."

"Thanks," Nathan managed with a wan smile.

"Anything else you need me to do? Happy to help, whatever it is," Donny added.

"I know, and I appreciate it. Where's Lizzie?"

"She and Steve had to handle something."

Nathan frowned.

"What aren't you telling me?" he snapped.

"I don't know anything about it, myself," Donny countered as gently as he could, "and even if I did, I wouldn't want to burden you with it right now anyway, Nathan. You have other, more important things you're dealing with lately."

Nathan sighed. "You're right. Sorry, man. I'm just.... everything is out of my control. I feel so helpless, and I freaking *hate* it. There's nothing I can do to help the most important person in the world to me. *Nothing.*"

"That's not true," Stacy chimed in. "You can take care of yourself, and of Charlie. It won't do Bella any good at all if she sees either of you run down and worn out, and you know it."

"I know. And she'll fuss at me," Nathan agreed, then sighed and continued, "I really want her to wake up and fuss at me, Stace."

She reached over and patted his hand.

"I know you do. And she will. She's tough as hell, remember? Just... give it a day or two, like the doctor said. Let her body heal itself some, and then we'll go from there."

"You're right. In the meantime," he said, looking at his son, "who's ready for a bath and a story?"

"Me!" Charlie answered with a lopsided grin.

"Okay, buddy. Let's go."

***

When they were a block from her home, the hair on the back of Lizzie's neck began to stand on end.

"I have a very bad feeling about this," she murmured to Steve, and he glanced over at her with a face filled with worry.

"How bad? Like, 'call for backup' level bad?"

"Yes. Call for backup."

She pulled to the curb while Steve called the Fort Worth Police Department and asked for assistance.

"They're on the way, and they'll be coming in quiet," he assured her, and she nodded, reaching down to undo the snap that secured her service weapon in its holster.

"Gonna roll up to the corner," she explained quietly. "We should be able to see my front door from there."

She crept the car's wheels forward slowly until she could just see her house before she put the transmission in park.

Her front door looked like it was standing wide open, but at such a distance, she didn't know for certain.

Donny's truck was sitting in the driveway. She couldn't tell from the angle, but it looked like perhaps the driver's side door was open.

"And now, we wait," Steve said, and Lizzie frowned but nodded her agreement.

Ten minutes later, a brief flash of red and blue in the rear-view let her know that the support they'd asked for had arrived, and Steve acknowledged their presence.

"Be right back," he said, and hustled out of the passenger seat to go confer with the squad car that was closest to them.

He returned in ninety seconds with news.

"Officer Jenkins says two more units are one street over that way," he told her, and pointed past her house. "Another one coming in from right in front of us, and SWAT is onsite, too. That should cover pretty well. He's going to let us know when everyone's in place."

"*Pete* Jenkins?"

"I'm not sure, he didn't tell me his first name."

"Huh," she said, and stepped out of the car to go see for herself.

"Hey, Pete," Lizzie said in greeting. "We about ready?"

"Hi, Liz," he replied. "Almost. Another minute or so. SWAT's getting into position."

Two minutes later Pete's radio chirped once then was silent.

"That's the signal. If you're ready, I need to send two chirps back."

"Do it."

Jenkins grinned and sent the confirmation.

"Now. Let's go see who decided the party was at *my* house," Lizzie growled.

She drew her weapon from its holster. A quick check to ensure that the safety was off, and she nodded to Steve.

Go, he gestured, and she took point, weapon trained on her own property, eyes sweeping left to right and back again for any threats lurking outside as she covered the distance from her parked car to the edge of her front yard.

In her periphery she saw Officer Jenkins and a SWAT team member closing in to her left, two more officers on her right, and she knew that others would be approaching the house from the back, as well.

Lizzie veered a bit, reached Donny's truck and quickly glanced inside. No one.

Taking a deep breath, she began to work her way forward at an angle toward the front door that she now could see clearly enough to confirm had definitely been smashed in. But the overpowering smell of natural gas wafted out to her and filled her nose just before she reached the bottom step of her front porch.

"Get back! Everybody back!" Lizzie screamed, then turned to run as fast as she could toward the street.

She only made it about halfway across her lawn before the air was sucked out of her lungs and she was lifted off the ground. Her last conscious thought was one of intense panic as a searing wave of heat chased her, and then, mercifully, all was dark and quiet.

CHAPTER TEN

He'd spent twenty minutes just lounging, munching slowly on pizza and channel surfing. It came as a huge shock when he heard a polite but firm knock on his motorhome's door.

He opened it to see Clint Asters standing there.

"May I come in for a moment?" the man asked.

"Sure," he mumbled, and shuffled to one side. "Want some pizza?"

"Thanks. Nice place, by the way."

"Um, thanks," he answered nervously, then handed his unexpected guest a paper plate and gestured to the dinette table.

"Help yourself," he said, trying his best to maintain a calm and cool exterior while his mind was racing along with his heartbeat.

Why is he here?

Clint claimed two pieces of pepperoni with extra cheese, sliding them over to his plate.

"I hate to barge in on you, but I need a favor," he began. "Out of the whole crew, you're one of the most senior guys we have. You've been with us, what, twenty years, give or take?"

Has it been that long since I was forced to go into hiding? Doesn't feel like it...

"That sounds about right."

"And I know you can run just about any station here as a result," Clint continued. "I'll be honest. We're in a hell of a mess right now. The new CEO is furious that we've been shut down, and he's breathing down my neck to 'minimize his financial losses'. Money is all he cares about."

A silence fell as Clint began to eat his first piece of pizza.

Oh, man... if you only knew that this mess is one hundred percent my doing...

"I don't see how," he finally said instead.

"He wants me to lay off some of the guys," Clint explained, his face turning red with anger. "Can you imagine that? A lot of these guys have families to feed, and it's not their fault that this has happened."

Like I really give a shit about that.

He really didn't want to, but he knew that to not ask would raise suspicion, so, he stayed in character, cleared his throat, and said, "How can I help, sir?"

"I'm not sure yet," Clint admitted once he'd chewed and swallowed the last bite of the first piece. "I'm racking my brain to think of a way that does not involve reducing the number of workers on this circuit. Firing people is the absolute last resort."

He's being sincere. Nice man. Under any other circumstances, I might actually like this guy.

"Well, hopefully whatever those people were looking for, they'll have an answer soon and we can keep going," he assured his new foreman.

I'm anxious to get moving, myself. I've got a bunch of towns to experiment on....

"I hope so. And I am going to keep thinking about all this to see if I can come up with a better solution. But if I can't, I need to know that I can count on you to run more than one station at a time if necessary."

So, the worst-case scenario is we become understaffed, which gives me unfettered access to and control of more than one area? Sign me up!

"You can count on me, sir," he answered, and was very proud of himself for keeping a straight face.

Clint sighed in relief and started in on his second slice.

"I really appreciate it. And thanks for sharing your dinner with me. It's really good."

When Clint was finished, he stood and threw away his paper plate.

Play this next part up, he reminded himself, then said, "Sir, I've got Jake's keys to the box trailer. Do you want them back?'

"Why do you have them?"

"Well, sir, when he got sick, I knew somebody needed to keep things running until you could get here. So, I picked up his keys, and made sure the sanitizer units got distributed and used, then put away again."

Clint tilted his head and watched him a moment, then quietly said, "And things like that are how I know I can count on you to stand in the gap with me during all this mess. I appreciate that more than you know. Hang on to those keys a while longer, please. I'd like you to remain in charge of that equipment for the time being. I've got enough on my plate right now."

He nodded. "Yes, sir. Happy to do that."

"See you in the morning," Clint told him as he opened the door and stepped down and out into the night air.

"Yes, sir, first thing," he answered, and watched his boss walk away into the slowly fading daylight.

Truly a nice man, he thought to himself as he closed and locked the door. *It's too bad, really. Something tells me he and I are going to be at odds at some point.*

It will be a damn shame when I have to kill him.

***

Steve watched in horror as Lizzie fell hard, then bounced and skidded all the way across the two-lane strip of asphalt, finally coming to rest face-down in the neighbor's grass directly across from her now demolished home.

"Somebody get some help down here!" Steve yelled, then sprinted to check on his fallen teammate.

He knelt down as soon as he got to her side.

"Lizzie? *Lizzie!*"

She moaned as her eyelids fluttered, then opened, and she turned her head to look at him and began to try to get up.

"Oh, thank God," he muttered, then told her, "Lizzie, stay down. Don't move around. You need to get checked out."

She frowned at him, and he heard her trying to draw in a decent lungful of air.

"You got the wind knocked out of you, I'm sure. Give it a second, and don't move."

She wrinkled her nose at him.

It was then that he noticed the thin trickle of blood seeping out of her left ear.

She can't hear me, Steve realized. *The force of the blast must have damaged her eardrums.*

Stay down, he motioned with his hands, and she managed a feeble nod before she laid her scraped right cheek back down onto the soft grass.

***

Lizzie could see Steve's mouth moving, but no sound was coming out. She was confused by that, and by the fact that someone seemed to be sitting on her upper back, making it almost impossible to breathe.

Wait. What's that smell?

It smelled... charred. Melted. Burnt.

I think my house blew up her conscious self finally summarized.

She raised her head again and saw Steve miming to her to stay down by holding his hands out parallel with the ground, palms down, and moving them downward.

That's weird. Why doesn't he just say so?

But she was too busy trying to catch her breath to argue or ponder it at the moment.

Exhausted, she lowered her head again and closed her eyes, enjoying the soothing cool of well-maintained St. Augustine grass against her throbbing skin.

Really hope whoever's sitting on me moves soon so I don't suffocate...

***

Once he was more confident that Lizzie would cooperate and remain still for a moment, Steve looked over his shoulder at the ruined, burning structure. In the fire's glow he could see that at least three other people had been injured in the blast as well.

A flurry of motion caught his attention, and he grimaced when he noticed two policemen starting CPR on someone lying not far away from what had been Donny's truck.

The melodic strain of sirens sounded in the distance, faint at first, then gradually growing louder as emergency crews approached the devastation.

"Come on, guys, get here," Steve muttered through gritted teeth, and turned his attention back to the battered agent by his side.

***

At Nathan's house, Charlie had been bathed and tucked into bed. As usual, Nathan had settled in at Charlie's side with his son's favorite book, *The Three Little Pigs*.

But as he'd opened the book to begin to read, a small voice asked him, "Where's Mommy?"

"Well," Nathan began, hoping that his voice sounded stronger than he felt, "Mommy's not feeling well, buddy, so she is at the hospital, and the doctor is helping her get better."

He paused, braced for more questions, and prayed for the strength and wisdom to answer them.

But after looking at his father intently for a moment Charlie had simply said, "She be better," with supreme confidence, then snuggled close for story time.

A shaky Nathan managed to get through the story and kiss his child goodnight.

Once he'd softly closed Charlie's bedroom door behind him, he'd wiped his eyes and whispered, "I hope so, buddy. I sure hope so," before he made his way back down the hall to where everyone else had gathered.

***

The group was sitting around in the living room talking, with the big screen turned on for background noise.

"I'll have to fly back in the next day or two," Stacy was saying to Jandy. "But I can certainly come back and stay longer once she's home from the hospital."

The breaking news story that appeared on the television set abruptly stopped all conversation.

"An explosion rocked a quiet east Fort Worth neighborhood this evening, all but leveling a single-story home. Information is still trickling in at this time, but fire and emergency crews have already arrived on scene. Let's go live to Kerri Smith who is on location."

Donny's jaw dropped open with disbelief when he saw where the on-scene reporter was standing.

"That's... that's our neighborhood... Holy hell.... That's our *house*," he confirmed, and leapt to his feet.

"I'll drive you," Rick said, and they hurried toward the door.

"Wait just a minute, please," Nathan told them, and pulled out his phone and tried to call Lizzie, but there was no answer.

He switched tactics and called Steve, pressing the speaker button as he did so that everyone could hear what was said.

"Steve. What the hell's going on? Why are we looking at what's left of Lizzie's house on the news?"

"We think the cartel figured out where Jones was," his boss told him, and Nathan, already overwhelmed from the day's events, went temporarily mute with shock amidst a collective gasp from the others.

"Lizzie?" he finally managed.

"Banged up pretty good, but she'll live," Steve relayed. "And some others with relatively minor injuries. I'm amazed that more weren't hurt, given what happened. But a Fort Worth officer and a SWAT team member weren't as lucky; they're in pretty bad shape, Nathan."

"Where's Jones?"

"We *think* he was inside the house, Nathan, but we still aren't sure of anything yet."

"I'm on my way."

"Nathan, you've got-" Steve started to say, but Nathan cut him off, and spoke frankly to his boss while he locked eyes with Donny.

"Lizzie's on my team. And the whole reason she's down here and on my team is because of *me,* Steve," he said quietly. "There's not much at all I can do to help my wife right now. But this? Investigating this is something I can work on. Something I can *do*. Let me do it, Steve. *Please.*"

Steve sighed.

"You want to meet here, or back at Harris? That's where they took Lizzie."

"I'll meet you onsite. We can head to Harris after that. If you're sure Lizzie's going to be okay, that is."

"Trust me, I'm sure. Once she finally caught her breath she kept saying, *'It's a few scrapes and burns and a bump on the head, for God's sake. Get the hell away from me'* when the paramedics were trying to convince her to let them treat her. She's not only definitely conscious and moving around under her own power, but she was also cussing a blue streak, *loudly*, if that tells you anything."

Despite the circumstances the group chuckled at that bit of news.

"Actually, it does," Nathan replied. "Okay, I'm on my way."

He hung up the phone, then stood and looked at Rick and Donny.

"You two," he directed firmly, "head to Harris. Lizzie is there. Like you just heard, she's going to be fine, but they insisted on checking her out completely."

"She's my best friend. I'm going too," Faith announced, and stood to move to Rick's side.

"Okay. We'll all meet back here. Donny, if you and Lizzie need a place to stay for a while, you're welcome to come here."

"I hadn't even thought about that part yet," Lizzie's fiancé admitted. "My primary concern is that she's all right."

As Nathan put his cell phone back into his pocket, he looked at his oldest sister.

"Charlie should be down for the night," he told Jandy. "And I'll be back, I'm just not sure when."

"Go. We've got things handled here," Jandy told him as she gestured to herself and Stacy.

***

His impromptu discussion with Clint had rendered him unable to go back to mindlessly surfing channels. He was much too excited to be lazy the rest of the night as he'd originally intended.

So, he switched off his television set and suited up, then entered his makeshift lab.

After all, our down time won't last long. Might as well mix and store up as much as I can. Things will be moving too quickly later to get much done.

"Hm, let me see... Ah! *That's* what I was looking for," he said as his right hand closed around his measuring spoons.

"I think.... Yes. Let's start with cherry, that's a popular one."

***

"Oh," Faith squeaked when she, Donny, and Rick entered the triage bay where Lizzie Zimmerman was being treated.

She was sitting on the side of the bed, draped in a hospital gown, as three nurses tended to her. Two stood behind her, carefully plucking shards of glass from her shoulders and the backs of her arms, while the third applied salve to the large, raw abrasions on each thigh and knee.

The angry softball-sized lump in the middle of her forehead was dramatically underscored by cuts and scrapes all the way from her chin to her hairline, and her skin had already begun to bruise from her ordeal.

"Hi," the patient said sullenly but carefully through swollen lips, then glared over her shoulder at the nurse working on her right arm.

"Ouch! You keep pinching me with those tweezers, and I swear..."

Donny stepped forward in an effort to both soothe and distract her.

"Looks like you had a long night, baby. What happened?"

"She can't hear you very well," the nurse applying salve revealed. "The blast ruptured both eardrums. She said a while ago that what little she *can* make out is very muffled, like she's deep underwater. You'll do better writing things down for her for the next week, at least."

Faith pulled a pen and small notepad out of her purse and wrote *What happened?* then showed it to Lizzie.

"Some jackass blew up our house, that's what happened," Lizzie snarled, then winced at the pain it caused. "Steve said I was thrown thirty feet, give or take. Damn good thing I had my vest on. Check it out."

She pointed to a corner of the room where her tattered clothes had been thrown.

Donny carefully picked up her bulletproof vest and held it high enough for all three of them to get a good look.

Several huge, sharp wedges of window glass were sticking out of the back of it like lethal spikes.

"Holy *crap*," Rick exclaimed, his eyes wide.

"Yeah," Lizzie quipped when she saw their stunned expressions. "If I hadn't had the vest on those things would have impaled me."

"She's going to need clothes," Faith pointed out as she glanced at the ruined shirt and pants lying in tatters beside the vest. "I'll bring her some of mine. We wear the same sizes."

I'm gonna run to my house and get some clothes for you, she scribbled, and Lizzie nodded.

"That's why I love you, Faith," she said, then gingerly poked her tongue out to touch the throbbing left corner of her mouth. "*Man*, I hurt all over... I didn't lose any teeth, did I?"

She tried her best to smile so they could see, and her relief was evident in her eyes when they all shook their heads no.

"Well, there's that, at least," Lizzie muttered, then frowned. "I need more aspirin. The first three haven't even put a dent in this headache."

"With a knot that big, I'm not surprised," Faith told the men as an aside. "It looks really painful."

"Donny, see if they will give you any updates on the others," Lizzie urged. "I know Pete Jenkins got hurt, and a SWAT guy. I saw both of them get loaded into ambulances. But I don't know what their status is, and I'm worried about them. And Jones. I don't know if Jones was there, or not."

"Tell her that I will see what I can find out," he replied, and Faith dutifully wrote, *he says he's on it* and showed it to her.

Lizzie gave a small thumbs-up.

"We'll be right back," Faith told Donny as she handed over the notepad and pen.

Donny held up a finger, then pointed out the door, and Lizzie nodded her understanding.

The three walked out and back toward the nurses' station.

"I don't know that they'll update me about any of the others, since I'm not related to them or on the job," Donny lamented. "I'll try. But Steve and Nathan may be the only ones that they share information with."

"I'll text Nathan and point that out," Faith answered.

***

Nathan couldn't find Steve at first. The scene was awash with firemen, members of the bomb squad, and policemen who'd set up a barricade to keep nosy neighbors and camera crews back at a safe distance.

He finally spotted his boss over to one side talking with the SWAT team leader and flashed his badge to be let through.

As he walked, his phone chirped. He plucked it from his pocket and read Faith's message.

Lizzie is beat up - one hell of a goose egg and can't hear anything - but she's awake and alert. And worried. She wants to know how the others are that were injured but we don't think they will tell us anything. You or Steve might have better luck with that.

I will make it a point to get more information on them when I get there, he typed back and hit 'send'.

"Steve," he called out as he put his phone away and closed the gap to where his supervisor stood. "What happened?"

"The short story is, all hell broke loose," came the wry answer. "We were about a block out when Lizzie's gut kicked in. We pulled over, called for backup, and then approached once they got here. It was obvious that her front door had been kicked in, but we never got a chance to go in and look for Jones. Lizzie was closest. Somehow, she knew something was wrong, and yelled out a warning to the rest of us to back up, then everybody started to run and the whole damn thing went up in a big fireball."

"How many were hurt?"

"Besides your agent? Five. Three of mine, and two patrolmen," the SWAT team leader replied softly with worry darkening his gray eyes. "The EMT's said one of my guys is critical. And so is Jenkins."

Nathan paled. "Pete Jenkins?"

Steve and the team leader both nodded soberly.

"Oh man. I know him," Nathan stammered, and ran a hand over his face.

Steve pivoted to acknowledge a firefighter that had walked over.

"Gas company shut off the flow twenty minutes ago. We've got the rest of the flames out now, but it's still too hot to go poking around in there," the newcomer said. "Not safe yet. We need to wait before we take a closer look."

"How long, you think?" Nathan asked.

"An hour, at least."

The two federal agents looked at each other.

"Change of plans, Steve," Nathan announced. "I think we should go check on everyone that was hurt. We can come back here afterward."

"I'll ride with you. I'd follow you over there, but I didn't think to get Lizzie's keys from her before the ambulance took off," Steve explained.

"I'll see you guys up there. I need to go talk to the rest of my team for a minute," the SWAT commander said before he walked away.

"We'll have lights set up when you guys get back. It's going to be a long night," the fireman told them, and left to return to his work.

***

At Rick's suggestion, she'd grabbed a pair of his sweatpants with a drawstring at the waist, and an oversized t-shirt from his side of their closet.

"Lizzie's not going to be able to wear anything form fitting that will rub up against those abrasions," he'd pointed out. "Loose clothes will be much more comfortable."

"I just can't believe this," Faith murmured as they climbed into Rick's truck to make the run back to the hospital. "First Bella. Now Lizzie. It's unreal. Like a really bad dream."

Rick reached over and took her hand.

"I'm feeling the same way," he admitted. "I keep expecting someone to jump out with a video camera and yell 'gotcha', or something. We just need to stay positive and trust that they're both going to be okay, honey."

She squeezed his hand but didn't reply, simply stared out the passenger window.

***

Meanwhile, Nathan and Steve had arrived at the hospital's emergency room and proceeded immediately to the intake desk. The waiting room was filled almost to overflowing with both on and off-duty police officers that had heard about or were present for the disaster and had come to support their injured teammates.

Nathan presented his badge and ID and said, "We're here to check on all of the law enforcement officers injured from tonight's house explosion."

The nurse checked his credentials, then nodded.

"We've got six casualties total that were brought in, and all of them are being treated by different physicians, Agent Thomas," she revealed. "Let me see if I can find Dr. Manning for you. He's the head of emergency medicine, and he should be able to tell you about each patient's condition. If you could have a seat in the room just to the right over there, please. It will be just a moment."

"Yes, ma'am. Thank you."

They turned and navigated through a sea of varying uniforms to enter the tiny auxiliary room that she'd spoken of, settling into the last two available chairs to wait.

Ten minutes passed, and a frazzled looking brown-haired, brown-eyed man in his late fifties opened the door and poked his head in.

"Agent Thomas?" he queried to the room, and Nathan and Steve stood and walked out into the hall to meet him.

"I'm Doctor Manning," he said briskly as he shook each of their hands. "If you'll follow me, please. We can talk in my office. There's quite a bit to go over."

Once they'd taken their seats in his visitors' chairs, Dr. Manning wasted no time at all.

"We had six patients brought in this evening," he began. "Agent Zimmerman has multiple lacerations and abrasions, a severe concussion, and ruptured eardrums. She'll need to be watched carefully over the next few days due to that concussion, but we expect a full recovery. She should regain her hearing within the next few weeks. Three others were brought in with injuries similar to Agent Zimmerman's, and I expect that they too will fully recover."

He took a deep breath, then continued.

"The last two patients that were brought to us had life-threatening injuries. I'm very sorry to have to tell you that one of them, a member of Fort Worth's tactical unit, died in surgery about twenty minutes ago."

There was a moment of silence for the fallen man.

"The other, Officer Jenkins, is still in surgery as we speak. Among other things, he's suffered an injury to his spinal cord, and I'm afraid there's no way to know yet whether he will fully recover or not."

"Meaning?" Nathan asked, hoping that his interpretation of the man's statement was wrong.

Dr. Manning gently cleared his throat, and the empathy showed in his eyes when he clarified his answer.

"Even if he survives this, he may never walk again, Agent Thomas. There's just no way to know for sure at this time."

CHAPTER ELEVEN

Nathan nodded his understanding but kept silent for just a few moments longer while he regained his composure. When he felt more in control of himself, he spoke.

"If you'd please keep me posted on Officer Jenkins' condition, I'd appreciate it," he told the physician, and handed him a business card as he and Steve rose to take their leave. "And I'd like to go see how Agent Zimmerman is doing now, if that's all right."

"I will, absolutely," Manning responded. "And by all means, go ahead. She's being looked after in triage bay fourteen, I believe. Go back down the hall to the waiting room, then go through the double doors. After that, turn left, and it should be the fifth doorway to the right."

The two agents thanked him for his time and left in search of Lizzie. On their way to find her, they saw the SWAT commander in the waiting room.

From the devastated look on the man's face, Nathan knew he'd just been told that someone he'd been responsible for had died in the line of duty.

I hope I never have to know what that feels like, Nathan thought to himself as he and Steve quietly offered their condolences, then walked to the room where Lizzie was being treated for her wounds.

***

"Hi," Donny called out from Lizzie's side, then patted her hand and pointed.

"Hey boss," Lizzie managed when Nathan and Steve appeared in front of her.

Nathan winced as he took in all the damage she'd suffered.

"I look that bad, huh?" she asked, and he nodded.

"Good news is, you should make a full recovery," he told her, then mirrored the frown that appeared on her face.

"She can't hear very well," Steve chimed in. "Ruptured eardrums, remember?"

Nathan pulled his cell phone and held it up with a questioning look.

"I'm not sure where mine is," she answered. "Check my pockets, I guess?"

She pointed to the remnants of clothing.

Nathan hissed in a breath when he saw the glass impaled in her vest.

"Dodged one there, didn't she?" he murmured to Steve.

"She really did."

Donny found her phone and handed it to her.

"Man," Lizzie exclaimed as she looked it over. "I'm really glad now I shelled out two hundred bucks for this hardcover case. This thing is barely even scratched. I'm impressed. Maybe I could write them an endorsement. You know. *'It's even blast-proof'*, or something."

She only missed seeing Donny's eye roll because she was looking down as she spoke. She pressed the button on the side to bring up the phone's home screen, then looked at Nathan.

Okay, this is how we'll communicate for the next couple of weeks since your hearing is shot, he texted her.

She read it, nodded, then asked, "Any word on Pete and the others?"

The fire marshal hasn't cleared the scene for us to get in there yet, so we still don't know if Jones was in your house or not. Five others hurt besides you. Three have minor injuries like yours. Pete Jenkins is still in surgery. The tactical unit member didn't make it.

Lizzie's hazel eyes flashed with grief for the fallen officer before she asked, "And? I get the feeling you're not telling me something. What is it?"

Nathan glanced at Steve, who shrugged and softly said, "She deserves to know."

Taking a deep breath, Nathan typed, *Pete has a spinal cord injury, Lizzie. If he survives this, he could be paralyzed. It's just too soon to know for sure.*

Reluctantly, he hit 'send', then watched and waited for her reaction.

The stifled sob that wrenched from his usually tough-as-nails teammate and friend broke his heart.

***

Not long afterward, the emergency room physician that been assigned to treat Lizzie entered the room.

"Okay, so," he began. "Not much we can do for her hearing. That should heal itself in the next couple of weeks. If it hasn't returned by then, we'll follow up. The scrapes and cuts will take time, as well. But because she's got a severe concussion, I'd like to keep her here overnight."

Donny relayed the doctor's comments via text, and she shook her head violently, then grimaced in pain.

"Nope, I've had a concussion before. No big. We can deal with that at home," Lizzie told her visitors, glaring in defiance at each of them in turn.

"I really think she should stay here, but I can't make her. She has every right to sign herself out," the doctor muttered, and Donny gave him an apologetic look.

"I'll look after her. I've had a concussion or two myself, so I know what to watch for."

The ER physician nodded. "Very well. I'm going to write out some prescriptions. One for pain, and the other for an ointment that she'll need to use on those abrasions. The nurse will be in shortly with them and her discharge paperwork."

He gave Lizzie the thumbs-up sign, turned on his heel, and left to go check on his next patient.

"Speaking of 'home', we need to figure out where we're going to stay," Donny said aloud to the group and via text to his fiancée.

"I don't suppose any of our clothes made it through the blast," Lizzie said with a sigh, looking from Donny to Steve to Nathan and back again.

No idea yet, Donny told her via message. *But I can go and see and load up anything that's still usable in my truck.*

"Um... yeah... no point to that, honey. I think your truck might be totaled," she told him when she looked up from her screen. "Right, Steve?"

He nodded his confirmation, then told Donny, "Sorry, buddy, but your home's hot water heater bounced off the front of the hood before it crushed the cab."

"Donny, my offer still stands," Nathan chimed in. "We have four bedrooms at my house. You and Lizzie can come stay with us as long as you need."

Donny passed along the offer to Lizzie, who glanced at Nathan.

"You sure? You've got quite a lot on your plate already," she told her boss.

Nathan smiled and nodded.

"Yes, I do. But I'd feel better if you guys stayed at the house. Please," he answered, and Donny relayed via messaging.

"Okay, then," Lizzie said quietly. "Thank you."

The conversation was interrupted by Faith walking into the room with a bag in her hand.

I brought you sweats and a t-shirt. Loose and comfortable, she scribbled on her notepad then showed her best friend.

***

Donny traveled back to the remains of Lizzie's house with Nathan and Steve. The moment he got close enough to see the destruction, he shook his head.

"We're going to assume nothing's left, except possibly what I had stored in my fireproof file cabinet," he told the two agents. "Whatever didn't get blown up or burnt up will have so much water damage that it's a complete loss."

"Sorry, man," Nathan said.

"Don't be. It was just stuff. I have Lizzie, and she's going to be all right. None of the rest of it matters at all," came the sincere reply. "See you back at your place."

And with that, Donny walked away to drive Lizzie's car back to the hospital to pick her up.

***

Nathan and Steve stood at the curb surveying the blast scene now bathed in bright lights.

"Ready?" the officer holding the recovery dog's leash asked.

"Yep," Nathan answered. "Let's get started."

The young man detached the leash from the gorgeous three-year-old brown Labrador's collar, then called out, "Molly, go find!"

Not even four minutes later she whined, sat, and looked over her shoulder at her trainer.

"Good girl, Molly! Good girl," her trainer crooned, then told the agents, "Molly's usually accurate to within eight inches. I'll put a flag there, and then have her keep searching."

Another twenty minutes passed but Molly found no other areas of interest. Her handler called her back and she bounded gaily to his side for a pat on the head and a treat before being loaded back into his car.

"Okay," Nathan murmured. "Let's see who's down there."

***

A single body, that of a male, was uncovered almost an hour and twenty minutes after the miniature crane was maneuvered onsite and hooked up to the first oversized piece of roof. From the body's position and the debris that had landed over and around it, investigators theorized the individual was in the center of the living room when the house exploded.

The crime scene techs immediately came forward to take detailed pictures and measurements before anyone touched the body. Once that was done, Dr. Broder squatted down and examined the dead man.

"Agent Thomas," the seasoned coroner called out. "Come take a look at this."

Nathan closed his eyes for a moment, forcibly expelling flashback scenes of the hospital bombing from his mind. He took a deep breath and willed his stomach to cooperate, then carefully picked his way through the broken landscape to close the distance.

"See that?" Broder pointed at the inside of the man's left wrist, which was pristine. "Looks like all the damage to him from the blast is on his back. We need to turn him over."

Nathan took three steps back as an assistant helped the coroner gently turn the body so that it lay face-up.

"Yep, check this out. Almost no marks at all, on him *or* the floor underneath him. This man was lying face-down right here when this place went up in flames. I'd bet money he was already dead."

"And that," Broder continued as he indicated the jagged wound on the side of the man's throat, "would be your cause of death."

Nathan stared intently at the dead man's face before he raised his eyes to meet the coroner's gaze.

"I need to know who this is as quickly as possible, Dr. Broder," he said quietly but firmly. "Because this is *not* Agent Jones."

***

He wasn't ready to stop mixing formula but realized he had no choice.

Dammit. I knew I should have bought another case of jars, the frustrated mad chemist grumbled to himself as he reluctantly stopped his production line for the night.

I'll go first thing in the morning and get more. Might as well pick up some other things too. It wouldn't do to get on the road again and run out of something at the wrong time.

He locked the lab door tightly before he climbed up into his bunk to get some sleep.

***

An exhausted Nathan Thomas pulled into his driveway a little after one in the morning. He'd offered Steve a ride back to Ben's place, but his boss had taken one hard look at him, then crossed his arms and shook his head.

"I'll find my way back to Ben's. You go home and get some sleep," Steve had replied.

"But-"

"Nathan," Steve said gently, "don't make me make this an official order instead of a polite request."

"Yes, sir. I'll talk to you tomorrow."

Nathan let himself into his house as quietly as he could, then jumped when a sleepy voice said, "Glad you're home safely."

"Jandy? What are you doing on the couch?"

"Stacy's in one room, Donny and Lizzie are in the other," she explained with a yawn. "Lizzie looks like hell, by the way. But it could have been a lot worse. She got lucky."

"Yes, she did. I feel bad you're sleeping on my couch, sis. Take my room. I don't know how much rest I'm going to get tonight anyway."

"Nope," was her firm response. "I'm fine right where I am, kiddo. Go try to get some sleep, Nathan. You need it."

"Yes, ma'am," he said with a chuckle and leaned down to kiss her cheek. "Love you."

"And I love you, baby brother."

He smiled at her before he made his way down the hall to Charlie's room, where he tiptoed in to kiss the child softly on the forehead, then continued to his and Bella's bedroom.

He wearily removed his clothes and set his alarm for seven a.m.

That will give me enough time to shower and get ready to go see Bella at nine, he thought, and lay back on the mattress.

Sleep took him mere moments later, but with it came no rest. Almost immediately his subconscious began to replay every single horrible image burned into his memory from the Phoenix scene.

***

Although the guest bedroom at Nathan's house featured a large and soft queen-sized bed, Lizzie Zimmerman could not get comfortable. Every single part of her body ached, even the ones that had been spared direct contact with the deceptively smooth-looking ribbon of asphalt in front of her property.

Beside her, Donny slept so soundly that he snored, totally oblivious.

So jealous of that right now, she thought as she felt each vibration of his sonorous breathing. *But I have to admit, I don't miss hearing it at all...*

That made her giggle a little, and she lightly put her hand over her swollen and bruised mouth so she wouldn't wake him as she lifted her head and looked past him at the clock.

Four-fifty-one.

Well, this is useless. Might as well get up.

She gently worked her battered legs over to the edge of the bed and sat up, pausing for a moment to let the silent scream of pain in her head work its way to completion before she attempted further movement.

I could really use a hot shower right now, Lizzie thought wistfully. *Too bad that's not possible.*

Coffee. I can still have coffee, at least. Thank God. I'll just have to sip it carefully.

She stood, leg muscles trembling in protest, and carefully shuffled into the bathroom to attend to other pressing matters first.

***

When he'd violently thrashed himself to wakefulness for the third time, Nathan muttered under his breath, scrubbed his hands over his face, and got out of bed, glancing over at the clock that seemed to mock him from the nightstand.

Five-twenty a.m.

Great.

He was almost to his bedroom door when he remembered that his oldest sister was camped out in his living room. Then he remembered that Stacy, Lizzie and Donny were *also* in his house.

That realization caused Nathan to detour over to the dresser, where he pulled pajama pants on over his briefs and added a t-shirt for good measure before he headed to the kitchen for some water.

He was surprised to see Lizzie sitting at the kitchen table staring morosely into a mug of coffee.

"Can't sleep either, huh?" she said as a greeting.

Nathan grabbed a bottle of water, rummaged for a notepad and pen in the junk drawer, then joined her at the table.

Nope. How are you feeling?

She chuckled, then winced.

"Like I was picked up and thrown thirty feet and landed on my face. You?"

Pretty much the mental version of what you just said, to be honest. Hey, aren't you supposed to avoid caffeine the first forty-eight hours after a concussion?

Lizzie wrapped her hands protectively around her mug and growled low in her throat at her boss.

He held up his hands in surrender.

All right, all right. Just, go easy on it.

She glanced at him and saw the pensive look.

"Nathan, what's on your mind?"

We found a body at your house, Liz. But it wasn't Jones.

Her brow furrowed as much as it was able to, given the huge knot still featured prominently in the center.

"It wasn't? Are you sure?"

I'm positive. And your mystery guest didn't die in the explosion, either. He took some sort of stab wound to the throat and was left lying on your living room floor.

"But how did they even know Jones was at my house? And where is he now?"

Million-dollar questions, Nathan wrote, then uncapped his bottle and took a long drink.

"Wherever he is, I hope like hell he's okay - and that he's got his burner phone with him," Lizzie said thoughtfully, her voice tinged with worry. "I'll send a text. Maybe we'll get lucky, and he will answer. I don't know what else to do."

Nathan's next response made her frown.

To be honest, Lizzie, I'm not sure, either.

***

By six a.m. Jandy and Donny had joined them in the kitchen. They took turns at the coffeepot.

"Is Lizzie all right?" Donny asked as he approached the table with his mug. "I didn't hear her get up."

Nathan watched with amusement as the tall blond man started to put his hand on his fiancée's shoulder, then hesitated.

"What's so funny?" Lizzie said when she noticed the twinkle of humor in Nathan's eyes.

He's not sure where to touch you since you're so banged up, Nathan wrote and showed her.

"Oh. Well, the backs of my legs and wherever the vest covered isn't all skinned up, if that helps," she told Donny, and he nodded, sat down next to her and lovingly caressed the middle of her back.

"Should she be having coffee? I thought with a concussion that caffeine and alcohol are no-go items for the first couple of days," Jandy pointed out as she pulled bacon and eggs out of the refrigerator.

"I've already mentioned it - and I got growled at," Nathan revealed, and Jandy and Donny both laughed.

"All right then. Guess we won't bring it up again," Donny quipped.

"I think that's smart. So, what do you two have planned today?'

"Well," Donny said, "no matter what ideas *she* might have to the contrary, I'm going to convince Lizzie that it's best that she stays here to rest and relax. I'm meeting the claims adjustor over at the house at eight-thirty to confirm what I already know - that it's a complete loss. After that, I need to go buy some things. All we own now is her car and whatever's in my wallet and her purse."

Lizzie tapped him on the shoulder, and when he turned his head, she told him, "I get a feeling you're talking about me. What did you just say?"

Oh, this ought to be good, Nathan thought with an ill-concealed grin as he scooted the notepad and pen over to Donny.

"There you go, dude. I'm not about to tell her what you just said about her staying put. You know she's going to fight you on that."

Donny sighed as he picked up the pen. "I know."

The lightning that flashed in Lizzie's eyes when she read what he'd written - *you are staying here today while I go handle some things* - made Nathan back his chair away from the table.

"I'm just gonna go get cleaned up," he murmured, and quickly left the room while Donny and Lizzie continued their half-silent, half-spoken conversation.

***

Nathan moved to his closet, selecting jeans and a t-shirt before grabbing socks and underwear and setting it all down on the top of his dresser. Then he entered the bathroom. It wasn't until after he'd turned on the showerhead then headed over to the double-sink vanity that he saw it - Bella's positive pregnancy test lying on the corner of the counter next to her hairbrush.

Oh, God. She knew.

Nathan Thomas numbly stripped down and stood under the shower's spray, head hanging down as the tears he thought he had run out of mingled with the water.

***

Twenty minutes later Stacy, still stretching and yawning, padded in to the kitchen in her pajamas and robe and paused to sniff the air.

"Bacon," she sighed. "That smells so good."

"Biscuits are just about ready to come out of the oven," Jandy announced, then glanced at a subdued Nathan who'd just rejoined them.

"Nathan, by the time you get Charlie in his chair we'll be ready to eat."

"On it," he said mechanically, and went to get his child.

Jandy raised an eyebrow and looked at the others. But everyone's faces held the same puzzled look. She shrugged and turned her attention back to the skillet of scrambled eggs on the stove as conversation resumed.

The growing buzz of activity as the breakfast items were brought to the kitchen table was interrupted by a loud shriek of shock.

"Oh no! Izzy!" Charlie exclaimed, huge tears welling up in his big brown eyes and rolling down his chubby cheeks. "Daddy! Izzy *hurt*!"

He wriggled out of his father's arms and made a beeline for Lizzie.

Although she couldn't hear his cry of distress, there was no way Lizzie could miss the stark worry in the little boy's face as he walked toward her.

"Hey, sweetie. I'm okay, I promise. Just a little banged up," she told him as she leaned down to be able to talk to him face-to-face.

Charlie slowly and carefully placed his hands lightly at her temples, then stood on tiptoe and very gently kissed the knot in the middle of her forehead.

"All better," he said matter-of-factly with a solemn and knowing look.

Every adult in the room suddenly found themselves a bit misty-eyed as Nathan picked up his little boy.

"You have such a big heart, little man," he told his son as he hugged him tightly, then set him in his highchair. "I love you."

CHAPTER TWELVE

Two mornings later, Nathan dropped Stacy off at DFW International Airport. He walked her into the terminal and hugged her goodbye.

"When she wakes up, you tell Bella that I love her, and that I will fly back out once she's home so I can help with things," Stacy told him, and Nathan nodded.

"Text me when you land, please."

"I will."

***

Further south, the square-jawed man leading the investigation into the strange illnesses in Midland, Texas was on the phone with the lab supervisor.

"Seriously? Not *anything*?" he asked, incredulous.

"No, sir. Not a single thing. Every one of the samples your people sent to us came back clean. I believe something definitely made those people sick, but whatever it was, it didn't happen there. There must be another common exposure point in your cases."

The man listening to her held the phone to his ear with his right hand while his left hand scrubbed his face in frustration.

"Very well," he finally replied. "Send me the official reports, please."

"You'll have them by this afternoon."

He thanked her and pressed the disconnect button, then immediately placed another call.

"Tell them they're free to go," he said without preamble. "The test results all came back negative. And gather the team, please. We'll meet in fifteen minutes and review everything. It's back to square one. We need to keep looking."

***

As he'd done for every visitation since her accident, Nathan arrived at the Neuro Critical Care unit's main doors two minutes early so that the moment the fifteen-minute window started, he could walk swiftly to Bella's bedside.

When he walked in, he greeted Dr. Adamal, who stood on the far side of the room reviewing both her chart and the screens that showed her pulse, blood pressure, and respiration rate.

"Morning, Doc. What's the word?"

"Good morning, Agent Thomas. I was hoping I'd be here when you arrived this morning. I've got some good news. The last CT scan showed that the swelling has diminished considerably," he told Nathan. "I am very pleased with what I'm seeing. We'll lighten the medication this morning, and hopefully by this afternoon we'll be able to wake her up easily."

"Is it too soon to know anything for sure?"

"It is. But based on what's happened so far, I'm very optimistic," Adamal replied with a smile. "Let's continue to hope for improvement. I'll be back at four p.m. to check her progress."

***

"Hey, kiddo. Good to see you're awake," Joe Wallace said gently as he entered the young policeman's hospital room to check on him.

He'd made it a point to come and see Pete as much as possible since he'd heard about the blast. But this was the first time the young man was awake and responsive, turning his head to see who had walked in.

Pete Jenkins had come through a difficult and delicate surgery well, but he still had a long way to go. The heavy, oversized chunk of debris that had slammed into his lower back and pinned him to the ground had severely damaged three vertebrae. No one knew for sure if he would ever regain the use of his legs.

"Hi, Joe," a pale Pete answered, and managed a weak smile from his hospital bed.

***

"That feels wonderful," Lizzie sighed as she leaned back and let Donny rinse the conditioner out of her long brown hair.

With Nathan's approval, Donny had made a small modification to his and Lizzie's temporary living quarters. He'd purchased a hand-held adjustable showerhead and installed it, along with a bath chair, in the guest bathroom's walk-in shower. It enabled Lizzie to enjoy some semblance of a normal bathing routine without exposing the majority of her abrasions to the water.

Jandy's husband Tony, the EMT, had also weighed in with his recommendations to make Lizzie's life easier until she fully healed.

"Tony said to get cast protectors," Jandy relayed to them.

"Cast protectors? What are those?"

"They're waterproof and reusable and made specifically to cover up casts, or in Lizzie's case, bandages. He also said that they make all kinds, including ones that go all the way up the leg to the hip. Kind of like waders."

Donny had immediately gone online and ordered a pair of them, and once they arrived Lizzie would be able to take a traditional stand-up shower. But in the meantime, he was thoroughly enjoying spoiling his bride-to-be as much as possible.

Donny heard Lizzie's cell phone chirping multiple times as he helped her to dry off her body and dress, then blow dry her hair. Once those tasks were complete and she'd pulled her hair back in a ponytail and brushed her teeth, he led the way to the dresser and pointed at her phone.

"Thanks, babe. I tell you what, this not being able to hear crap is getting old. How long did the doctor say until it comes back?"

Donny held up two fingers and she rolled her eyes.

"Let's hope it doesn't take two whole weeks," she retorted, then scanned the four incoming messages she'd just received.

She whooped loudly and showed them to Donny before she texted Nathan.

***

"How is she this morning?" Jandy asked as soon as Nathan arrived home.

"Doctor Adamal seems to think she'll be awake sometime this afternoon, actually," Nathan revealed with a hopeful grin. "The swelling on her brain has gone down enough that he feels comfortable bringing her out of the coma."

"Oh, honey! That's wonderful!" his sister exclaimed as she hugged him.

"I thought so," he agreed, and his grin faded as he stepped back. "We just don't know how much she'll remember. Her memory could be a hundred percent intact, or she may not even know who I am. If she does remember everything, she'll be devastated about losing the baby. But if she doesn't..."

"If she doesn't, you'll have to tell her all of it, the good *and* the bad," Jandy surmised earnestly. "Because keeping secrets in a marriage isn't good. *Especially* ones that big. She deserves to know, Nathan."

He nodded, and she reached over and took both of his hands in hers.

"And you two will love and support each other through whatever comes after that, kiddo."

She smiled at him gently, then said, "Now then. I was thinking keep it simple for lunch. How about sandwiches? You think Charlie will like grilled cheese?"

Nathan chuckled. "That kid's pretty picky lately, but if it's got cheese in it, it might actually stand a chance."

***

Meanwhile, a jubilant Clint Asters called his crew together.

"I just got off the phone with the Department of Health. We've been given permission to leave, finally," he announced with a beaming smile. "Let's get the hell out of here. Straight to Fort Stockton, no stops."

A cheer went up from his workers as they scrambled to get the caravan rolling as soon as possible.

While he took great pains to keep it well-hidden, one employee in particular was extraordinarily happy at the news.

About time. I was running out of storage space.

***

"Nathan, big news," Lizzie said as she rushed into the room. "Did you see my text?"

He shook his head no, then pulled out his phone and read what she'd sent him.

He looked up at her with wide eyes, then texted back.

When?

"About fifteen minutes ago," she said. "Donny's going with me."

"Actually, Donny is *driving* her," Donny said from behind her, making Nathan smirk.

"How far away is it?" Nathan asked.

"Couple of hours."

Nathan addressed his next question directly to the agent under his command.

Are you sure it's not a trap? he texted.

Lizzie read it, then looked into his eyes as she replied, her tone full of conviction.

"Positive."

Nathan raised an eyebrow and held her gaze intently. *You'd better be damn sure,* his expression read loud and clear.

"Nathan. I'm sure," Lizzie said quietly.

"I'd go with you, but the next time I can see Bella is at one o'clock, and I'm not missing it. For the record, I don't feel good at all about a civilian being involved in this, but I can see from the looks on your faces that I'm not going to convince either of you to stand down," Nathan grumbled to Donny.

"Nope. You and I both know we won't talk her out of going," Donny agreed. "And I am damn sure not letting her go alone."

Nathan pinched the bridge of his nose and took a deep breath to realign both his thoughts and his patience.

"Fine," he finally said in exasperation. "One stipulation. You're taking Ben and Annie with you. Stop at the office and pick them up. I'll reach out to Steve and read him in. And I want you two to come straight back here when you're done, all right?"

"You got it," Donny assured him, then moved to where Lizzie could see him, and motioned for her to head to the car.

Lizzie. Take your sidearm, just in case, Nathan texted.

She read his directive, then patted her handbag, smiled at him, and confided, "And Donny's packing, too."

***

He tapped the steering wheel of his Coachmen Leprechaun, keeping time to the rhythm of an old rock classic filling his traveling home with soothing notes as he waited his turn to fall into line. As usual, he preferred to ride toward the back of the procession of company vehicles, completely content to bring up the rear.

And as he waited, he charted out the next steps of his plan in his head.

Let's see. We should be in Fort Stockton around two, give or take. Broad daylight. Not exactly the best time to put things in place.

But tonight, after we close up?

Game on.

Within forty minutes his motorhome left the huge grassy lot and traveled south two miles, then made a sweeping right turn to head southwest on Interstate 20.

***

"Oh, *wow*," Annie cried out the moment she saw Lizzie's face.

Lizzie immediately noticed her co-worker's distress.

"I'm okay, just a little rough looking still," she assured the younger woman. "Actually, I look a lot better than I did two days ago. But I still can't hear worth a damn yet, so if you wanna talk to me you're gonna need to text me."

Annie gave her a thumbs-up just as Ben strolled over.

"Holy shit, Lizzie, it looks like you fought a weed whacker and lost," Ben blurted out before he could stop himself.

Lizzie watched as a look of sheer surprise followed by one of utter contempt rolled across Annie's visage. She had no idea what Ben had said to cause Annie to make those faces, but she doubled up her fist and punched him in the shoulder as hard as she could anyway.

"Ow!" he exclaimed and looked at Annie for sympathy.

"Nuh uh," she retorted, trying her best not to laugh. "You earned that after the weed whacker comment. Just be glad she didn't actually *hear* you."

"Let's get moving," Lizzie announced. "It's about a two-hour trip."

***

At the one o'clock visiting session, Nathan could already see a change in his wife. Her eyes darted back and forth behind closed eyelids, and her delicate hands kept clenching into fists so tight that her knuckles briefly turned white before her body relaxed again.

"Has Dr. Adamal been back by?" Nathan asked.

"Not yet," came the reply. "But it's my understanding he planned to be here at four to check on her and speak with you."

Nathan nodded in determination.

"Let's hope that she's awake by then."

***

"We take a left at the second stoplight," Lizzie directed as the team pulled into Emory, Texas. "The pizza place will be on the right-hand side, and the thrift store on the left."

The sharp alertness of the three agents with him as they drove to their destination hit Donny like a tidal wave, and he found himself clenching the steering wheel more tightly than before.

As they turned into the parking lot Lizzie saw a figure poke his head out from around the corner of the brightly painted brick structure.

"There he is," Lizzie murmured, and Donny angled the SUV to pull up to a smooth stop just long enough for an obviously tense and exhausted Agent Jones to pile into the backseat next to Annie.

"Man, am I glad to see you guys. I made sure I wasn't followed," Jones rasped in relief as he set a small plastic bag on the floorboard between his feet. "But get me the hell out of here anyway."

***

While Donny drove the SUV back toward the FBI's Dallas office, a caravan five hundred and twenty miles to the southwest slowed to a crawl then turned into the huge open space that would serve as their base of operations in Fort Stockton, Texas.

Once they'd parked and Clint Asters had confirmed that all were present and accounted for, he nodded in approval.

"Get it set up," was all he had to say, and his crew sprang into action.

***

It was one minute past four when Nathan entered her room and saw his lovely bride looking back at him.

"Hi, honey," he said, tears almost obscuring his vision as he made his way to her side.

"Hi," Bella managed in a rough, raw whisper.

Nathan barely registered Doctor Adamal's presence in the room before the man spoke.

"She's been awake for almost an hour," Adamal revealed, "and when she tried to take the breathing tube out herself, we thought it best to go ahead and get her off the respirator."

Bella's blue eyes flashed with both temper and humor, warming Nathan's heart.

"And that's why she sounds so raspy. It'll improve in a day or so," the neurologist continued with an infectious grin.

"What comes next as far as tests?" Nathan asked.

"We've done some preliminary ones just now to establish the baseline," Adamal answered. "Motor skills, speech, and memory."

"And?"

"I did good," Bella blurted out, with a stern look on her face that plainly said *ask me, I'm right here, for crying out loud.*

Nathan couldn't help himself.

"Do you know who I am?"

Her face softened and her eyes filled with recognition and love.

"You're my husband. Nathan Thomas."

She's going to be okay. Oh, thank you, God. She's going to be okay, repeated over and over in his head in a joyful chorus as Nathan sat down in the chair right next to his wife's bedside, took her hand, and kissed it.

***

It wasn't until they pulled into the parking garage and got out of the car and into the elevator that Jones got a really good look at Lizzie.

"What the hell happened to you?" he exclaimed.

"She still can't hear very well," Donny cut in. "But the short version is, she was in the front yard when they blew up our house."

Jones swung his head and his jaw dropped as he gawked at Donny.

"That explains what that guy was doing in the kitchen, then."

"What do you mean 'that guy'? Was there more than one?"

The elevator door opened just as Donny asked the question. Steve was standing there.

"My assumption is that he's talking about the same guy whose body was found lying on your living room floor," Steve interjected. "But why don't we all go sit down first and get comfortable so we can all get up to speed at the same time?"

He turned on his heel and led the way to the conference room.

***

When four-fifteen came, Nathan stood, reluctant to leave her.

"Visiting hours are over," he told her somberly, and Bella frowned and looked over at the man directly responsible for her recovery.

"Then get me out of here and into a regular room so he can stay longer," she stressed.

Dr. Adamal grinned and patted the hand that Nathan wasn't holding.

"I can let him stay another half-hour or so," he told her. "I want to get another CT scan done before I release you to a regular room, though."

Bella considered it, then nodded. "Okay. Let's get it done then."

Her laser focus made Adamal belly-laugh.

"You're a bit stubborn, Mrs. Thomas," he said, "and that will serve you very well, because you've got quite a bit of physical therapy ahead of you. But something tells me you're going to do just fine."

To Nathan he said, "Can we talk for a moment?"

"Sure," Nathan replied, then turned to Bella and said, "I'll be right back, honey."

"Take your time, I'm not going anywhere," she quipped and made him smile.

"We'll take her for another scan right around five o'clock. Once I get those results, we should be able to get her transferred," Dr. Adamal said the moment they were in the hall.

"Okay," was Nathan's confused response. "Not sure why we had to step out here to talk about that, but..."

"I wanted to let you know - while her memory seems to be fine so far, she hasn't asked about the baby at all. I don't know yet if that signals some sort of permanent short-term memory loss, or if she's just been so overwhelmed with all the physical trauma and subsequent medication that it hasn't occurred to her yet."

***

Steve looked over at Jones once they'd all gathered around the table.

"Nice to see you in one piece," he observed. "Now, walk us through what happened."

Jones blew out a long breath.

"Well, I'd taken Donny up to the hospital to meet Lizzie," he began. "I went back to their house and hopped in the shower. I got out and had just gone to my room to get dressed when I heard voices. At first, I thought it was Lizzie and Donny - which surprised me because Donny had filled me in on what happened to Nathan's wife, and I found it strange that they would be home again so soon."

He accepted the bottle of water Ben offered him and took a sip.

"I finished getting dressed, and I started to go out to the living room. But as soon as I opened the bedroom door, I could hear the voices more clearly, and I realized it was two men speaking to each other in Spanish. The voice I could hear the best sounded frustrated and the other sounded like it was far away but really pissed. I don't know very much Spanish, but the little bit I could understand I recognized as curse words."

"I thought about going out the back door but realized I couldn't. My phone and the keys to Donny's truck were in the living room. I crept down the hallway, trying to figure out how to get past them long enough to grab what I needed. It wasn't until the living room came into my line of sight that I realized it was only one guy in the house. He was on a phone call and had it on speaker phone. He went into the kitchen, and I eased my way forward and grabbed my phone from the coffee table. But then it got quiet. Before I could pick up the keys to Donny's truck or hide again, he came back to the living room, saw me, pulled a switchblade and came at me. We fought, and I managed to get the knife away from him and stab him in the neck with it."

He turned pale with the memory, and took another, longer drink from the bottle that trembled in his hands. Donny took advantage of the break in speaking to furiously text Lizzie a summation of what had been revealed to that point.

She scanned the lengthy message, then raised her eyes to Jones and motioned for him to continue.

"I went back to my room just long enough to put my shoes on and grab my wallet and my gun, then I picked up Donny's keys and headed outside. By that point I was on high alert and it occurred to me that he might have sabotaged the truck, so I got down and looked underneath it. I couldn't tell for sure if anybody had messed with it or not, but I wasn't about to take any chances. I went back inside and rummaged through the guy's pockets and got the keys to *his* car instead. By then I could smell gas. I didn't even try to find out what he'd done in the kitchen. I just knew I needed to get the hell out of there, so I hauled ass."

"Why wait almost three days to make contact?" Annie asked.

"Because at first, I was completely and totally freaked out. I have no idea how they found me at Lizzie's. *None.* Not a clue," Jones responded. "I wasn't exactly eager to broadcast the fact that I was okay, much less where I was because I didn't know if there was still a threat. And I had obviously endangered Lizzie enough already. So, I just left and headed east. I figured I'd text her and warn her about the guy I left on her floor once I was safely out of the area, but my phone's battery died, and I didn't have a way to charge it."

"What made you decide to stop in Emory, Texas?" Steve asked.

"The idiot who tried to kill me has a shitty car, that's what," Jones explained. "I was trying to get to my great-uncle's place in Louisiana. He has over two thousand acres I could have disappeared on and been just fine. But that freaking car broke down on me three miles east of Emory, and I've been laying low since. I don't usually carry any cash and I didn't think it was smart to use any of my credit cards, so, I've been roughing it the past two days. The thrift store owner noticed me hanging around this morning and took pity on me. She fed me and gave me another set of clothes and let me borrow her charger. The moment my phone had enough battery to stay powered on, I messaged Lizzie."

The room was silent as Donny updated Lizzie again.

The moment she got done reading she looked at Jones again, and said, "I'm proud as hell of the way you handled all that. I'm not happy that we feared the worst for a while, but under the circumstances

I can definitely see how difficult it was for you to make contact. I'm just glad small-town Texas hospitality kicked in."

She leaned forward.

"And I can *also* see the guilt you feel because you took another life," Lizzie continued softly. "But you had no choice, Jones. I know you didn't go looking for trouble. But he put you in an impossible situation, just like the guy in Chicago did. Remember that. And remember that it was either them or you."

Jones glanced at each of them, and they all nodded with sympathetic understanding.

"I know," he answered, his voice strained, his youthful face contorted with raw emotion. "I just... I don't know if I can live with that."

***

He was sitting at her side holding her hand and waiting for the techs to come get her for the CT scan when Bella's eyes went wide, and she gasped.

"Oh - the baby!"

She whipped her head to the right to look at him.

"I took a pregnancy test, and it was positive, but I didn't tell you yet because I wanted to have a doctor's appointment," she began.

"I know about the pregnancy, Bella," he told her gently, but couldn't keep the pain out of his eyes, and she noticed it.

"I lost the baby, didn't I?" she whispered. "Because my injuries were too much."

Nathan nodded sadly, then leaned over and wrapped his arms around his wife as she began to cry.

Once she'd composed herself, she sniffled, "Are we still going to be able to have more kids, or..."

"They haven't told me anything like that, so my assumption is that you're going to heal and be just fine, honey."

"Okay," she managed, slow tears still trickling, and Nathan reached up and gently wiped them away.

"And either way, I love you," he added. "And I always will."

"I love you too," she whispered.

A brisk knock at the door preceded two techs entering the room.

"Hello," one said brightly. "It's time to take you for another scan."

"That's my cue, baby," Nathan told Bella. "But the minute they let me see you again, I'm there."

He held her hand as they wheeled her bed to the oversized elevator used to transport patients between floors, then kissed her goodnight before he headed home.

***

"What's next?" Jones asked. "What happens now?"

"I think we need to try to figure out how it is that the cartel located you down here," Steve said matter-of-factly. "Given that only Lizzie, Nathan and Donny knew you were staying at Lizzie's, I'm thinking that it had to be a tracking device of some sort."

CHAPTER THIRTEEN

Jones' jaw dropped in surprise and it took him a moment to gather himself enough to speak.

"Tracking device?"

"Yes. What did you bring down here with you?"

"My wallet, my gun, and my ready bag."

"And was that ready bag out of your sight at any time before you got on the plane to fly down here?"

"I keep it in the backseat of my car. The afternoon I flew out I went down to the parking garage and got it."

Steve frowned.

"I'll need to reach out to the director in Chicago and ask him to take a look at his security tapes. I'm wondering if someone with clearance to be in the garage planted that tracker when the cartel realized that they weren't going to be able to intercept you at your apartment."

Donny typed *Steve thinks someone planted a tracker in Jones' duffel bag* and showed it to Lizzie.

"Smart thinking," she told the group. "They'd have tried his apartment, and when they couldn't find him, it makes perfect sense that they would have shifted focus to his workplace to try to find some point of access. Especially if someone up there's been bribed to give them information. It's not a far stretch at all to think that their insider could also be persuaded to plant the device."

"I don't understand. Why let me leave town at all? Why not just rig my car to explode or something?" Jones asked.

"While it's sitting in the garage of a federal building? I think they're much smarter than that," Steve retorted. "It's easier, not to mention much more subtle, to get someone who's already got access to the employee garage to plant a simple tracker. Then they just follow the beacon and make their move when they have the best chance of not getting caught."

"But there's no way to prove that theory," Annie interjected, "unless his bag *wasn't* completely demolished when the house blew up."

"Well, we can go look," Ben told her. "It can't hurt to try."

"Donny and Lizzie can go do that," Steve directed. "They already know what his ready bag looks like, and anyone watching will just think that Lizzie is checking out the damage to her property."

Donny shrugged. "She's been wanting to go look at it anyway. Might as well see if we can find anything while we're there."

You think we have enough light left to go look for Jones' bag tonight? Donny messaged her, and Lizzie nodded.

"We should, yes. Sun won't go down for another two or three hours. Plenty of time - if we leave now."

I'm going to let Nathan know where we're going and that we'll be at his place afterward, he told her, and Lizzie gave him a thumbs-up.

"What about me?" Jones asked Steve.

"Until we figure out how they found you, *you* are not going anywhere. You're gonna stay right here at this office," Steve answered firmly. "We have round-the-clock security, a lounge with a sofa, a cafeteria, and shower facilities onsite. The only thing you'll still need is clothes, and I bet Ben and Annie can help you out with that."

"That's a safe bet," Ben acknowledged.

"Okay, let's get moving," Steve said as he stood up. "I'll call the director in Chicago and read him in. Something tells me reviewing that video will help him plug the leak he's got."

***

He passed out the benign sprayers to his co-workers right on schedule, then locked the trailer again and shuffled to his workstation.

As soon as they opened for business, patrons swarmed the grounds like a tidal wave.

Geez, you'd think they've never seen us before, the way they're packing this place. Wish I'd known that ahead of time. Could have kicked off our first night here with a real bang.

Oh, well. Something tells me I'll have plenty of test subjects the next two days. Which means I'd better move damn quickly tonight to make sure it's all set and ready to go come morning.

***

"Wow," Lizzie gasped when they turned the corner and she saw the carnage left behind on the lot where her childhood home once stood proudly. "I... it's just.... *wow.*"

Donny nodded in commiseration.

"I knew it had blown up, and that probably nothing was left, but to see it in person..." Lizzie managed to tell him, then swallowed hard.

He squeezed her hand before they got out of the car, ducked underneath the barrier tape, and walked slowly up the narrow strip of concrete toward where the front porch should have been.

"They cleared the scene, right? It's okay for us to be here?" Lizzie asked as she glanced at him.

He nodded again and motioned her forward.

She moved slowly, taking it all in. To the left of her front door, the kitchen windows - the entire street-facing kitchen wall, for that matter, as well as the roof above it - were completely gone, only a huge gaping hole left in place that enabled anyone passing by to stare straight into the interior.

Not that there's anything left in there, her psyche said mournfully.

She slowly pivoted her head to her left, noticing that the water heater that had totaled Donny's truck still lay across the top of the cab where it had come to rest three days earlier.

Lizzie turned her head to the right to ask Donny something and noticed he'd left her side. When she looked back toward the street, she saw Nathan walking beside Donny back over to where she was standing. The two were in deep discussion as they closed her position.

Donny's filling him in on how our trip went, she realized.

"Hey boss," she said calmly, and waved an arm at the destruction. "It's a bit of a fixer-upper now, I guess."

Nathan grinned sympathetically at that before he texted, *I think you should look at this the same way Jandy did when her place caught fire. If you wanted to make any renovations, now's the perfect time.*

She read, then mulled over, his message.

"Makes sense. And yes, we're rebuilding, so, we have a chance to change things. A fireplace would be good, for starters."

Then she saw the extra twinkle in her boss's eyes.

"You got good news about Bella, didn't you," she guessed. "Am I right?"

Nathan's small grin morphed into an enormous smile as he typed furiously.

She's awake - and no damage at all to her brain that we can tell so far.

"That's such good news!" Lizzie squealed, and completely surprised both men by hugging Nathan tightly.

"Sorry, couldn't help myself," she confessed when she finally turned him loose and took a step back. "I've just been so worried about her - *and* you."

Nathan put a hand on his heart to show he appreciated her sentiment, before he pointed to his eyes and then the ruined structure in front of them.

"Right. Back to the task at hand," she agreed. "Jones' bag. It was an Army-style duffel bag, but black, not green."

Fire department used a crane to remove big pieces of the roof that had fallen inward, then stabilized any walls that they felt were in danger of collapse, Nathan told her. *Fire marshal has cleared us to go ahead and enter and have a look around, as long as we are careful. But we have to wear these, just in case.*

Lizzie gave him the 'okay' sign, put on the hardhat he'd handed her, then stepped over the blackened threshold.

Thank God it's on a slab, was her immediate thought as she made her way into the soot-covered and water-damaged living room and felt rather than heard the vibrations of each loud creak happening with every step she took. *Otherwise, I'd be in danger of falling through the floor.*

The wall separating the kitchen from the living room had also been obliterated, but that only held her attention for a moment.

Makes sense. Kitchen is where the gas line came into the house.

She already knew that looking in what was left of the kitchen would be a wasted effort, so she focused her attention on trying to make it across the living room area to the hallway leading to the bedrooms. It was somehow more somber to see that pretty much only rusted, charred springs remained of her loveseat, couch, and her father's recliner.

As she started down the ruined hallway, she was marginally encouraged.

Blast damage isn't so bad back here. Smoke and water damage, on the other hand...

The door to the guest room was open and blackened, as was the entire back side of the antique six-drawer dresser now lying face-down on the floor beside the scorched remains of the beautifully carved matching wooden bedframe.

That bedroom set was in the family for four generations, she thought sadly. *It's irreplaceable.*

But her pulse quickened when she spied a sliver of what looked like black canvas protruding out from underneath the side of the dresser.

"Hey, guys," she called out. "Come take a look at this."

When Nathan and Donny approached, she pointed.

"That looks like it could be part of the bag's strap," she told them.

Donny nodded, then motioned for her to move out of the way. He and Nathan got on either side of the dresser and lifted it long enough for Lizzie to dart forward, grab the bag, and pull it out of its hiding place.

Once they'd gently laid the dresser down again, Nathan stepped around it. He pulled latex gloves out of his pocket and put them on, then crouched and opened Jones' bag.

"I have no idea what a tracking device would look like," Donny admitted as he watched Nathan start to search the bag's contents.

"It could be anything, really," Nathan told him. "Something embedded in a belt buckle, or a watch, or any number of things. Some trackers are amazingly small."

Suddenly he stopped and looked up.

"Let's get Jones on the phone. I can call out items in the bag, and he can tell us if there's something here he doesn't recognize."

Donny nodded, then told Lizzie, *need to get Jones on the line.*

"So that he can vet what's his, right?" she asked, and Nathan smiled.

"His phone won't be charged enough yet. I'll call Ben," she announced as she pulled out her phone and dialed, then handed it to Donny.

"Ben. Hey, it's Donny. Is Jones nearby?"

"He's right here. Hang on a second."

When Jones came on the line Donny put it on speakerphone.

"Okay, we have your bag," Donny told him. "Nathan's going to call out items in the bag, and you tell us if he mentions something that doesn't belong to you."

"Got it."

The verbal parade began with *tennis shoes* and *jeans*. *Socks* and *underwear* were mentioned next, then *shirts*, followed by *a comb* and *deodorant*.

Jones answered each one in the exact same way - "Mine".

It wasn't until Nathan said, "We have what's left of a mechanical pencil, but it's been smashed up pretty good, so I don't think it's usable anymore," that there was a pause on the other end of the call.

"I don't ever use mechanical pencils, so I damn sure didn't put one in my ready bag," Jones announced solemnly. "That's the bug. Gotta be."

"Do me a favor and let Steve know we found it," Nathan said. "I'm on my way to the office once I confirm with Mitch how to make sure this thing isn't still transmitting."

"Will do."

When the call was disconnected Donny handed her phone back to Lizzie.

"You guys coming?" Nathan asked as he peeled off his gloves and got out his own phone to contact Mitch.

"That's completely up to her," Donny answered, and asked Lizzie via text, *do you want to go with Nathan to your office?*

She thought a moment.

"Actually, I'm hungry - and tired," she confessed. "I still can't sleep worth a damn, and it's catching up to me. I think I'd rather eat and then lie down. But update us when you get back, okay?"

"I will," Nathan assured Donny, then nodded at her, and put his phone to his ear.

As Donny took Lizzie by the hand and led her back to their SUV, he heard Nathan say, "Hey there, buddy. Tracker in a mechanical pencil. How do you know if it's still working or not?"

***

"Mom, I've gotta *go*," eight-year-old Josh sang out loud and clear from the backseat, and his mother rolled her eyes.

"Told you we should have made him use the bathroom when we stopped for gas," her husband murmured. "He does this every time."

"Can you hold it until we get there?"

"No."

She sighed.

"Fine. Honey, pull over, please. This won't take long."

The father, biting back a chuckle, maneuvered the car to a stop on the shoulder, and Josh hopped out to relieve himself.

"Mom! Dad!" they heard Josh screech moments later, and quickly exited the car.

"What, honey?"

Josh, trembling so hard he couldn't speak, extended an arm and pointed down the slope.

His mother turned to see what he was pointing at and screamed as his father grabbed for the cell phone in his pocket.

"911, what's your emergency?"

"There's a body in the drainage ditch on US-87 just north of Wayside."

***

The moment he arrived at the office Nathan gathered with the rest of his team to update them.

"Mitch was able to walk me through what to look for," Nathan revealed. "No way that this thing is still working."

He pulled a baggie out of his jacket pocket and laid the ruined pencil down on the conference table.

"That's pretty slick, I have to admit," Steve said. "Such an ordinary object that it wouldn't be out of place at all."

"Lucky for us I hate those damn things," Jones said with a smile. "I tried using them a long time ago. Damn lead kept breaking, so I switched back to regular pencils."

"And that was the last thing in the bag that I called out to you," Nathan told him. "We'd already confirmed everything else. I think you're in the clear. Question is, what to do with you. I think it's safe for you to travel. But where?"

"I'd really like to get to my great-uncle's place in Louisiana," Jones answered. "I'll be safe there. It's a huge tract of land, and a lot of it is rough, not cleared at all. I know that property like the back of my hand. Trust me, no one will find me out there unless I *want* them to. And more importantly, no one else will be at risk anymore because of me, like Lizzie and Donny were."

He paused, and his face clouded.

"Or *you*, Nathan," he continued. "Don't think it hasn't occurred to me that you welcomed me into your home where your wife and child were, and that I stayed there almost an hour, with an active tracker in my bag right there in your driveway. I am so grateful that the cartel didn't try anything then."

Nathan looked him directly in the eyes and murmured, "Me too. More than you know."

"And another thing," Jones pressed. "How do we know for sure that all of you aren't still in danger because of me?"

"We don't," Steve said quietly, and glanced at Nathan. "What does your gut tell you?"

"To hope that the cartel thinks he died in the explosion and that's why the tracker wasn't moving," Nathan replied, his jaw tight with tension. "But to plan for contingencies, just in case they don't fall for that and decide to try again."

"Which means..." Steve trailed off in understanding.

"Which means," Nathan said in a grim tone, "that to keep my wife and child safe, I need to come up with a battle plan to deal with this. I need to figure out other housing arrangements for Lizzie and Donny. And for Bella and Charlie too, to be honest. My place may no longer be safe for *any* of us."

A solemn silence lingered among the agents for a moment before Steve directed his attention back to the man in the cartel's crosshairs.

"Jones," he said, "let's get you some wheels so you can get going."

***

When the emergency crew and Lynn County sheriff's deputies arrived, the shell-shocked family of three were questioned briefly, then allowed to continue on their trip while emergency staffers made their way to the body lying face-down in the shallow ditch.

In keeping with established protocols, the lead EMT on scene sent the required notification back to Dispatch requesting the presence of the Justice of the Peace and/or someone from the coroner's office to officially pronounce death. Both were dispatched in that direction.

The Justice of the Peace, a short, stocky middle-aged man imbued with the power to proclaim for the record what in this case was obvious, arrived first.

With a nod to the deputies, he carefully navigated his bulky frame down the steep slope. Not even a minute passed before he traversed the incline again and paused, winded, on the gravel shoulder.

It took a few minutes, but once he finally caught his breath again, he signed the EMT's paperwork, walked the fifteen feet back to his car, and left.

It was another ten minutes before the hired van pulled up to handle transport, but they had to wait their turn while the crime scene tech took measurements and photographs.

***

"Colorado," Donny said the moment Nathan got home and told him his concerns.

"Beg pardon?"

"My place up in Vail," Donny reminded him. "If push comes to shove Lizzie and I can go there for a while. We're damn sure not about to put you and Bella and Charlie in harm's way."

"What's going on?" Lizzie asked as she and Jandy joined them in the kitchen.

Nathan's concerned that the cartel won't be convinced Jones is dead, and that they could show up here, Donny explained in a message.

"We need to leave, then," Lizzie said immediately with a steely look in her eyes. "We've got to keep your family safe, Nathan. *Especially* Charlie. If anything happened to that sweet, wonderful little boy....".

Her voice trailed off and she cleared her throat.

"I'll be sending Charlie to your house tonight, and when Bella gets out of the hospital, she'll go there, too, if that's all right," Nathan revealed to Jandy. "Because while I'm hopeful, I'm also realistic. I don't think this place is safe for any of us for a while."

Jandy's eyes shone with concern when she said, "I admit I'm not really clear on what's happening, but from the little bit that I caught just now, I absolutely agree. Charlie and Bella need to come stay with me - and you do, too."

"I will join you there the moment Bella is discharged. In the meantime, I'll be staying here so I'm closer to her," Nathan replied, and his firm tone let his big sister know it wasn't up for discussion.

She raised her eyebrows but remained silent.

Meanwhile, Donny relayed Nathan's words to Lizzie via text, then added, *You and I can go to my place in Vail,* and she shook her head.

"Not Vail. Not at first, anyway," she told him. "I still have a job to do, and I can't just bail on my team. We need to stay somewhere in the area. If that means an extended stay hotel or something, then so be it."

I'm on it, he texted her. *Let me make a couple of calls.*

And he walked away, already dialing.

Lizzie turned to Nathan.

"I'm going to go pack up so Donny and I can get moving," she announced.

***

Since Lynn County didn't have its own coroner, the body found north of Wayside was transported all the way to the Lubbock County Medical Examiner's office.

"Drawer number three, please," an exhausted Dr. Rachelle Overtin pointed with a yawn.

The previous Sunday afternoon a fisherman with an attitude - who also, it turned out, had had *way* too much to drink - rammed his bass boat into an overloaded party barge on Buffalo Springs Lake. The result was eleven people injured and five fatalities. Four of the victims' bodies had been recovered almost immediately, but the search for the fifth - the fisherman's nephew - was not successful until just after daybreak Wednesday morning.

"Long day, Doc?" one of the transport drivers asked as he and his partner gently maneuvered the black bag onto the long steel pull-out slab, then slid it back into place and shut the door.

"Long week, actually," came the reply. "Double shifts. I'm just now finishing up everything from Sunday's boating accident. I'll get started on the new arrival first thing tomorrow."

***

At long last the crowds dispersed, and the grounds were quiet.

He methodically cleaned and closed down his area in preparation for the next day's bratty horde, then strode with purpose to his motorhome.

Dinner was simple, a box of mac and cheese with a couple of hot links diced up and thrown into the mix. After he ate, he turned his focus to carefully measuring out smaller portions of his variety of cocktails he'd mixed up for distribution.

He reviewed his stock and selected the five flavors that he knew from his research would be very heavily favored by the site's visitors. He slowly filled the first glass vial - roughly the size of a tube of toothpaste - with the grape-flavored mixture, capped it, then nestled it carefully down into the bag he'd customized with a foam insert for transport. He repeated the exercise four times more, and vials of cherry, blue raspberry, tiger's blood, and watermelon-flavored death joined the first vial in his bag.

"Now for the other," he murmured, and picked up the clear, tasteless variant to fill three more vials.

The last thing he placed into his bag was a handful of three-milliliter syringes to aid him in dispensing his product.

Once that was accomplished, all that was left to do was wait. With an impatient grunt he sat back and surfed TV channels, keeping one ear trained on the steadily diminishing noises around him as one after another co-worker turned in for the night.

It was after one a.m. before he was certain that no one else in the group was awake and it was safe to make his move.

He stood, stretched his lanky frame to work out the kinks that had settled in from sitting for a while, then moved to his lab to retrieve his workbag and a pair of surgical gloves.

Armed with his syringes, the flavored and plain versions of his lethal mixture, and his penlight, he crept through the entire setup, focused on reaching the twelve beverage stations scattered throughout and adding his poisons to as many of them as he possibly could.

By the time he'd finished with the third station, he'd found his rhythm - altering the flavored syrups first, then polluting the icemakers before moving to the gallon-size box-covered bags of soft drink syrups. A tiny needle prick near the nozzle of each of those proved to be invisible to spot afterward, and he grinned.

He moved quickly but quietly, aided by the unexpected bonus of possessing Jake's master key that gave him unfettered access to every single station since all twelve locks were keyed the same.

***

Donny and the claims adjustor were working on locating something more feasible long-term while Lizzie's property was put back together. But nothing had been confirmed, so for the short-term, Donny had booked a hotel room.

On the bedside table, Lizzie's phone trilled once and was silent again. She couldn't hear it, but Donny did, and sat up, rubbing his eyes in disbelief at the time displayed on the alarm clock.

Seriously? Who texts at two a.m.?

He got up, walked around the bed to her side, and picked up her phone to read the two sentences left for her.

Made it here safely and settled in. Signing off for a while. - J.

"Good luck, kid," Donny mumbled under his breath as he set the phone down and crawled back into bed.

***

Just before five-thirty he made the return trip to his house on wheels, moving with urgency to avoid being seen; he knew all too well that a few in the group were early risers. It wasn't until his trailer door closed behind him that he sighed in relief.

He put the workbag with its now empty transport containers back in his lab, peeled off and threw away his surgical gloves, and locked the door before setting his alarm and climbing into his bunk for a nap.

But sleep didn't come immediately. He was too excited, his mind racing with the inevitable outcomes that were now just a matter of time.

CHAPTER FOURTEEN

The unfamiliar clock shrieking loudly not far from his ear resulted in a startled Donny bolting upright in bed at six a.m. His abrupt movements shook and woke Lizzie.

"I'm guessing the alarm went off," she murmured as she yawned and stretched, then smiled when her fiancé turned to her with a scowl and nodded his head.

He reached for the little notepad and pen that he'd left on the nightstand, wrote *that thing's volume must have been turned all the way up, too,* and showed it to her.

She laughed, sat up, then leaned over and kissed him.

"Come on, grumpy. Let's take a shower and then go find breakfast."

***

In his hospital room, Pete Jenkins was already wide awake. The thoughts bombarding his brain had chased away any hope of rest.

No one's come out and said it yet. I wonder why. Are they really not sure, or do they already know and they're all just too scared to tell me that I'm never going to walk again?

He sighed and looked down at his feet, focusing with all his might.

"Move, *please,*" he whispered brokenly, then concentrated hard, and waited.

Nothing.

Just the way it had been every single time Doctor Adamal ran more sensation testing and asked, "Can you feel this?" as he pressed a blunted object first against the sole of Pete's right foot, then his left, then moved to calves, shins, knees, and finally thighs.

190

If Pete hadn't seen the man pressing against his skin with his own eyes, he would never have known. Because he hadn't felt a damn thing. His body had simply gone to sleep from the hips down, only there was no pins-and-needles-tingling happening as it reawakened. Just... silence.

And stillness. An unbearably heavy, soul-crushing stillness.

I'll never be a detective now, Pete thought bitterly, lifting a hand to wipe away silent tears that coursed unbidden down his cheeks. *My life is over.*

***

"Morning, Doctor Overtin," her assistant called out as he walked into the breakroom of the Lubbock County Medical Examiner's building. "I brought donuts."

"You're a lifesaver, Cleve."

They sat at the dinette table to enjoy coffee and the sugary snacks in peace for a few minutes.

"Maybe today will be closer to normal," Cleve observed between bites. "I know you've been running ragged this week."

The pathologist sighed.

"Been rough," she agreed softly. "Especially when one person's stupidity causes so much suffering."

"I heard that."

Dr. Overtin took one last sip to empty her paper cup of its contents, then smiled at Cleve.

"Ready to get going?"

"Lead the way, Doc."

Fifteen minutes later the as yet unidentified body of the young male found discarded in a drainage ditch was lying on the steel table in the middle of the room for closer inspection.

"Recorder on, please, Cleve," Dr. Overtin said briskly, and began her official examination.

***

Doctor Adamal's tests confirmed a severe concussion but no brain damage, and on a brilliantly sunny and warm Friday morning Bella Thomas was released from the Neuro Critical Care unit to spend her second week in the hospital in a regular patient room.

After she'd been transitioned out of Adamal's care Dr. Mesa, the man who'd originally made contact with Nathan in the surgical waiting room, took point on her treatment.

"I won't try to downplay this. The next few months might be a challenge," he'd told her and Nathan honestly. "Pelvic fractures can take as long as six months to heal. You've got that *and* your busted leg to contend with. Slow and steady is the key, but not too slow - we don't want to lose muscle tone. And we will line up the best physical therapists around to help get you through this. Do what they tell you, when and how they tell you, Mrs. Thomas, and you'll see great results, I promise."

"How much longer will I have to stay in here?"

"I believe we might be able to discharge you within a week or so. The only question is where you go once you leave here. Some patients find it easier to maintain their physical therapy regimens in an inpatient rehab facility. And some patients' injuries are such that an inpatient environment is the only viable option to ensure they get the help they need to fully recover. In your case, we might be able to arrange in-home physical therapy. Let's talk more about that over the next several days, and we'll see where things are at that point. I want to at least make sure that the pins and plates you have are stabilized before we get you up and moving too much."

She thanked him and let out a long sigh when Dr. Mesa left the room.

"I really want to go home, honey," Bella said plaintively.

"I know you do," Nathan soothed. "But here's a thought to cheer you up. Now that there's longer, less restrictive visiting hours, I can bring Charlie up this afternoon."

Bella didn't have to speak. Her dazzling smile and teary eyes said it all.

***

"No luck at all with getting a usable set of fingerprints the usual way, Cleve. They're seriously degraded. He was outside for too long. The good news is, I think he's an ideal candidate for thanatopractical processing," Overtin revealed. "Maybe we'll catch a break."

"Agreed. I can take point on getting that started as well as making dental impressions, if you like, and hopefully we'll get some leads to try to match them up with sooner rather than later. I'll reach out to the police department and ask about any missing persons cases in the area, too. How long for toxicology, you think?" Cleve asked Dr. Overtin.

"I'm hoping by tomorrow afternoon, since I put a rush on it. I *really* want to know what caused that damage in his esophagus and stomach. They looked like burns of some sort. I've never seen anything like it in my entire career."

"Neither have I. That *was* really strange, wasn't it?"

"Yes, very."

"I have an idea," Cleve said suddenly. "I have a professional network group that I participate in. I won't give specifics about the victim, of course, but I'm thinking if I post a general question, someone in that group might be able to shed some light on what might have caused those burns."

Dr. Overtin considered it, then nodded. "Be discreet, but yes, go ahead. Maybe someone can help."

***

Though it was only eleven a.m., it was already a typical hot, humid mid-July day in North Texas. Ben and Annie had opted to spend their day off together staying out of the oppressive heat and binge-watching movies.

Ten minutes in, Ben paused the DVD they'd just started to field a call from his friend Brody with Fort Worth's Gang Unit.

"Hey, that tattoo picture you sent me. You got any info on the victim? I have a couple of informants I work with and my best one has gone missing. I'd hoped he'd gone back to his parents' house. But now I'm wondering if his disappearance is related at all to what you were working on."

"Deputy Greisen sent me over the entire file. I can make a copy of it for you," Ben offered.

"That works. Let's meet for dinner and I can get it from you. I'll buy."

"Deal. Usual place? Six?"

"Let's make it six-thirty. See you then."

Ben hung up, checked his watch, and looked over at Annie.

"I'm meeting Brody for dinner. Want to go with me and have some really excellent barbeque?"

"Sure. What's going on?"

"It sounds like we might have a lead on who Wise County victim number three is."

***

"I think it's getting better," Lizzie mused aloud, then glanced over at Donny as he drove them to the apartment complex's office to sign a six-month lease on the furnished unit that the adjustor had helped them find.

He looked back at her with a puzzled expression.

"My hearing," she elaborated. "I think it's starting to come back."

She stared at him until he parked the SUV and turned his head toward her.

"Say something," she prodded.

"Like what?" he blurted.

Lizzie grinned.

"You said 'like what' didn't you? I heard it. It was very, very faint, but I heard it."

***

Nathan had just pulled into the driveway at Jandy's to pick up Charlie when the call to his cell phone rang through his car's speakers, courtesy of his hand-free setup.

"Thomas," Nathan said as he answered.

"Hey," Steve answered. "Just heard back from Chicago. They've identified the source of the leak, and she's being questioned now."

"Who was it?"

"Alicia Merris. She's got basic security clearance only, thank God, so she doesn't have access to anything huge, but she was able to see enough to give her handlers Michelson's address, at the very least. I'll keep you posted as I know more."

***

He had no way of knowing just how well his plan had worked so far, but by the time the company began setting up operations in El Paso, over two hundred people had unknowingly ingested enough of his formula to develop symptoms from visiting the Fort Stockton site.

Of those, almost half were children younger than eight, and many of them were sick enough that their parents rushed them to local emergency clinics.

Unlike the Midland cases, the Fort Stockton patients were scattered over a much larger region. Each local provider simply chalked the new cases up to the same culprit - a strong variant of stomach flu that had ravaged the area all summer - not realizing that the problem was more widespread and much more sinister.

After two hectic days the group wrapped up in El Paso and headed east again toward San Angelo. By then, his favored dispensing method had already claimed twenty-two young lives, with another eighty-three small children dangerously ill. The total number of people who drank a quantity big enough to become sick climbed to well over two thousand - and continued to grow.

El Paso, a much larger city, had a higher concentration of sick people showing up in one facility - and by the time medical staff at Kindred Hospital realized they weren't dealing with any sort of communicable infection, the contamination point common to all of their patients was long gone.

The troupe made good time to San Angelo and went straight to work, setting up shop in the oversized parking lot next to the high school football stadium.

He unpacked and assembled his area while he also planned out his next trip through the gauntlet to refill depleted stations. The flavored versions had moved more quickly than he'd thought in both Fort Stockton and El Paso - so much so that he'd scrambled each night to make sure another round was in place and ready to go the following morning.

And I think this stop will be just as busy. Good thing I stockpiled while we were stuck in Midland, otherwise I'd never get ahead of it. Plus, the layout here is spread out more. I'm going to have to really hustle to keep up with it all.

He shrugged his shoulders in response to that last thought.
Sometimes being brilliant requires sacrifices. So be it.

***

At one p.m. Nathan tapped on Bella's hospital room door.

"Hi, sweetheart," he called out to her as he walked in the room with their son in his arms.

When Charlie saw Bella lying in her hospital bed, he was very quiet at first, his brown eyes wide as he gazed intently at her.

"Mommy better?" he finally said, and she nodded.

"I missed you so much, kiddo. Come here."

Nathan gently set Charlie on the bed next to Bella and watched as their son threw his arms around her neck and laid his head on her chest.

"Missed you too," her little boy said, and they both cried.

"We go home, Mommy," Charlie prompted when he finally lifted his head to kiss her cheek. "Wanna go home now."

"I agree, sweetie, but it's not up to me," she told him with a wan smile. "Maybe in a few more days."

The pout that flashed across his face made her giggle.

"I know, Charlie. I feel that way, too. But I can't leave here until the doctor says I am well enough to go home."

"'Kay," the toddler grumbled, clearly not impressed with having to wait.

***

"Hey, buddy. Good to see ya," Ben called out as he and Brody shook hands then did their usual 'bro hug' thing.

"Brody, I'd like you to meet Annie, a team member of mine. Annie, this is Brody. We go way back."

Team member? That's it? After we've talked about moving in together? Annie thought to herself in irritation. *That's how you wanna play this, fine. Game on.*

She smiled her brightest smile at the man she'd just met and made sure her voice held just the right amount of sultry when she extended her hand and said, "It's so nice to meet you, Brody."

Annie could feel a wave of shocked displeasure emanating from Ben when Brody took her hand and with a twinkle in his eye replied, "The pleasure's all mine."

"Anyway," Ben cut in with a terse tone and a frown, "I brought that file you needed. Let's take a seat."

He spun on his heel and approached the hostess station.

Brody looked at Annie with a raised eyebrow.

"Let me guess. You're not just team members and he's in the dog-house now, right?" he whispered to her.

Her eyes widened with surprise and respect.

"Got it in one," she confirmed.

Brody grinned, showing perfect white teeth.

"Wanna make him suffer a little? All in fun, of course."

She nodded and held back a chuckle.

"After you, then," Brody replied, sweeping one hand out in front of them while he deliberately placed the other at the small of her back.

By the tight set to Ben's jaw as Brody and Annie passed him, Annie knew Ben was aggravated.

Brought it on yourself, honey.

After they were seated and the waitress had brought their drinks and taken their order, Ben handed Brody the file, then casually leaned back and draped his arm across the back of Annie's chair. Brody noticed it immediately and winked at Annie before he turned his attention to the file's contents.

But when he saw the pictures, all traces of humor fled from both Brody's face and his voice.

"Aw, man," he said bitterly. "Dammit. I *knew* it, but I was hoping I'd be wrong. That's Mouse."

"Mouse?"

"It's the code name I gave him when I brought him on as a confidential informant. His full name is Estencio Garza. Good kid. Couple minor scrapes in Mexico but nothing big. He migrated up here about four years ago and fell in with the wrong crowd. But he's been very careful. Never been in trouble here, so his prints aren't on file. Otherwise, Wise County would have identified him by now," Brody explained.

He closed the file and leaned forward with his elbows on the table.

"When he went missing, I started digging around a little bit trying to find something out. Last I'd heard, my other informant said something about some bigshot from Mexico coming through the area had taken a shine to Mouse's girlfriend. I'm guessing that had something to do with this."

"What's next, then?" Annie asked.

"I'll be making a trip up to the morgue in Wise County in the morning so I can formally identify him," Brody answered. "And I'll give them some contact information so they can reach out to his family and let them know. His four older sisters and his parents still live in Mexico."

Ben nodded, lost in thought, then blurted out, "That bigshot from Mexico. He got a name?"

Annie glanced over at him. "Why?"

"Just a hunch. I'm wondering if this doesn't all tie back to what happened with our co-worker," he told her, then turned back to Brody, who threw him a puzzled look.

"One of our people got cross-wise with a Mexican cartel recently," Ben revealed, "and landed himself on their radar in a big way about two weeks after your guy Mouse was killed. I'm just curious to know if this is all connected. That's why I asked."

"My guy never mentioned him by name, just referred to him as 'big boss'. But I can find out and let you know," Brody confirmed. "Might take me a bit, though. We have a pattern set up. I'm not supposed to make contact for another four days."

"No rush on my account. I could be completely wrong; the two events might not have anything to do with each other. And I don't want you to break your routine to reach out to your guy, either. Don't do anything that outs him," Ben replied, then fell silent as their server appeared with their meals.

***

When Bella yawned, Nathan said gently, "Honey, you could use some more rest, so we're going to go now."

"Are you sure?" she asked sleepily, her chin resting against Charlie's head as he snuggled further into her arms.

Her husband nodded.

"You're right. I'll see you both in the morning," she decided. "It's better to keep Charlie's sleep schedule as normal as we can."

"Come on, little man. Give Mommy goodnight kisses. We'll see her again tomorrow. You need your dinner and a bath."

Gonna have to tell her at some point that Charlie's been staying with Jandy - and why, Nathan acknowledged as he and Charlie walked back toward the elevator. *But now isn't the time.*

He sighed.

Not looking forward to that talk at all.

"I wonder what Jandy's made for dinner?" he asked his son.

Charlie threw up his hands and squealed, "Pizza!"

"Probably not, buddy. But let's go find out."

***

When Ben and Annie got back to his apartment complex's parking lot, he was surprised to see her pull her keys out of her purse. The moment his truck stopped, she climbed out and headed over to her car.

"Annie, where are you going? I thought you were staying the night?"

"Nope, I'm gonna head on home. Good night, *team member.*"

He watched, completely baffled, as she drove away.

***

He opted to dress in black from head to toe before he grabbed his gloves, penlight, and the replenished workbag with a full complement of death in it.

He checked his clock as he pulled on the gloves.

One-oh-eight a.m.

"Time to go," he whispered to an empty trailer, then slipped outside into the darkness and closed and locked the door behind him.

His trek through the compound was fully illuminated; a full moon had appeared to keep him company, but it also had the unfortunate effect of spotlighting him, and he grimaced.

Need to hurry and get this done.

He picked up his pace to a fast stride.

***

Ralph just couldn't get comfortable. He'd gone to bed at eleven just like always but tossed and turned instead of falling straight to sleep. That was unusual for him, and he didn't know what to do about it.

Just after one a.m. he sighed and got up.

"Guess I need to burn off some energy, maybe," he muttered as he searched in the dark without success for his shoes.

He snarled, out of patience with himself, and finally opted to turn on his bedside lamp so he could locate his sneakers before he tripped over them.

Ralph put them on, stood, stretched, and stepped down out of his camper into a warm still night.

Couple laps around the place ought to do it, he assured himself, and set out on his unwanted and unwelcome dead of night stroll.

He'd just reached the edge of the setup when he saw motion ahead and to the left. Startled, Ralph ducked behind the closest structure - a ticket booth - then peeked carefully around its corner.

What the hell is he doing?

And why is he dressed like a cat burglar?

Ralph was equal parts afraid and curious, but after a moment's hesitation, curiosity proved to be the much stronger of the two. He crept forward quietly, keeping to the sides of the natural funnel the group's setup had formed, and ducking behind structures to hide himself when he thought the figure ahead of him might be looking his direction.

And Ralph noticed something extremely odd. His co-worker only seemed to be focused on certain stations in the setup.

Wait, what? He's not even looking at anything else... just the beverage stations...

The sudden deep shock that hit him as he worked through the implications of what he was seeing made him gasp aloud. Terrified, he dove behind the nearest solid object - a row of enclosed portable toilets - for cover, convinced the sound had carried and revealed his presence. Ralph shut his eyes and silently counted to thirty before he even dared to risk taking another peek.

The figure had vanished.

Oh, thank God. I don't want to know anything about what he's up to. I'm gonna go back to my trailer and lie down and forget every single bit of this.

He stood on trembling legs and willed them to stop shaking before he pivoted to sneak back the direction he'd come from.

One gloved hand slammed across his mouth and nose as the other grabbed him by the throat and began to squeeze. He started to struggle, but the taller, thinner man's wiry strength took him completely by surprise, and Ralph found himself pinned to the ground next to the portable toilets, unable to escape or even cry out in distress.

"You know what they say about curiosity and the cat, right?" his assailant asked him softly, and Ralph's eyes bulged in pure panic as he stared up at the man he'd worked with for years and saw no trace of humanity. Tears streamed down his face as he clawed at his attacker's hands, trying desperately to breathe.

Just as Ralph began to black out from his airway being compromised, he felt the pressure ease. He was about to express his gratitude at being spared when a thin sliver of cold, hard steel invaded his skin just below his jawbone, then pierced his rapidly thrumming carotid artery.

"Haven't had a chance to try injections yet," his nightmare solemnly whispered to him. "It's full strength, too. Lucky you. Let's see how well it works, shall we?"

Ralph began to buck his hips wildly, trying to throw the other man's weight off of him, but it was no use. An immense burning, a bone-deep, painful scorching, started in his neck and spread, the undiluted three milliliters of toxins he'd been dosed with riding the superhighway of his blood stream for maximum effect. With each heartbeat the poison coursed further and further through his body, a relentless surge of white-hot lava obliterating every cell it encountered.

"Aw, Ralph. You look... *uncomfortable.* Here, let me help you out with that," came a rough teasing whisper in his right ear.

It was the last thing that Ralph was conscious enough to understand before the assault on his oxygen supply began again in earnest - and in that last moment of clarity, Ralph knew for certain *exactly* what had happened to Jake.

***

He held his deadly grip on Ralph's throat, nose and mouth until he saw the man's eyes glaze over, then close.

I don't necessarily need him dead just yet, only knocked out long enough for me to move him.

He thought briefly about stashing Ralph in one of the portable toilets, then dismissed the idea.

I really do want to see what happens when it's injected. Can't do that if I leave him here.

He checked Ralph's pulse and nodded in satisfaction before he hoisted him up into a fireman's carry and worked his way back to his motorhome.

Damn his nosiness. I only got one of them done. Gonna have to really hustle now to get the rest before sunup, he grumbled to himself as he walked, his long legs closing the distance easily.

He got his door unlocked and stepped up and into his home, then laid both his workbag and Ralph down.

Restraints. I need restraints just in case it doesn't kill him quickly...

He stepped outside only long enough to retrieve his toolkit from the storage compartment. He brought it inside, opened it, rummaged through it, and smiled.

Moments later Ralph's wrists were zip-tied together behind his back as he lay face-down in the middle of the floor. His legs were also zip-tied together at the ankles, and a wide swath of duct tape had been applied all the way around his head to keep him quiet.

Not that he's gonna be doing much talking, he thought with smug satisfaction.

He knelt and felt for Ralph's pulse again.

Almost done.

"It's too bad, Ralph. You weren't completely annoying to be around. But you were rude and interrupted my work, so now, here we are," he reprimanded, then clucked his tongue.

He settled into his bunk to watch and wait.

This shouldn't take long, he thought to himself. *Half-hour, forty-five minutes, tops.*

He was still thinking about dosages and timeframes when he drifted off to sleep.

CHAPTER FIFTEEN

The sun was already on its way up when he jolted himself awake.

Dammit. Fell asleep and didn't get my work done.

As soon as he looked down at Ralph, he knew his formula had worked its magic to the ultimate conclusion.

Great. Missed that, too. Oh, well.

Still, he climbed down from his bunk and checked the man's pulse, just to be safe.

Nothing.

Well, then. Guess I need to get that tarp out of storage to wrap him in until I can figure out when and where to dump him.

Way to go, brainiac. Why didn't you take him back to his own camper in the first place? came the immediate response from the logical left of his brain. *Then you wouldn't have to deal with this at all. But it's okay, there's still time. You can make it look like he died in his sleep. You have twenty minutes until it's fully daylight, and his camper isn't far. Get moving.*

He paused only long enough to exchange his black shirt for a light blue one - *being dressed all in black might draw attention first thing in the morning*, he realized - then removed Ralph's tape and zip ties. He hauled the body upward to as much of a standing position as he could, flung Ralph's left arm around his shoulders and wrapped his right arm around Ralph's waist.

This will work - right?

Shut up and get going.

He was just about to open his door and try to maneuver Ralph down the narrow metal stairs when he froze.

Other people in the group were already awake. He could hear them talking and moving around outside.

Dammit. Back to the tarp idea.

206

"Sorry, Ralph," he said mirthlessly in a low murmur as he lay the body back on the floor. "Looks like you get to hang out with me a little longer."

Once the voices outside his window faded, he risked another trip outside and retrieved the tarp he owned.

Better think of something more permanent soon though, he realized as he spread the big blue tarp out as much as possible in the tiny space, then rolled Ralph's body onto it. *A deep freezer, maybe? Just until I can figure things out. Wonder what one of those would cost?*

First of all, there's zero room in here for a freezer, his pride chimed in. *But there* is *just enough space in the lab back there for a fifty-five-gallon drum. And second, I am a brilliant chemist. All I need is a drum and a couple of ingredients and I can solve this, no problem.*

What about the fact that people will notice that he's disappeared but all his stuff, including his camper and his car, are still here? Boy. For such a genius you sure as hell lack common sense sometimes, don't you? his logical side clapped back against his pride and made him scowl. *Stop making things more difficult than they have to be. Put him back in his own place as soon as possible - and for God's sake remember to act surprised when he's found. Should be easy enough for such a smart fellow as yourself.*

A sudden booming rap on his door nearly made him jump out of his skin with fright.

"Yes?" he called out, taking care to put the slow drawl in his voice.

"Boss called a meeting at the main ticket booth."

"Okay, thanks, I'll be right there."

He crept to his window and watched as everyone around his motorhome walked away toward the setup to hear what Clint Asters might have to say. When the last one passed out of sight, he took a deep breath.

It's now or never. I can't leave him on my floor all damn day.

He hefted the tarp-wrapped body over his shoulder, stepped outside, and moved as fast as he could to put Ralph back where he belonged.

It was an effort, handling so much awkwardly packaged dead weight for the ninety-yard dash to Ralph's camper, but he managed to get there and then wrestle the corpse inside without being seen. He quickly arranged Ralph's body on his mattress and slipped away, scurrying back to his own space.

Man, that was much too close, he told himself as he stashed the tarp in the exterior storage compartment then hurried to change into fresh clothing before he ran toward where the group had gathered.

Clint noticed his late arrival immediately, and a frown of concern creased his face.

"You all right?"

"Yes, sir, I'm fine. Sorry I'm late. Spilled coffee all over myself and had to change right quick."

Clint nodded once in acknowledgement, then resumed speaking to his crew.

"Like I was saying, we had a near-miss accident yesterday. I know we're all busy and we've got a lot of towns on this circuit, but we've got to do things the right way, the safe way, each and every time. The last thing we need is to have anyone hurt - customers *or* employees."

Too late, he almost blurted out but caught himself and turned the noise into a brief, quiet cough as the site foreman continued his pep talk.

"So, stay sharp and pay attention. Any questions?"

No one spoke.

"Good. It's gonna be a long Saturday, gentlemen. We open for business in one hour. Let's get to it," Clint concluded, and closed the meeting.

A long day, but oh, such a good one, the killer hiding in plain sight among them mused as he hurried back to his motorhome for a quick shower and food.

***

Two days later, Bella Thomas was finally cleared by Dr. Mesa to leave the hospital.

While they waited on her discharge papers, Nathan told her about the young agent, Jones, and his run-in with the Mexican cartel. He also told her about Lizzie's house being destroyed - and his concern that the cartel might pay the Thomas residence a visit, as well.

"So, Charlie's been staying at Jandy's," he concluded. "And I'm taking you there, too."

When he was finished speaking, she gazed at him intently.

"I think if they were going to do something like show up at our house, they would have already done it," she said calmly. "Think about it. It's been what, two weeks now, at least? Cartel members don't strike me as the patient type."

"You could be right," he answered.

"And *you've* been staying there this whole time. Anything weird happen? Unfamiliar cars coming around? Any unexpected packages dropped off or strangers knocking on the door?"

"Well, no, actually," he admitted, "but I don't want to take that chance with Charlie - or you."

"And yet you're not concerned enough about your own safety to have someone there with you to watch *your* back?" she challenged, arms crossed over her chest and left eyebrow arched.

He had no good answer for that one, so Nathan opted to remain silent.

"Okay, so, if it's such a concern for me and Charlie to stay there, then line up agents to come stay with us," Bella argued. "But I'm not going to your sister's house. It's not fair to Jandy and Tony to have their house overrun, and I'm beyond ready to sleep in *our* bed again."

"But what if -"

"Nathan," she said firmly, "you and I both know that we cannot base the rest of our lives on 'what if'. If we do that, we're not really living."

She reached for his hand and gentled her tone.

"I love you, and I know you worry, honey. You're trying to keep us safe. I get that. But in this case, I don't believe it's warranted, I really don't. Now, please take me home. Please."

He sighed and relented.

"Okay. We'll go home instead. And I'll call Jandy and ask her to bring Charlie over."

When his cell phone buzzed, he grimaced.

"Take that," Bella encouraged. "Nothing else to do right now, anyway. I can't leave until she brings the paperwork and takes this damn IV out."

He grinned as he answered the phone.

"Hey Steve, what's up?'

"Got more data on Alicia Merris."

Nathan's face took on his 'work mode' expression.

"And?"

"Evidently her old man emptied their bank accounts and took off about seven months ago, leaving her with a critically ill child and no way to pay for his treatments," Steve told him. "She didn't tell anyone, too proud."

"But not too proud to turn on her fellow agents, I suppose."

Steve sighed. "The branch director told me she seemed to be genuinely surprised and remorseful when she realized that her giving out information most likely led to Abes and Michelson's deaths. He's decided to keep her in play but control what her handlers receive from her."

"Counterintelligence?"

"*Precisely.*"

***

"We have a match on the prints," Cleve said as he poked his head in Dr. Overtin's office doorway a little after one in the afternoon.

"Already? That was quick. *Almost* as fast as the completely normal tox screen results - but a lot more useful."

Cleve grinned at her sarcastic tone.

"Yep. Matched to a Toby Duane Bryton, twenty-one years old, and he's from Amarillo. He got arrested last year for an unpaid speeding ticket that went to a warrant, otherwise his prints wouldn't have been on file at all. And get this - his parents filed a missing person report after his truck was found abandoned here in Lubbock about ten days ago."

"Well, then," she said as she picked up her desk phone's receiver, "I guess I need to let Amarillo PD know we found him so they can make notifications."

***

Dr. Heming, the Tom Green County coroner, was completely stumped.

His latest case was a thirty-six-year-old male. He had arrived at the morgue two days earlier, after he'd been discovered dead in his camper by his site foreman, Clint Asters. But the backlog Heming had been working through had delayed Ralph's progression from the cold storage locker to the examination table.

At first, the highly experienced coroner thought it would be another routine autopsy of a victim found dead in their bed - drug overdose, maybe, or an undiagnosed heart condition, or perhaps even an aneurysm.

But he'd been completely unprepared for what he saw when he began his examination.

"Corrosion - there's no other word for it. It looks like he's been hosed down with battery acid, only on the inside rather than the outside," Heming lamented to his co-worker. "I've never seen anything like this, and I've been in this line of work for quite a while now."

"Wait a minute," Chad, his longtime assistant, said. "I seem to remember.... Hang on, I'll be right back."

And he dashed out of the autopsy room before Heming could question what he was up to.

Five minutes later Chad was back, cell phone in hand.

"I knew it. Check this out," he announced to his confused boss. "I'm in a private networking group, and a member named Cleve that works at the Lubbock County coroner's office posted something recently about a case with internal burns that they couldn't figure out."

Chad scrolled and found the post and read it aloud.

"That does sound a lot like what we're seeing here," Heming agreed, and moved to the stainless-steel sink to remove his elbow-length gloves and dispose of them before he scrubbed his hands. "I need to make a call to Lubbock County so we can compare notes. Who's the lead up there? Overtin?"

"Yes, sir. Rachelle Overtin," Chad confirmed.

"I'll call her now. In the meantime - would you please collect samples of that sticky residue in his hair? It's all over the back of his head. Need to get that tested."

***

"Hey, Doc," Cleve said when he poked his head through Rachelle Overtin's open office doorway. "Dr. Heming with Tom Green County is holding for you on line three."

"Thanks, Cleve," she replied before pressing the button on her desk phone to retrieve the parked call.

"Hello, Anthony, how have you been?"

A chuckle floated across the line.

"I've been good, Rachelle. Busy, but good. Hey, a couple of days ago you guys had a weird one come through, right? With what looked like internal burns?"

"Yes, we did," she answered immediately, all her senses on high alert. "Why? Have you heard of that before?"

"Not until today," he admitted. "But the case I just started sure sounds a lot like yours."

"I can send you some video and pictures we took," she offered. "For comparison."

"I was just about to ask you to do that. And I can send you mine," Heming confirmed. "I'll be honest, I've been doing this for almost twenty-five years, and this is the first I've ever *heard* of this, much less seen it."

"I'm not too far behind you, Anthony, and I've never seen or heard of it, either."

Cleve rushed into her office, waving a piece of paper to get her attention.

"Hold on just a moment, please, Anthony," Dr. Overtin advised, and placed her hand over the speaker end of the receiver. "What's going on, Cleve?"

"The forum," he blurted out. "Somebody else just answered my question. Three other cases, all in Midland. Same burns."

She stretched out her hand and he gave her the page.

"Anthony," she said into her phone, "my assistant just brought to my attention that there are other cases like ours in the area. What do you suggest?"

"I know just the man that can help us figure out what's happening," Heming replied immediately. "There's an FBI profiler that investigated a case down here earlier this year. I believe his last name is Thomas, and if memory serves me correctly, I think he's based up in

Dallas. I'll reach out to the detectives here that worked with him and get his contact information."

"I'm going to forward you my entire case file," Overtin decided. "And you might want to reach out to Barry Gillespie, too - he just took over the coroner's spot for Midland County a couple of months ago. Let me know what else I can do to help."

***

Nathan had just gotten Bella out of the passenger seat and settled into the wheelchair he'd bought for her to use at home when his phone rang.

"Don't you need to answer that?" she asked.

"Not until I get you situated, I don't."

"Take the brakes off this thing. I can roll myself around while you take that call," she huffed.

Jandy's van pulled into the driveway just as Nathan was about to argue his point.

"See? Jandy's here now. She can help me if I need it," Bella pointed out, her tone a bit softer. "I'm injured, Nathan, but not completely helpless. And I'm not made of glass. So, would you please stop hovering over me and answer the damn phone?"

He glared at her but took the call.

"Thomas."

"Agent Thomas, my name is Dr. Heming, and I'm the coroner down here in Tom Green County. I got your number from Detective Perez, and I know you helped solve the Edward Baker case earlier this year. Do you have a moment to talk?"

Go on, Bella urged silently, gesturing with her hands.

He threw his free hand up in the air in surrender and led Charlie into the house while Jandy took up station behind Bella's wheelchair.

"Give me just a moment, Dr. Heming. Let me get to my office right quick," he told the caller, then whispered to Charlie, "Go play in your room, all right? I'll be there in just a few minutes."

"Okay," his son replied with a cheeky grin, and ran to his bedroom.

Nathan walked into his home office and shut the door.

"Sorry about that, Dr. Heming," he told the man as he reached for a notebook and pen. "Now, how may I help you?"

***

It was a full thirty minutes before Nathan's call concluded with, "Yes, sir. Send me everything you have as soon as possible, please. Yes, sir, I'll be in touch. Goodbye, Dr. Heming."

He set the cell phone down on his desk and scanned the notes he'd scribbled during their conversation, his mind reeling.

Five cases total, spread out from Lubbock to San Angelo...

He stood and walked out of his office to go find Bella.

***

In the FBI's Dallas office, Ben sat at his desk, trying not to stare at the captivating woman sitting mere feet from him who was acting like he didn't exist.

Man, she sure can hold a grudge, he thought bitterly.

Annie had given no quarter since his major gaffe in front of his friend. She'd kept every interaction between them strictly professional and deflected all of Ben's attempts to talk to her outside of working hours.

His desk phone rang, and he pounced on it, supremely grateful for the distraction.

"Hey, buddy," he heard Brody say. "Got some news for you."

"Hi, Brody," he replied, then stiffened and frowned when he noticed Annie lift her head to look his way. "What's up?"

"I finally had a chance to talk to my informant," came the reply. "The guy that was chasing after Mouse's girlfriend is named Izan."

Ben made a note of it, then said, "I appreciate it. I'll keep you posted."

He hung up the phone and paused for a moment.

Maybe this will get her to talk to me.

He forged ahead.

"Hey, what was that guy's name that Jones shot in Chicago?"

Annie looked at him with an eyebrow raised and a *get it yourself* expression but remained silent.

Just when he thought he'd need to find and ask Steve instead, she finally pressed some keys, casually scanned her screen, and drawled, "Izan Cortinas."

"*Gotta* be the same guy," Ben blurted out, and launched himself out of his chair to go find Steve. He caught up to him in the breakroom.

"I just heard from my contact with Fort Worth PD," Ben announced. "And I think the guy Jones shot in Chicago might be the same one that killed that other guy in Boyd."

At Steve's puzzled look, Ben grinned.

"Sorry, let me start from the top."

Ben got partway through his story when Steve interrupted.

"Did you just say *Izan Cortinas*?"

"Yes. You know him?"

"You could say that. I've been working a cold case the last three months that I believe ties directly back to him and his father's cartel - I just can't prove it. *Yet.*"

***

"So, what's going on?" Bella asked when Nathan came into the living room.

Jandy had wheeled her to the ladies' room, and then out to the oversized recliner chair, where she currently sat with her feet propped up and a glass of tea in her hand.

"You caught a case, didn't you?"

He nodded. "Five victims with very similar - and unusual - injuries. I'll know more once I get the files."

He took a seat on the couch closest to her chair.

"How are we going to do this?" he asked her earnestly. "Make no mistake, Bella. You and Charlie are my first priority. I'd already arranged for a leave of absence, so..."

"There's no need for that," she said simply. "Yes, I've got some broken bones and yes, it will be a long road until I'm back to a hundred percent, but otherwise, I'm fine. And we've got a home office, remember? You can work from here just as well as you can in Dallas."

"That's true," he agreed.

"Jandy's already said she's happy to stay with us during the day, and I just got off the phone with Stacy. She said she and Brad and Emily can fly out here anytime we need them to. I've also got home health care and physical therapists scheduled to come every day starting on Monday. Trust me, Charlie and I will *not* be by ourselves. So please don't feel like you have to neglect your job, because you don't."

Now she leaned toward him a bit and teased, "Besides, if you take a leave from work, what will you do all day? Sit around and stare at me? That won't help me heal any faster, and to be honest, it will really get on my nerves after a while."

Nathan chuckled. "I see your point."

"Good. Because the look on your face just now after that phone call told me two very important things."

"Which are?"

"That other people are having trouble finding out who's responsible for those deaths - and that *you* have the power to figure out who the killer is and stop them. So, get your ass back to work and stop them, Agent Thomas. Don't you dare hold back on my account."

He looked into her eyes and saw a quiet, determined strength there.

"Yes, ma'am."

"Then it's settled. I'm glad. Now, can you bring me my laptop? I know you said you contacted my professors, but I need to check in and make arrangements to catch up on what I missed."

***

"How long do I have to stay here?" Pete Jenkins growled at the nurse charged with settling him into his room at the inpatient rehab facility that Dr. Adamal had chosen for him. "And what's the point, anyway? Why can't I just go be a cripple in the privacy of my own home?"

The even-tempered nurse, accustomed to such outbursts, calmly replied, "Doctor Adamal believes that being here will help you. So, you're here."

Pete scoffed. "Whatever."

"I know you're upset, but -"

"But what? Let me guess. You were going to say something like, 'but I know how you feel.' News flash, lady. *You don't.* You're still whole. You can get up and walk around and do whatever you want. You haven't had your dreams *and* your body stolen from you."

He turned his head away from her to look at the wall.

"Please go away now."

"Hey," she said softly, then waited.

When Pete finally swiveled his gaze back to her, his mouth dropped wide open. She'd pulled up the right pant leg of her scrubs so that her prosthetic limb was clearly visible.

"You're angry at the world right now. Trust me, I totally get it," she told him, her eyes locked with his. "Once that passes, we'll talk. Because your life isn't over - despite what you think."

***

It was almost time to head home for the day when Ben's desk phone trilled again.

"I just thought you'd like to know where things stand," Deputy Greisen told him. "And that your profile was pretty much spot on. All we're waiting on is the warrant so we can go pick her up."

"That's good news," Ben replied. "I'm glad we could help."

He hung up and told Annie, "Sounds like maybe our friends in Wise County caught their killer. I wonder who it turned out to be?"

"Good for them," she responded in clipped tones.

Enough already, Ben thought in exasperation before he moved to deliberately perch his backside on the corner of her desk.

"What are you doing?" she whispered, eyes narrowed.

"Invading your space so you'll at least give me the time of day," he whispered back.

She frowned and started to reply but Lizzie returning to her own desk stopped the exchange.

"Tank used to do that and it would crack me up," Lizzie told Ben. "It made quite the picture, this great big guy balancing himself on a teeny tiny sliver of furniture. Good times."

She paused and glanced between the two of them.

"All right, you guys. This has gone on long enough. Seriously," she admonished. "I don't know what happened between you, and I really don't care to know. But you two had better call a truce or something, because this is getting old. Don't make me knock your heads together."

And with that parting shot, Lizzie picked up her keys and purse and headed to the elevator.

Ben watched her leave then turned his attention back to Annie.

"All I want to do is talk, Annie. Can we go out to dinner or something? *Please?*"

He felt like she made him wait a year before she finally shrugged her shoulders and nodded her head.

Oh, thank God, he thought to himself with relief.

Annie was almost to the elevator before she looked over her shoulder at him.

"But *you're* buying."

***

The following morning, after a very busy two-day run in New Braunfels, Clint Asters' crew loaded up for the eighty-two-mile trek to Round Rock, the next stop on their summer circuit.

By the time the last transport left the lot and headed north on Interstate 35 the anonymous killer had left quite an impressive set of numbers in his wake. In addition to the five victims that had landed on FBI agent Nathan Thomas' radar, he'd caused another fifty-one deaths along the roughly four-hundred-twenty mile stretch from El Paso to San Angelo. Most of the fatalities were children under the age of ten.

There were three other children in the New Braunfels area whose untimely deaths would later be attributed to the same killer.

CHAPTER SIXTEEN

It wasn't until Monday that the five case files Dr. Heming and Nathan had talked about arrived at the Dallas branch office. The sudden and unexpected delivery of a large box of paperwork surprised his team - as did Nathan's mid-morning appearance.

"Hey there! How's Bella?" Annie asked when she saw Nathan step off the elevator.

"She's doing so well that I've been banished to working here," he responded with a grin. "Evidently, I'm already on her last nerve because I am, and I'm quoting here, *'hovering over her too much'*, or something."

Annie laughed.

"Although in fairness, Bella did forecast that might happen. Anyway," he continued briskly, "I'm expecting a set of files from-"

"They showed up just after nine o'clock," Annie confirmed. "I put them on your desk."

"Good. Please round up the team and let's get started in the conference room in fifteen minutes," he directed. "There's a *lot* to go over here, and we need to get up to speed very quickly."

***

As Nathan's team members prepared to gather in Dallas, the ghost they were about to chase was ninety minutes south in Waco, Texas. He took deep breaths in and out, in and out, trying to talk himself down from a full-blown panic attack.

I don't believe this. I just don't believe this...

He'd been so excited to execute his plan that he never even considered pacing himself on its implementation. Two solid weeks of spending his nights rebaiting his traps instead of getting enough sleep had come back to bite him.

221

His exhaustion had rendered him inattentive. The end result of his lapse in concentration was that he had let himself run completely out of his single most important ingredient, the one that formed the basis for his entire scheme.

He scrubbed his face with his hands, then wearily counted his existing pre-mixed inventory again.

I might have enough to get through our Dallas/Fort Worth stops - but maybe not. And there's not a way to get any more. If I were closer to the border, I might have a chance, but not now... I don't have a choice. Going to have to scale back. There's no other way.

Dammit. I knew I should have made a run while we were in El Paso.

Okay, so, his logical side soothed. *Instead of whining about what you can't change, look ahead and plan. Research the next towns on the schedule and choose which ones will be included in the experiment and which ones won't. Simple as that.*

"Yes, that will work. I may still have to ration, too, to get through it," he whispered to himself. "But I'm smart. I can do this."

But his logic had one final parting shot for his bruised pride.

And while you're at it, how about you build some time into your grand design to get some sleep?

***

Nathan kicked off the discussion once his team had settled in around the conference table.

"Dr. Heming, the Tom Green County coroner, called me this past Wednesday," he began. "He had a case come to him that was... unusual. After doing a bit of research, he and two other pathologists in the region discovered a total of five very similar cases across three different counties. This isn't just a profile work-up. Our job is to figure out what's going on, and if the source of it is malicious, to find and capture the person or persons responsible."

He indicated the five thick manilla folders laying side-by-side in the center of the conference room.

"Let's each take one case file, and review them," he directed. "Then we'll reconvene in here at noon and plot out each case's pertinent details on the whiteboard. It will be a working lunch today. I've already made arrangements to have sandwiches delivered. Make sure you give your order to the unit secretary within the next ten minutes, please."

***

After Lizzie, Ben, and Annie had selected their files to work on, Steve grinned at Nathan.

"Which one you want?"

Nathan shrugged, projecting an air of nonchalance that he did not feel. "I'm good with either one."

Steve made his selection and slid the other folder over to Nathan.

When Nathan opened the file he'd be working on, his heart sank. It was Timmy Steward, the six-year-old, by far the youngest victim.

Not too much older than Charlie, he remembered sadly, and swallowed hard. *I don't know if I can do this.*

The other team members had already left the conference room, but Steve had lingered, and he immediately noticed the completely distraught look that washed over his employee's face.

"We can trade, you know," Steve said softly. "Some cases are more difficult or hit closer to home than others. There's no shame in it."

Without a word, Nathan Thomas closed the file in his hands and gratefully passed it over to his boss in exchange for the Toby Bryton file.

***

He put down his pen and looked at the list of cities and population sizes, thought a moment, then nodded and picked up his pen again.

Okay, he mumbled internally, *Hillsboro and Corsicana are definitely out, since there isn't even thirty-five thousand people total between the two.*

He crossed them off of his list.

Same for Waxahachie. It's not much bigger.

It too had a line drawn through it.

Decatur's official population is a lot smaller than I thought it would be, but it's the county seat and every year our setup there is jam packed, so, it stays.

He leaned back and scanned the rest of his list.

Every other place left on the schedule has a hundred thousand residents or more, so, those are my targets to focus on. And if I back my application down to one night only in each place, that should give me just enough formula to be able to complete the circuit.

"Well. Would you look at that. Unexpected bonus," he said aloud once he noticed that adjusting his plan of attack also resulted in no overnight activity for the next week.

Sweet. I'll be good and rested by the time we reach Dallas.

***

The team reassembled at noon. Each member retrieved their lunch order from the credenza against the far wall before moving to their seats around the long conference table.

"As we eat, I'd like each of you to write out your case's bullet points on the board. Then we'll discuss all this. Sound good?" Nathan asked, and received confirmations from everyone.

"Who'd like to begin?" Steve prompted.

"I'll start," Annie volunteered, and left her chair to move to the whiteboard. She recorded the highlights of Elaine Steward's case in a neat script, then retook her seat.

Ben came next, adding the main points for Jake Morgan. He was followed by Lizzie contributing what she'd gleaned from Ralph's file. After that, Steve wrote out Timmy's information, and Nathan finalized the whiteboard's contents with salient data for Toby Bryton.

The team deliberately kept the conversation confined to neutral, everyday topics while they ate; it was a means of enjoying the calm before the impending storm.

Twenty minutes later the empty wrappers were cleared away, and the entire atmosphere in the room shifted and took on a determined concentration.

"Let's get rolling," Nathan announced, glancing at the whiteboard's contents. "I'll lead off."

He stood and moved back over to the board.

"Toby Duane Bryton, aged twenty-one, a native of Amarillo, Texas. His vehicle was found abandoned in Lubbock, Texas the afternoon of July thirteenth and was towed to the police department's impound yard. His parents reported their son missing on July sixteenth."

After a small sip of water, Nathan continued.

"His body was found in a drainage ditch alongside US-87 just north of Wayside, Texas on July twenty-second," he added, then placed a pin on the map of Texas that had been tacked up beside the whiteboard.

"The coroner's notes indicate that he'd been dead approximately ten to twelve days. She wasn't able to narrow it down much beyond that due to the body's deteriorated condition. She also lists his cause of death as 'undetermined'. His toxicology report came back clean, and she found no signs of obvious physical injury or adverse health conditions. The single anomaly in Toby Bryton's autopsy were some burns all along his esophagus and down into his digestive tract. Dr. Overtin indicated her belief that whatever caused them likely played a prominent role in his death but has been unable to identify the source."

With that, Nathan resumed his seat at the table.

"Okay, based on the whiteboard data, Ben's case comes next."

Ben took position next to the map.

"Jake Morgan, thirty-seven, hometown unknown. He was found unresponsive in his travel trailer by a co-worker named Ralph Smith and was transported by ambulance to the hospital in Midland, Texas the morning of July fourteenth."

He paused to place his location's pin, then started to resume his verbal report to the group.

"*Ralph Smith*?" Lizzie blurted out, and when everyone looked at her, she pointed to the board where she'd added her notes about the case file she'd reviewed.

"Interesting," Nathan mused aloud. "We'll get to that shortly. Keep going, Ben."

"Jake Morgan was taken to the emergency room around seven a.m. and was pronounced dead around three that afternoon. Dr. Gillespie, the Midland County coroner, made notes in Jake's file that pretty much mirror what Dr. Overtin had to say about Toby Bryton. Nothing on toxicology, no obvious health issues, no physical trauma, just some strange burns in the sinuses and throat, as well as in his lungs. Cause of death is 'undetermined.'"

Steve went next.

"The case I reviewed is also out of Midland, Texas," he revealed, then placed a pin on the map. "Local resident Timmy Steward, aged six, was brought to the emergency room by his mother when he experienced extreme nausea and vomiting, then became unresponsive. His toxicology came back as positive for nicotine and three other unknown substances. He arrived at the hospital around eleven p.m. the night of July fourteenth and was pronounced dead at around three-thirty a.m. on July fifteenth."

"Dr. Gillespie's notes don't indicate any pre-existing conditions or obvious injuries, and he found no burns in the airway or esophageal tract, but Gillespie *does* mention 'deep subcutaneous burns' over a large majority of the body, as well as 'burn-like or corrosive striations covering muscle tissue'. I wasn't sure precisely what that meant so I called the home office and asked our lead pathologist. In layman's terms, the body had deep and extensive burns on the *inside*, underneath the skin. Gillespie listed his cause of death as 'nicotine poisoning, pending further investigation,'" Steve concluded.

Annie stepped onto the presentation stage and placed a third pin on Midland once Steve was seated.

"Elaine Steward, thirty-two. Timmy's mother. As Steve said, she brought Timmy to the hospital the night of July fourteenth. She became ill to the point of collapsing around three-forty-five a.m. and was admitted to triage immediately. Her condition deteriorated throughout the morning and she was pronounced dead just before noon the same day. Her tox screens tested positive for three unknown substances, but no nicotine. Gillespie noted the exact same types of burns on her body that Timmy's had. Her cause of death is listed as 'undetermined', as well."

When Annie sat down again, Lizzie made her way to the whiteboard.

"Ralph Smith, aged thirty-six, hometown unknown, died in San Angelo, Texas," she announced, and stuck a pin in the map to indicate location.

"He was found unresponsive in his trailer by his boss, a Clint Asters, and was transported by ambulance to the city hospital where he was pronounced dead on July twenty-fourth. Coroner's notes estimated he'd been dead roughly thirty-six hours prior to discovery. His toxicology panel came back clean, but unlike the others, Ralph's body *did* show outward signs of trauma. He had bruising around his wrists and ankles consistent with being restrained, and tape residue was found both in his hair and on the skin on his face. Slight bruising across his throat was also documented. Heming mentions in his notes that he believes that Ralph died somewhere else, and that his body was later moved and staged in his bed, based on the pattern of mottling on his skin."

"And this next part I found especially interesting," she continued after a slight pause. "Dr. Heming's report notes, quote, *the presence of a high level of corrosion, spreading outward from the victim's major blood vessels and into surrounding tissue.* He listed his case's cause of death as 'undetermined - pending further review.'"

"So those are the case highlights, but I also have some personal observations to add in here," Lizzie stated. "The guy who found Jake Morgan being named Ralph Smith is not suspicious in and of itself. But the fact that both Morgan and the Smith in this case file were found unresponsive in their mobile living quarters, and that both had weird internal burns? There's no way in hell that's coincidental. I think the 'Ralph Smith' mentioned in Jake Morgan's file is the *exact same one* that's on our whiteboard. I think Jake Morgan and Ralph Smith not only knew each other, but that Ralph saw or heard something he shouldn't have, and *that's* what got him tied up, then killed."

"Yes, I agree," Nathan confirmed immediately. "My gut says it's the same Ralph Smith."

He looked at each of his team members.

"Excellent run down to get us started, guys. Now we get to start digging further. Here's what needs to happen next. I want each of us to travel to our respective file's site and do a full on-scene investigation. That means I'm headed out to Lubbock to talk with Dr. Overtin, then to Amarillo to speak to Toby's family. Lizzie, start your search in San Angelo with Dr. Heming. Steve, you, Annie and Ben get to make a road trip down to Midland."

"When would you like us to leave?" Lizzie asked.

"Tomorrow morning is fine. Reach out to your respective points of contact and let them know you're coming to meet with them."

***

"Daddy!"

As was his custom, Charlie ran full tilt at his father the moment Nathan walked through the front door, and as usual, Nathan scooped him up and hugged him.

"How was your day?" Bella asked when Nathan smiled and walked her direction.

"Well, things are heating up quickly, for sure. I have to make a run out to Lubbock, then Amarillo. I need to leave in the morning," he answered, then closed the distance and leaned down to kiss her tenderly. "But I *also* feel the need to double-check and make sure you're one hundred percent okay with my traveling right now."

"Honey. I thought we covered this."

"We did. And you've got plenty of help around - for stuff during the day. But what happens if I need to be gone overnight? You're making great strides, Bella, you really are. But you're still not able to maneuver yourself out of bed on your own yet, either. So yeah. I really worry about being gone overnight."

"You have a point," she conceded with a frown.

"I know," he replied with a grin, and she grinned back even as she lightly punched him in the shoulder.

"Just for the record, if I have a couple of hours' advance notice, I can usually stay overnight," Jandy offered as she came into the living room to join them. "And on the off chance I can't for some reason, I bet Faith would be willing to help out. So, consider that question answered, all right?"

"Yes, ma'am," Nathan told his big sister.

"You hungry? I made spaghetti."

"That sounds great. Bella, I'm gonna put our little man in his highchair right quick, then come get you."

"No need. Look what I've *already* gotten much better at," she proudly said, and wheeled herself swiftly past him and into the kitchen.

"Not bad, Speedy," he teased. "Next thing I know you'll be popping wheelies."

***

After the previous week's dinner - during which Annie had let Ben grovel quite a bit before she actually told him he was forgiven - they'd resumed their relationship, including their standing Monday night date at their favorite restaurant.

"What a day, huh?" Ben asked as they dug into the appetizer they always ordered.

"Agreed. *So* many similarities in those five deaths. It's eerie," Annie said before taking another sip of her daquiri. "And I don't think they were caused by anything natural at all. It's a serial killer, I just *know* it. And that got me wondering..."

"About what?" Ben responded once he'd finished his first mozzarella stick.

"Well, the last death was July twenty-third, right?"

"Right."

"And today's the eighth of August, right?"

"Yep."

"So, why did they stop? I mean, we know that most serial killers don't stop on their own, right? They only stop because they get caught. Not only that, why the long space between the three deaths in Midland and Ralph Smith in San Angelo? There's eight days in between, and the last one was over two weeks ago. All that just strikes me as odd. There's no set length of time in between victims. At all."

Ben's eyes went wide.

"Holy crap, Annie."

"What?"

"What if you're wrong?"

She scowled, and he winced.

"No, sorry, that didn't come out right. I didn't mean it like *that,*" he explained. "What I'm trying to say is, what if there *aren't* any gaps at all."

"Meaning?"

"Meaning, there's *not* any long spaces. Just more victims that we don't even know about yet."

"How would we even find that out?"

"I'm not sure," Ben admitted. "The only thing I can think of is ask around once we're down in Midland, maybe?"

"You know what I'm thinking?" Annie said quietly. "I'm thinking we ought to run this theory by Nathan and get his take on it. Because I have a very bad feeling that you could be absolutely right."

***

"Hey Ben. What's up?"

"Nathan, I've got you on speakerphone, and I've got Annie with me. We wanted to run something past you and get your input on it. You got a minute?"

"Hang on, let me get into my office."

Nathan glanced at Bella. "Be right back."

He walked quickly to his home office, plugged his headset into his cell phone so he could have both hands free, and grabbed a notepad.

"I'm ready. Whatcha got?"

"Well, I started thinking about those five cases," Annie told him, "and I wondered why there's such a big gap in time between the three in Midland and the one in San Angelo - especially if Lizzie is right and the two men knew each other. I mentioned that, and the fact that the last death was more than fourteen days ago, to Ben. Because serial killers..."

The hairs on the back of Nathan's neck stood on end.

"Because serials don't tend to stop their activities on their own," Nathan finished for her. "You're absolutely right. They don't. They may take a break temporarily if something interrupts them or the police get too close, but usually they only stop once they're caught."

"Exactly. And then Ben thought that perhaps there are more victims out there that happened in between the Midland and San Angelo deaths, and we just haven't heard about them yet. So, we decided to call you. We wanted to get your take on our theory."

There was a long pause while Nathan mulled it over before he spoke.

"I think," he said very carefully, "that it's a very strong possibility. So, here's what you need to do when you get to Midland tomorrow. Go talk to the coroner, absolutely. But also go to the hospital and see if you can't make contact with the doctors that treated Jake Morgan and Elaine and Timmy Steward. They may know something that didn't make it into the coroner's reports that could help us rule more victims in or out."

***

"I'm making a drive down to San Angelo in the morning," Lizzie told Donny as they settled in on the couch. "Should be a day trip."

"Want some company?" Donny asked. "I've got a couple of prospective clients based down there that I can interact with while you're doing your thing."

"Sure," she said, then raised her eyebrow as her phone buzzed.

"It's Nathan," she announced, and Donny muted the television as she answered.

"Hey, boss. What's going on?" she asked, then listened, and Donny could measure the intensity of what she was hearing by the way she frowned at first.

"Wow," Lizzie managed. "The possibilities there are.... well, they're frightening, actually. Yes... I agree... so what's the plan?"

She listened intently for another minute or two, then answered, "I'll scope out the hospital in San Angelo as well, then. You bet. 'Night."

"Should we plan for it to be an overnight stay, instead?" Donny asked her once she hung up the phone.

Lizzie chewed her bottom lip for a bit before she replied, "Possibly. I'm just not sure yet."

***

Pete Jenkins spent part of his evening talking in depth with Barbara, the nurse who'd understood his situation much more than he'd given her credit for.

"I'd wanted to be an Olympic cross-country runner since I was ten years old," she confided with a soft smile. "I was eighteen, and in the best shape of my life. I'd been training night and day, for *years*, for my chance to fulfill my dream."

"About two weeks before the national trials that year, I was lying in bed being lazy on a Sunday morning, trying to work up the motivation to get myself up and go out for a run. I finally talked myself into it, so, I got up and put on my running gear and I went. And about three miles in, I got hit from behind by a car that was passing on the shoulder of the road around a blind curve."

Pete shuddered.

"I realized much later how lucky I am to even still *be* here," Barbara revealed. "But I didn't see it that way for a long, long time. Spent five weeks in a coma, among other things. I didn't even realize I'd lost my right leg from the knee down until I came out of it and the pain meds wore off a bit."

Her eyes misted over with the memory, and she paused to regain her composure.

"And like you, I felt cheated, and I was pissed off, all the way down to my *core*. I hated everyone and everything that crossed my path."

Pete nodded solemnly, his own eyes brimming.

"Then one day, I had a new physical therapist start working with me who absolutely *refused* to allow me to wallow any more. 'Girl,' she'd say, 'your life ain't over, just different. Now get your ass up out of that bed and let's walk some'. And at first, I *hated* her, with a capital 'H'. But Shirley just wouldn't let me give up on myself, and eventually I came to realize that she was absolutely right. My life wasn't over. Not by a long shot."

Barbara looked at him and smiled.

"So, I stopped feeling sorry for myself, and I went to college and got my Bachelors' degree in nursing and my Masters in rehabilitative therapy. That was almost twenty years ago, and now, I pay Shirley's gift to me forward as much as I can."

***

Nathan was just about to turn in for the night when his cell phone rang again.

"Hey," Steve said. "Just wanted to let you know that something's come up and I need to get back to D.C. tonight. I'm sure Ben and Annie can handle Midland just fine without me."

"Is everything all right?"

"Yep, and with a bit of luck it's about to be even better. There's been a big break on that cold case I've been working for the last few months. But keep me posted on what you guys find out, because I'm curious as hell to know what caused those burns."

"That makes two of us. You need a ride to the airport?'

"Ben just dropped me off."

"Okay. Good luck with your case, Steve. I'll let you know what happens down here."

***

After they closed down for the night, he retreated to his motorhome.

He revisited the highlights of the remaining stops on the circuit, then did some more calculations and realized that he would have to give up a second round of dosing in Waco, as well.

But it will be worth it, he reminded himself. *I've got to use my remaining formula where it will be the most effective.*

He fixed himself a light meal, ate, and washed and put away his solitary plate and fork before he sat down again. And for the first time in two weeks or more, he found himself without a single thing to do other than tapping his fingers impatiently on the dinette table.

I didn't do it for very long at all, but I got really used to constantly being on the go lately, he realized. *Now that I've got some down time in my schedule again, I'm not entirely sure what to do with myself. I'm kind of bored, actually...*

His shoulders gradually dropped in relaxation as he picked up his remote and flipped channels. He narrowed his choices down to three before he finally decided on a classic movie that he'd never seen, but always wanted to watch. With the remote still in his hand, he moved from the table up to his bunk, stretched out comfortably, and settled in for some television.

He was sound asleep within the first fifteen minutes.

CHAPTER SEVENTEEN

Nathan was scheduled to meet Dr. Rachelle Overtin at her office in Lubbock at ten a.m., so he was up before sunrise. He packed a small bag, kissed Bella tenderly, and went down the hall to kiss a still sleeping Charlie on the forehead before he headed to his car to enter the Lubbock County Medical Examiner's address into his navigation system.

It's a five-hour drive, he confirmed when his GPS displayed its search results. *Better stop on the way and get coffee and breakfast.*

A brief detour through the closest open drive-thru netted him both. He took a moment to rearrange his breakfast sandwich's wrapper to make it easier to eat while driving, then pulled out of the lot and back into the slowly increasing early morning traffic.

***

With Steve's sudden return to D.C. came the unexpected opportunity for Annie to spend the night at Ben's place without dealing with any awkward interactions with their boss's boss.

Ben woke before she did and lured her from her sound sleep a little before six a.m. with the tantalizing aroma of freshly brewed coffee and warm cinnamon rolls. After breakfast they dressed and grabbed their ready bags.

"It's about a five-hour drive, right?" she asked.

"Three hundred and thirty miles, so yes, roughly five hours," Ben confirmed as he locked the door to his apartment.

Annie tilted her head. "And we're meeting with Dr. Gillespie at noon, right?"

"Yep. We'll have time for one quick stop in between here and there but that's about it."

"Unless you let me drive," she teased. "*I* can get us there in four."

He pondered it, then tossed her the keys.

**

Lizzie and Donny's trip to investigate the San Angelo victim's death was the shortest distance to travel - a mere two-hundred-forty miles. But when she called him, Doctor Heming hadn't been able to commit to meeting and talking with Lizzie until at least one in the afternoon.

"I'm so sorry, Agent Zimmerman. I have a deposition starting at nine o'clock in the morning, and I have no idea how long it might last. We can try for one p.m. and see how it goes. That's the best I can do at the moment," the coroner told her apologetically.

To which Lizzie replied, "I completely understand, sir. How about this. I'll give you my cell phone number, and you can call me whenever you're ready. I'll make sure I'm in San Angelo by noon, just in case."

As a result, compared to her teammates, she and Donny had the relative luxury of sleeping in until seven-thirty a.m. before they left Arlington.

After a light breakfast they got underway, heading west on Interstate 20 for the first ninety minutes of their drive.

**

By comparison, the killer's sleep schedule was even more luxurious. With nothing to booby-trap in the near future, he was able to sleep soundly until almost ten a.m. before he slowly stretched his lanky frame, then descended from his bunk to brew himself some coffee.

**

Nathan made excellent time, arriving ten minutes ahead of schedule, and introduced himself to Cleve.

"Nice to meet you, Agent Thomas. Right this way. Doc said to bring you on back when you got here."

"Thanks, Cleve," Nathan said when the man stopped beside a door down the hall to the right of the lobby area and gestured for the federal agent to pass through.

"Good morning, Agent Thomas," Dr. Overtin said from behind her desk as she typed furiously. "Bear with me just a moment as I wrap up this email. Go ahead and have a seat anywhere you'd like."

"By all means," he replied, and selected the right-hand visitor's chair in front of him.

A couple of minutes passed while she continued her typing, and Nathan seized the opportunity to quickly scan his own emails for any urgent items. Finding none, he relegated his cell phone back to his pocket.

"And, done. Sorry about that," Overtin told him with a warm smile. "Bureaucracy. You know the drill."

"I do. Fun, isn't it?"

She laughed. "Not in the slightest. Now, the Toby Bryton case. What would you like to know?"

He pulled his legal pad and pen out of his briefcase and answered, "For starters, can you clarify for me which Wayside, Texas the body was found in? When I tried to look it up, I found *two* of them - one north of here, and one to the south."

"The southern one. About twenty minutes from here. He was found around mile marker 314, to be exact. And that Wayside is pretty much a ghost town. Nothing around out there but a few farms and ranches, so, it's a good area to do things like leave a body and not be seen doing it, I suppose."

Nathan made a note about the location before he asked, "Can you please describe the burns you found in more detail?"

***

While Annie didn't match her boasted time of four hours, she did manage to shave twenty-eight minutes off of the trip. Annie and Ben had a bit of a wait when they reached the Midland County Medical Examiner's office as a result.

They signed in at the visitor's desk and took seats in the sparsely appointed lobby.

"Dr. Gillespie might be running a bit behind," the receptionist informed them. "There was an accident overnight that he was called in for."

"That's fine, thank you," Annie replied.

Ten minutes later the receptionist's phone rang. After a brief conversation, she hung up and looked at the agents occupying two of her chairs.

"Dr. Gillespie's asked me to let you know he needs to postpone your meeting until two p.m.," she announced. "I'm terribly sorry."

"It's all right," Ben assured her. "We can take a lunch break and come back. Is there a place nearby that you'd recommend?"

***

"Okay, gang, last day in Waco," Clint Asters told his crew at what the madman in their midst had begun to think of as the 'pre-opening pep rally' meetings.

"We had a great turnout yesterday, and I expect another busy one today," the site foreman announced. "We had a bit of a stutter-step, getting hung up in Midland like we did, but we've made up for it, and I appreciate each and every one of you for helping me make that happen. We only have three more weeks on this circuit, and then we all get to go home to our families."

Well, not all *of us,* the man responsible for two team members' untimely demises thought to himself sarcastically before he returned his attention to Clint's motivational speech.

"So, everybody stay safe today and keep that momentum going. We'll lock it down tonight at eleven o'clock sharp, and we'll roll out in the morning at nine a.m. Any questions?"

When his query was met with silence, Clint nodded to the group.

"You know what to do."

I do, actually.

Too bad I have to wait until we get to Dallas.

***

As planned, Lizzie and Donny's SUV was passing the San Angelo city limits sign two minutes before noon.

"How about we find someplace to eat, then go from there," Donny suggested. "And once Heming calls you, I can drop you off if you want. Bert said his schedule is wide open, so I can meet him pretty much anytime today, and it shouldn't take long at all."

They found a mom-and-pop style café not far from their destination and stopped for a leisurely lunch. It was just after the waitress had cleared their empty plates that Lizzie's phone rang.

"Good afternoon, Agent Zimmerman," Heming said. "I just got out of court. Let me grab a quick bite and I can meet you at one-fifteen, if that's all right."

"That's fine, sir. See you then."

She looked at Donny.

"He can meet in about twenty minutes, and his office is only about four blocks from here."

"What are you thinking?"

"I'm thinking walk it."

"Lizzie. It's August. In Texas. It's *already* ninety-eight degrees outside."

"Pardon my interruption, but we haven't even hit the high today yet. Weatherman said it's supposed to be a hundred and four degrees by three o'clock," the waitress chimed in as she put their slices of pie on the table in front of them. "With a heat index of a hundred and *twelve*. I'm not trying to poke my nose in your business, ma'am, but if it were me? I wouldn't walk *anywhere* in this heat if I didn't absolutely have to."

Lizzie grimaced, crinkling her nose.

"Good point. I didn't even think about that," she admitted. "Ugh. Yeah, never mind."

The waitress chuckled before she subtly put their check on the table and walked away.

Lizzie shrugged her shoulders.

"Guess I spent too long in Seattle," she confided to a grinning Donny. "I forgot how hot it can get down here."

***

By the time Lizzie and Donny finished their apple pie, Nathan Thomas had wrapped up his conversation with a friendly and helpful Dr. Overtin and made the twenty-mile journey south to mile marker 314, three miles north of the former small town of Wayside, Texas.

He pulled over, parked, and stepped out of his car, immediately missing the blasts of cool air he'd been surrounded by inside the vehicle.

Nathan eased to the edge and looked down at the drainage ditch some thirty feet below the shoulder of the road. Not much rain at all had come through the region since Toby's body had been found, so traces of the biodegradable pink spray paint sometimes used by crime scene techs at outdoor scenes remained.

After surveying the slope for a moment, he opted to proceed downward at an angle rather than attempting to move straight down the steep pitch.

I need to go really slowly here. Can't solve anything at all if I break my freaking neck out here in the middle of nowhere, he thought as he gingerly made his way to the drainage ditch, breathing a sigh of relief when he reached the bottom.

Overtin said she believes whatever killed him was ingested, he recalled as he looked around and swatted at the horde of gnats that had him surrounded. *But I don't see anything here at all. No bottles, cans, or wrappers of any sort - at least, none that haven't obviously been here for months before Toby got here. I agree with her that he was killed elsewhere and dumped here.*

But there's no telling where *he actually died. That could have happened anywhere in a two-hundred-mile radius,* he thought wistfully as he eyeballed the steep slope again, plotting his return topside.

"Guess I'll talk to the police in Lubbock about his truck getting towed, and see where that leads," Nathan grunted aloud as he chose his steps carefully across the face of the slope and slowly worked his way up.

He paused to catch his breath and wiped his sweaty face with a small towel from his ready bag once he was standing beside his car again.

I need to start exercising more. I thought I was in pretty good shape, but that wore me out.

He sat behind the wheel for a few minutes letting himself cool off before he made a U-turn to return to Lubbock and ask more questions.

***

"Call me when you're ready," Donny said, and Lizzie nodded, then shut the passenger door and walked into the Tom Green County Medical Examiner's office building.

She was greeted almost immediately by the pathologist himself.

"Hi there! You must be Agent Zimmerman. It's so nice to meet you. Come right this way and let's get started," the short brown-haired man with friendly eyes said. "I'm sorry that you had to wait on me."

"It was no problem," she replied sincerely. "Betty's Place has really good food."

Heming chuckled. "They absolutely do, and I myself eat way too much of it. Especially the apple pie. You tried it, right?"

"I did," she confirmed. "And yes, it was pretty good."

They walked side by side into a small conference room.

"I thought we'd set up in here. My office is cramped, but also a bit of a mess," he revealed, his cheeks turning pink with the admission.

They settled in at the table, and Lizzie pulled out her notepad.

"So, I reviewed the file copy on Ralph Smith's autopsy," she began, "but I wanted to come talk to you in person, maybe get some details or impressions that reading a file wouldn't provide."

"Completely understandable. What would you like to know?"

They walked through the Smith case slowly and in-depth, but Lizzie wasn't gleaning anything new until Heming mentioned, "He was most likely injected with whatever killed him. There was a small spot of blood under his jawline, at his carotid. When I cleaned it off there was a clear, very tiny puncture mark."

"Do you have pictures?"

"He's still here, actually. You can see it for yourself up close, if you like. We still haven't made contact with his family," Heming explained.

"Yes, please."

They walked down the narrow hallway to the examination room, where Heming pulled open a cold storage drawer and slid the metal gurney out a bit, then lifted the plastic sheet and pointed.

"There, on the right side."

Unfazed, Lizzie bent over and looked closely.

"Yep, that's definitely from a needle," she agreed. "I've seen marks like that before when I was with Seattle PD. Worked a few overdose cases. But in those cases, the tox screens still popped positive for the substances involved. I know your notes said his tox screen came back clean. Must have been something that the body metabolizes very rapidly."

Heming nodded, impressed. "It would have to have an extremely short half-life for no trace to remain after twenty-four hours."

He frowned as a realization hit.

"Or," he said carefully, "it's a substance that is naturally metabolized as a function of death... that's... interesting...".

"Let me ask you this," Lizzie interjected. "In one of the other cases involved here, the victim tested positive for nicotine. Could nicotine be the cause of these burns we're talking about?"

"Absolutely not," Heming responded without hesitation. "Whatever caused the burns was either *extremely* acidic or extremely basic on the pH scale, and the result was that it acted as a corrosive as it traveled through the body. By that I mean the substance's pH level would have been lower than two-point-five or higher than twelve-point-five. Nicotine in its popular commercially available 'liquid vape' form ranges in pH between five and nine, by comparison."

"The case with the nicotine," Lizzie said. "Those burns were subcutaneous. If the mystery substance is that corrosive, why weren't there any burns on the *outer* layers of skin?"

Heming's eyebrows raised.

"Seriously?"

"That's what Dr. Gillespie's notes said."

"Interesting," the pathologist said again, deep in thought. "So, it's something corrosive that's obviously lethal in a big enough dose, yet it doesn't leave any exterior damage on the skin? Hm. The only thing I can think of is that it might have been mixed with something to lessen - or increase - its pH long enough to be administered."

He glanced up and smiled at Lizzie's confused look.

"Almost some sort of binding agent, or a buffer, for lack of a better term," Heming explained, then continued his line of reasoning. "And once it's in, the interaction with certain naturally occurring chemicals in the body would break up and remove that binding agent, and set the substance loose, so to speak. Then once death happens, the substance is cleared out rapidly during the initial post-mortem stages... But I've never even *heard* of anything like that at all..."

Lizzie scribbled furiously on her notepad as she listened to him talk out the possibility, her pen going still when he grew quiet for a long moment.

"Well. I can definitely say that while I don't know yet what killed Ralph Smith, I *do* know for certain he didn't die in his bed," Heming announced suddenly, changing the focus of their discussion back to the body lying on a metal slab between them. "Take a look at this."

He gently lifted Ralph's right arm to show her what he was talking about.

"See how this is mottled? Not consistent at all with the way he was found. He was found lying on his back, with his arms down by his sides, so this mottling should have been on the *underside* of the arms, not this side. But this pattern, coupled with the bruising around his wrists, tells me that he died with his hands bound together behind his back, and most likely he was also lying face-down, giving the pooling in his upper torso, neck, and face. Similar patterns elsewhere on the body further prove that he was moved and staged after he died. You can't erase or alter the effects of gravitational pooling, no matter what."

"I don't suppose you have any copies of the crime scene photos?"

"I do, but I think you'd get more out of it to be able to walk through it in person, don't you? After all, his car and camper are still at the impound yard. Like I said, no one's been able to reach his family yet."

Lizzie's ears perked up at that statement.

"That's a lucky break. I figured they would have already been long gone."

"Nope. Not yet anyway. Technically, family involved or not, they actually had to wait on *me* to release the scene before they could even tow it to the impound yard in the first place," Heming confessed. "Because there was nothing natural at all about Ralph Smith's death, so at first I refused to let the police touch a single thing until I get some solid answers as to what happened to him. But it was parked right next to our high school's football stadium, and the team's two-a-day practices started this week, so I finally relented and let them move it. Didn't want anybody breaking into the camper."

"When might I be able to go take a look?"

"Happy to take you over to the impound yard right now, if you're ready. Just let me tidy up and get my keys."

He deftly arranged the plastic sheet over Ralph Smith's remains and moved the gurney back into its refrigerated slot, then closed the small square door before he stepped over to the steel sink to wash his hands thoroughly.

***

In Lubbock, Texas, Nathan Thomas wrapped up his queries at the police department and retreated to his car. He entered the address for Toby's parents into his GPS, and sighed.

Another hundred and fifty miles to drive.

His stomach rumbling loudly reminded him that breakfast had happened too many hours ago, and he recalled passing a string of fast-food joints on his way to the police station. He pulled out of the visitor's parking lot and drove back the way he'd come in, taking his place in line at the closest burger chain's drive-through.

Once he'd traded money for food, he pulled over into the first empty parking spot available and nibbled on French fries as he dialed the number the police had provided for Marty and Helen Bryton.

A few minutes later Nathan confirmed their meeting time of five p.m., then thanked Helen for taking his call. After he hung up, he purposely cleared his mind and focused solely on eating his meal while it was still warm.

***

Meanwhile, Annie and Ben were introducing themselves to a very tired-looking Barry Gillespie down in Midland's Medical Examiner office complex.

"Sorry I had to push out our meeting," he said as he stifled a yawn. "I got called out to a scene just after midnight, and I've been going full-steam on it since."

"Been there," Ben told him. "We understand."

"Now, refresh my memory. You've come down here about three cases, correct?"

"Yes, sir," Annie confirmed. "Jake Morgan, and Elaine and Timmy Steward."

"Weird burns, on all three of them," the pathologist commented as he rubbed his eyes. "And the strangest part was, while all the burns looked exactly the same, Mr. Morgan's burns were in a different location. Which tells me the method of exposure was different. His was primarily in his nose, throat, bronchial tubes and lungs, which points straight to inhalation. And the Stewards both had burns throughout their bodies - pretty much everywhere *but* the respiratory tract. I thought maybe at first theirs was a topical exposure. But there were little to no disruptions on the epidermis. Strangest thing I've ever seen - and I've seen a lot."

"Disruptions?"

"Marks, burns. Damage of any sort. The only thing I noticed was that their skin looked a bit pink, like they'd gotten a mild sunburn. Not surprising for July in Texas, and they were both very fair-skinned, so, it could have been as simple as that. But even a third-degree sunburn wouldn't have done *that* kind of internal damage."

Ben and Annie asked a few more questions to clarify a couple of points, including the names of the physicians who'd treated each patient at the hospital.

"Those are in my supplemental notes. Hang on just a sec," Gillespie replied, and pulled up the case files on his computer.

"Here we go.... All right. The lead on Morgan's treatment was Ed Howerton. Andrew Maunrey was the pediatrician that treated Timmy, and.... yes, here it is. Gabrielle Marshall was the primary on Elaine Steward's case."

When the man yawned again, Ben glanced over at Annie, and when she nodded her agreement, he told the pathologist, "I believe we've got what we need, for now. Thank you for your time, Dr. Gillespie."

***

Once they'd parted company with Dr. Gillespie and retreated to the car, Annie turned to Ben.

"What do you think? Go check things out at the hospital first, or talk to Mark Steward first?"

"Not sure, actually," Ben responded. "I was leaning toward taking on the hospital next, but now, I'm thinking that getting what I am sure will be a difficult conversation with Mr. Steward done and over with is a good idea."

"I agree," Annie said softly. "He's been through enough. We'll keep it simple and short, and head to the hospital afterward."

***

Mark Steward sat in his living room across from the agents. He was pale and gaunt, his grief marring usually handsome features and haunting his sky-blue eyes.

"They were my entire world," he said listlessly. "Elaine and I have been together since our sophomore year of high school, and we got married right after we graduated college."

He swallowed hard.

"Our life together was perfect, except for one thing. We tried for years to have kids. But after several miscarriages, we'd given up hope. Timmy..."

Mark's voice broke, and he closed his eyes and fell silent for a moment.

"Timmy was a miracle baby," he finally managed in a rough whisper filled with deep, raw pain. "Our child... our precious little boy that we thought we would never get to have..."

He opened his eyes and looked at Annie and Ben.

"I'm sorry. I can't help you. I have no idea who would have harmed them, or why. Elaine could be a little overzealous when it came to Timmy, but that doesn't justify hurting either one of them."

Mark Steward slowly rose from his chair, tears streaming freely, and softly said, "I can't help you, and I really don't want to talk about this anymore. Please excuse me."

Before they could offer their condolences, he turned and left the living room, and a somber Ben and Annie quietly saw themselves out.

***

They were almost to the hospital before Annie found her voice to break the oppressive silence.

"That poor, poor man," was all she could get out before she broke down.

Ben pulled over to the curb, parked the truck, and tried his best to comfort her as she wept.

"I know, Annie. I know."

After a few minutes she wiped her face with some napkins from the stash Ben kept in his glove compartment. When she turned to look at him, Ben could see the steely glare in her green eyes and determined set to her jaw.

"Whoever did this needs to pay," she announced. "So, let's get moving. We have a killer to catch."

CHAPTER EIGHTEEN

When Lizzie finally called Donny to come pick her up, he asked, "So I guess it went well?"

"Very well. I'll tell you all about it when I see you. Speaking of which, how far away are you?"

"Be there in the next fifteen minutes."

When Donny pulled up Lizzie got in the SUV and immediately dialed Nathan's number.

"How's it going in Lubbock?" she asked when he picked up the call.

"It went well. Got some more data from Dr. Overtin, then went to walk the site where Toby Bryton was found. After that I talked to the folks at the police department about his abandoned truck, and now, I'm heading to Amarillo for the interview with Toby's family. How are things in San Angelo?"

"Dr. Heming is a wealth of information, seriously," Lizzie shared. "He found a puncture mark on Ralph Smith's right carotid that leads us to believe whatever killed the man was *injected*, not inhaled or eaten. I asked Heming about the nicotine level that showed up in the little boy's tox screen and asked him if nicotine would leave burns like this. He said, very clearly, that there was no way that nicotine could have caused those burns on *any* of the victims, because the pH simply isn't high or low enough to be corrosive. Smart cookie. He's even got some theories as to why the two deaths in Midland with interior burns didn't have any damage to their skin. I learned a lot that I think will really help us with all this."

"Sounds like it."

"I wonder how things are going in Midland. Have you heard from Ben and Annie?"

"No," Nathan replied. "I was about to call and check on them."

"Anything else you need me to do? I'd still planned on swinging by the hospital here, but with Ralph Smith being pronounced DOA, I don't know how much more intel I'll be able to get that will be useful."

"Due diligence," came the response. "Let's cover all our bases, just in case. After that, if no new leads surface, then head home. We'll meet up in the morning and pool our data."

"Roger that. Bye."

"Okay, then. Let me drive you to the hospital, and after that it sounds like we're free to leave," Donny commented as he backed out of his parking space.

***

Ben and Annie's arrival to the hospital in Midland was well-timed for the most part; both Andrew Maunrey, the pediatrician, and Gabrielle Marshall, who'd attended Elaine Steward, were on shift. But it was Dr. Howerton's day off.

They found a youthful-looking sandy-haired Andrew Maunrey in the lounge area refilling his coffee mug. He smiled and shook hands with each of them upon introduction.

"But please, call me Andy," he said. "I was wondering when you guys would show up."

"You were expecting us?"

Now the pediatrician was confused.

"Department of Health didn't call you in?"

"No. Dr. Heming with Tom Green County brought five very similar cases to our attention."

"Oh," Maunrey said, startled. "That's weird. I thought you were here to ask about the wave of strange cases we had around here in mid-July."

Ben and Annie exchanged puzzled looks.

"Andy," Ben said solemnly, "I think the three of us had better find a quieter place to talk. It sounds like there's a *lot* that we aren't aware of."

"I think so too. Let me fill my department head in on what's going on and ask her to join us. Can you guys wait right here for me? I'll be right back."

"Sure. One thing, though," Annie chimed in as she flipped through her small notepad to locate the names Gillespie had given them. "We also need to talk to a Dr. Marshall and a Dr. Howerton, and we were just told that Dr. Howerton is off today. Any chance of getting both of them to join us, as well?"

"Dr. Marshall's a given - she's our department head," Maunrey relayed with a friendly grin. "And let me see what I can do about getting Ed to come up here. Hang tight. Help yourself to some coffee, if you like. I just made it."

As Dr. Maunrey left the lounge, Annie pulled out her cell phone. "I'm going to call Nathan," she said, and Ben nodded.

***

"I was just about to call and see how the investigation in Midland was coming along," Nathan said when Annie's voice came to him through his hands-free setup.

"Look, we think there's more to all this than just the five cases Heming called you about. Andy Maunrey, the man who treated Timmy Steward, just asked us if we were here to talk about, quote, 'the *wave* of strange cases in mid-July'. He's rounding up the other doctors as we speak so we can all sit down together and figure out what the hell's going on."

"I just got off the phone with Lizzie. Interestingly enough, she said Heming had some theories about the Steward cases," Nathan revealed. "If it's possible at all, I'd like for you to conference Lizzie and me in once your group there is assembled. Something tells me we're going to need to be able to exchange information on the fly here."

"Will do."

"And I'm going to call Lizzie and get her to go back to Dr. Heming's office for the meeting. I'd like him to be involved, as well."

"Good idea. Hang on just a second," Annie said when Dr. Maunrey came back to the lounge.

"Ed will be here in twenty minutes," he told the agents, and Annie relayed the timeframe to Nathan.

"Get it set up, then call me. I'll make sure I'm pulled over somewhere," Nathan directed.

"You got it, boss. I'll talk to you shortly."

***

"Change of plans," Nathan told Lizzie over the phone as she exited through the hospital's front doors. "I need you and Dr. Heming both on a call that's going to happen in the next twenty to thirty minutes."

"Sounds ominous," Lizzie replied, and heard him sigh.

"I hope not, but yeah. I think this thing's about to blow up. Be ready."

She hung up the phone, then called the pathologist.

"Dr. Heming," she began, "I think there's about to be a major development, and we're going to need your input. I'm on my way back to your office as we speak. You and I both need to be a part of a conference call here shortly."

"I'm glad to help. See you soon."

"Back we go, please," she said to Donny when she got back to the SUV. "I need to go see Heming again."

***

A half-hour later, Ben, Annie, and the three physicians had gathered around a conference speaker system perched on an oval-shaped table on the second floor of the administration building adjacent to the hospital. As promised, Nathan had found a safe place to park to be able to participate in the call, and Lizzie and Dr. Heming were sitting side-by-side at his conference room's table in San Angelo.

"There," the Midland hospital's IT staffer announced. "Everybody should be on the line now."

"Hello," Nathan's voice came clearly through the speakers. "I'm Nathan Thomas, and I'm a profiler with the FBI's Behavioral Analysis Unit. My team members are at your sites today in Midland and San Angelo because Dr. Heming, the Tom Green County pathologist, brought five very similar cases to our attention. I've asked the Midland group to include me, my agent in San Angelo, and Dr. Heming in this meeting to discuss new evidence that could assist in our investigations."

Gabrielle Marshall took point, and after introducing herself said, "We're happy to assist in any way we can. Initially, we believed your agents to be here due to the total of thirty-one unusual cases that came through our emergency department in a thirty-six-hour period on July fourteenth and fifteenth. Of those cases, three were fatalities - Jake Morgan, and Elaine and Timmy Steward. But now, it's our understanding that *only* the three fatal cases were brought to the FBI's attention."

"Yes, ma'am, that is correct," Nathan answered. "And the five cases that we knew about, all fatalities, are spread over three towns - Lubbock, Midland, and San Angelo. Can you please give us an overview of the remaining cases you treated at your facility?"

Gabrielle gestured to Andy Maunrey.

"Hello, Agent Thomas, Dr. Heming. I'm Andy Maunrey, the pediatrician who was working the night Timmy Steward was brought in. Once we discovered nicotine in his system, and I realized that we'd had seven other cases present within an hour of Timmy with very similar symptoms, we ran toxicology screens on *all* of them. Every single one of those first seven cases tested positive for nicotine and three other unknown substances. Patients who arrived later in that thirty-six-hour period all tested negative for nicotine, but still had those three other substances appear in their tox results, albeit in smaller quantities."

"Dr. Heming here. Your thirty-one cases - did they all appear to have a mild sunburn anywhere on them?"

The Midland doctors conferred quietly for a moment.

"Yes, Dr. Heming, as a matter of fact, they did. I personally didn't think much of it at the time," Maunrey said. "It's summertime in Texas. Lots of folks get mild sunburns, so that just didn't stick out to me as odd. But given the tox results, I did call the local health department and let them know that I thought we had a public health emergency going on."

"Interesting. Did you ever get any feedback as to what they found out?" Nathan asked.

"Well, we knew that every patient had attended the carnival that was in town on the fourteenth. I believe the theory was that some food or beverage at the carnival was what made everyone sick. But no two patients had exactly all the same things to eat and drink, and five of them that I am personally aware of didn't eat or drink anything at the carnival at *all*," Gabrielle Marshall chimed in. "The Department of Health did due diligence and went and collected samples of every type of food and drink at the carnival, and every single sample came back negative. I've not heard yet if they've made any other strides in their investigation, but I can tell you that we've not had any more cases here in Midland since July fifteenth."

"Thank you for sharing that. Dr. Heming," Nathan prompted, "will you please share your theories about the substance and the delivery methods?"

"Happy to. I believe that the level of corrosive burning each autopsy revealed is a marker of the substances that killed these five people. I also believe that for the patients in Midland, the delivery method was topical - through skin absorption. That would explain what might look like a mild sunburn - only it's actually the milder initial effects of being exposed to an aerosol that's corrosive. Now, for something that caused that much internal damage to not decimate the epidermis would be unheard of - *unless* the corrosive substance being used was mixed with a binding agent to neutralize its effects at first."

"It becomes a sleeper, basically, isn't that what you're saying, Dr. Heming?" Dr. Howerton interjected. "The binding agent keeps the adverse properties of the substance at bay until it reaches a certain depth in the tissue, perhaps?"

"Precisely. Think of the binding agent a bit like a gelatin capsule. It contains the corrosive substance at first, but eventually it breaks down."

Ben spoke up. "That's right. The coroner here in Midland, Dr. Gillespie, indicated in both Elaine's and Timmy's autopsy notes that all their burns were widespread - but *subcutaneous*."

"Agent Lizzie Zimmerman here. I have a question for the doctors on the call. If there were thirty-one people in Midland, all exposed to the same mystery substance, why weren't there thirty-one fatalities? What was different about Jake Morgan and the Stewards that meant they died but the others lived? Any variations in their treatments, comparative to the others?"

"Oh, dear God," Andy Maunrey said suddenly.

A chorus of "What?" came at him from around the room and across the speakers.

"Of the thirty-one cases treated at this facility," he said slowly and carefully, "only three of them developed respiratory distress to the point that they had to be intubated to make certain they were getting enough oxygen. Those three cases? Jake Morgan, Timmy Steward, and Elaine Steward."

"If I'm hearing you correctly," a solemn Dr. Heming said, "what that means is that the corrosive properties of this substance, whatever it is, are *amplified* by oxygen?"

"That's what I'm saying," Maunrey confirmed.

"But that's a basic tenet of emergency medicine!" Gabrielle exclaimed. "It's an established protocol when a patient is in respiratory distress. If we don't intubate when a patient desperately needs it to help them breathe, then..."

All were quiet as they wrestled with the revelation.

"So, in trying to help them by intubating them, we inadvertently magnified the effects of whatever they'd been exposed to," Howerton said morosely.

"Not to mention, it seems whoever is exposing people to this stuff figured out more than one way to do it, and still have serious effects," Annie pointed out. "Through the skin, by swallowing it, or by inhaling it."

"Here's a question. Is it possible in the case of absorption through the skin that it wouldn't have to *stay* an aerosol to be effective? What I mean is, if it's sprayed, can it still be dangerous if a person comes into contact with it afterward?" Nathan asked.

"You mean like touching a surface that it's been sprayed on?" Dr. Heming answered. "With the evidence we're talking about, I'd say yes, that's exactly what happened in Midland. Unless it can be confirmed that all thirty-one patients did something that put them in direct contact with it still in aerosol form, like stand under a misting tent to cool off."

"None of them mentioned misting tents, at all, during their intake questioning," Gabrielle confirmed. "But every single one of them got on at least one ride at the carnival."

When Nathan spoke again, it was with a deadly calm, and only his agents knew by his clipped tones that he was pissed off to his core.

"Dr. Marshall, if you could please pass along the name of who I need to speak with regarding the testing done at the carnival, I'd appreciate it. Two final questions for the group. Does anyone happen to know the name of the carnival company, and where they were heading when they left Midland, Texas?"

Gabrielle Marshall supplied the point of contact that he'd requested.

As for Nathan's two questions, no one could say.

***

"Holy crap," Lizzie exclaimed, her wide-eyed gaze locked with Dr. Heming's once the call ended.

"Indeed. I think it would serve your investigation very well to expand your search parameters across a *much* larger geographical area."

He pressed the intercom button.

"Chad, could you join us for a moment?"

While they waited for Chad to appear, Lizzie checked her phone to find a new text from Nathan.

We're going to have another call in twenty minutes to talk more about what we just learned. I'll call and connect you in - N.

"He is super pissed," she confided when Heming looked at her with a raised eyebrow.

"I don't blame him. Forgive my phrasing, but it sure sounds like whoever took the samples at that carnival had an excellent chance of stopping this right then - had they not half-assed it."

Heming's blunt comment had Lizzie grinning, despite the circumstances.

"That's pretty much *exactly* what I was just thinking, sir. I just wasn't going to say it out loud."

Heming returned her grin.

"Yes, sir?" Chad asked as he walked in.

"That networking group of yours," Heming prodded. "Any new messages in there lately about all this?"

"I haven't checked lately, to be honest."

"Can you, please? It's quite important."

"Yes, sir, I'll be right back."

"One other thing that just occurred to me, Agent Zimmerman," Heming said after Chad left. "Whatever this stuff is, it's powerful, and it doesn't take much to cause some very serious issues. That means there is a very specific demographic of your typical carnival-going crowd that is at extremely high risk of serious illness or death."

When she raised her eyebrows, he elaborated, and his words hung heavy in the air between them like a malevolent omen.

"Children," he said softly, concern darkening his eyes. "And I'd say especially those weighing less than eighty pounds would be the most vulnerable here."

***

"Thanks again for all the information," Ben said as he and Annie stood and shook hands with Dr. Marshall, Dr. Maunrey, and Dr. Howerton.

"Good luck," Maunrey told them sincerely. "And let us know how it turns out."

They were walking down the stairs to the ground floor when Annie's phone chimed. She paused, scanned the message, then read it aloud to Ben.

We're going to have another call in twenty minutes to talk more about what we just learned. I'll call and connect you in - N.

"Yep, he's furious," was Ben's immediate comment. "I feel really sorry for whoever he gets hold of at the health department."

***

Technically, Nathan could have assembled his team for the call right away.

But I need to fill Steve in, and I also need some time to try and calm down some. This could have damn well been stopped in Midland, and it wasn't - all because of a piss-poor job of investigating. And now, there's no telling how many other people were exposed...

He gripped his steering wheel so tightly that his knuckles turned white as he counted down from three hundred in his head.

Nathan Thomas was only slightly calmer when he got to 'one' and dialed his boss's number.

"Are you sitting down? If not, you might want to, because you're not gonna *believe* this," was the phrase he used to start his conversation with Steve Brown.

***

He called Lizzie first and then brought Annie and Ben into the call, after which Nathan immediately launched straight into his plan.

"As of now, per home office, this is an official full-scale FBI investigation, using any and all resources available, and this team is running the entire show all the way through to the end. Matter of fact, our top lab techs are coming down to Dallas. They will arrive in the morning. Here's what needs to happen next. Ben, I need you and Annie digging and finding out what the hell carnival company that is. I want as much as you can find - company name, address, who owns it, how many employees, years in business, the works."

"Yes, sir," they answered him in unison.

"Lizzie, I want you doing a statewide search at this point - any case at all within the last three months where the victim had unexplained burns."

"On it, boss."

"I'm going to get in touch with whoever at the health department decided it was okay to *not* test every square inch of the environment in question and let them know that I'm pulling rank. Get yourselves back home. We meet in the conference room at seven a.m. sharp. Any questions?"

"Nathan, Dr. Heming said something to me just now, after our conference call, that all of you really need to know," Lizzie said gently. "His strong opinion is that children, particularly those weighing less than eighty pounds, are at the highest risk of dying if they come into contact with whatever this stuff is."

They all clearly heard Nathan's sharp, reactive inhale, and no one spoke.

"Thanks for the info, Liz. I'll see everyone in the morning," he finally managed to say, and hung up.

***

Donny swiveled his head to the right to gape at his fiancée.

"*Wow*," he exclaimed, having witnessed Nathan's acidic tone first-hand due to the SUV auto-synching Lizzie's phone to the hands-free feature.

"I don't think I've ever heard him anywhere *close* to being that mad before. Have you?"

"No, I haven't," Lizzie confirmed. "And I hope like hell that *I'm* never the reason he sounds that way. Let's go home, honey."

"You got it."

She leaned back against the padded headrest and gazed out the passenger window, suddenly exhausted to her core. Because deep down, she knew *exactly* why Nathan had gasped like that after she'd shared Heming's last observation with the group.

He immediately thought of Charlie... just like I did.

***

Nathan had to reset his temper by counting down again after he finished his call to the health department that had so badly botched things. It wasn't until he was roughly five miles from his destination in Amarillo that his blood pressure returned to normal. He took several deep breaths and realigned his focus before he rang the doorbell of Marty and Helen Bryton's home.

His conversation with Toby's parents was heartbreaking; they'd had him later in life, and Toby had been an only child. But a single detail passed on by them - the names of two of Toby's closest friends - paid dividends.

Nathan Thomas finally found Blake and Jason at the local watering hole, relaxing after a long day of hauling hay.

"I'd like to ask you a few questions about Toby, if you don't mind," he said when he joined them at their table.

At first, the two friends didn't have much to say that was useful. But once the conversation turned to hauling hay versus other summer endeavors Nathan caught a huge break.

"Yeah, Toby was all excited about his summer gig," Jason said sadly, staring into his mug of beer. "He'd met this guy Jake who took him on as a temporary laborer and was gonna pay him cash under the table. He was really rubbing it in that we were still stuck out in the hayfields."

"Jake hired him to do what, exactly?"

"Be a carnie."

Nathan did a mental double take.

What are the chances that 'this guy Jake' had the last name Morgan?

"Beg pardon?"

"A *carnie*. You know, working at a carnival?" Blake parroted Jason's answer. "Eat cotton candy, ride the rides, pop the balloon and win a stuffed zebra. That kind of thing. Said he was gonna make big money, too."

"Did he mention anyone else specifically besides this Jake guy?"

"There was that one old dude he talked about the last time we saw him. We were here, playing pool and hanging out with him for his last night in town," Jason recalled, then squeezed his eyes shut briefly as he searched his memory before he gazed at Nathan again. "But I don't think he ever mentioned him by name, though. Toby just called him 'Pops' and said he was creepy as hell, but fun to mess with."

After a few more questions Nathan thanked them, expressed his condolences at the loss of their friend, and walked out to his car for the five-hour drive back to his wife and child.

It was half-past one on Wednesday morning when a mentally and physically exhausted Nathan Thomas wearily pulled into the driveway at his home in Pantego, Texas.

CHAPTER NINETEEN

They still met at seven as scheduled, although with the shortened amount of sleep he got Nathan regretted setting the time so early in the morning.

To compensate, he poured himself a generous amount of coffee before he walked down the hall to the conference room and took the seat at the head of the table at six-fifty-eight a.m.

He took a long sip of his coffee before he reluctantly set it down again.

"Quite a few discoveries made yesterday," he mentioned. "Let's review what we have so far."

Lizzie, Ben, and Annie shared the details of their on-site investigations and their impressions on the conference call that had yielded so much information.

Then it was Nathan's turn.

"I didn't get much out of speaking to Toby's parents," he began, "other than some background on him that's not really germane to the case. But they *did* point me in the direction of two friends of his, Blake and Jason - and my conversation with them took an extremely interesting turn."

He relayed the information they'd shared with him to his team.

"That's *gotta* be the same Jake," Ben muttered.

"I feel that it is. But we still need to be able to connect the dots with zero wiggle room. To do that, we've *got* to be able to say definitively that yes, it was the exact same carnival company operating in Amarillo as it was in Midland."

"If Toby was paid under the table, then he wouldn't show up on a list of employees," Annie pointed out.

"True," Lizzie interjected. "But an employee roster will still show Jake Morgan and Ralph Smith, if our theory is right."

"When we got back last night, we surfed the net a bit. Did you know that there are at least thirteen traveling carnival companies based in Texas alone?" Ben told the group. "Mind you, those are just the ones based *here*. Nationwide, that number jumps to well over a hundred and fifty. And conceivably *any* of them could be operating in Texas this summer. Even if we disregard the companies based farther than four states away, we're still talking a good chunk of data to wade through."

Silence reigned as they mulled over what he'd said.

"Maybe not," Lizzie said.

"What do you mean?" Ben asked.

"Well... think about it. They can't just blow into town and set up, right? Because it involves oversized transport and needing a certain amount of square footage to set up and safety guidelines and everything else. So, they'd *have* to make arrangements ahead of time with the cities they operate in. And I'd guess that those arrangements are made weeks, if not months, in advance."

"Stands to reason," Nathan agreed.

"So, if they make arrangements, they'd need some sort of paperwork to *prove* they've gone through the right channels and are where they're supposed to be, right? Like an operating permit of some sort," Lizzie offered. "I don't know about *every* town in Texas, but I know for sure you have to have a permit in Pantego to even have a garage sale. I would think there'd be a *huge* paper trail for traveling carnivals."

"Wow. Forest for the trees, I guess. I was totally overthinking this. Thanks, Lizzie. That's going to streamline things quite a bit," Ben admitted sheepishly. "And we already know three towns involved - Lubbock, Midland, and San Angelo - that we can reach out to, and go from there."

"You're welcome," Lizzie rejoined with a teasing grin.

"Nice! Lizzie, did you set up the search for like cases?" Nathan asked.

"I got it up and running when I got here this morning. Statewide, the last ninety days, the whole deal, just like we talked about. But I *also* went ahead and built an all-points bulletin, flagged it as 'priority', added in our office's main phone number, and asked anyone with like cases to please give us a call. Hopefully one or both of those things will pop."

***

By that afternoon, things had not just popped, they'd exploded.

On top of the usually high volume of inbound telephone calls, the FBI's Dallas office receptionist had been completely over-whelmed with a flood of additional calls from city and county med-ical examiners and police precincts stretching from El Paso, Texas all the way to New Braunfels, thanks to Lizzie's priority bulletin blast.

When it began around ten a.m., Ben, Lizzie, and Annie stepped up to help capture the deluge of information rolling in, speaking with caller after caller and scribbling furiously as they listened.

By lunchtime, Agent Grace Womack had been unceremoniously drafted to help as well. She was quickly read in, given a list of names and phone numbers, and tasked with helping return the calls that had rolled straight to the primary line's group voicemail inbox.

At around two p.m., after the wave of calls had slowed back down to a trickle, the team switched gears and began to compare the data they'd been given from the phone conversations against the plentiful results that had come back from Lizzie's statewide search.

***

A little after four, a normally calm and unflappable Lizzie appeared, wide-eyed, in Nathan's office. One look at her expression had Nathan raising both eyebrows in concern.

"We've spent the last two hours cross-referencing all the data from the inbound calls with my database search's results. Nathan, we've gotten notifications of...." she glanced at the notes she held in a trembling hand, "fifty-four deaths that are highly probable matches to our five cases."

His jaw dropped open.

"Did you just say *fifty-four*?"

She nodded, looking dazed. "And all of them occurred within the last three weeks. From New Braunfels all the way out to El Paso."

There was a long pause before she spoke again.

"But that's not all. It gets worse," she said softly, almost in disbelief. "*Much* worse."

"Please don't tell me..." his voice trailed off.

Tears came to Lizzie's eyes as she confirmed Nathan Thomas' worst fear.

"Doctor Heming was right. Most of them were little kids, Nathan."

His face drained of color, and his next words came out shaky despite his best efforts to rein in his madly swirling emotions.

"Conference room in fifteen minutes... our team plus Womack, Davis, and Calloway. You'll need to read them in... and shut my door on your way out, please."

She solemnly nodded once in acknowledgement, then quietly left to do as he asked.

***

Once he'd gathered himself, Nathan left his office and headed to the conference room where his team had already assembled.

The room was tense and silent as he joined them at the table.

"Did Lizzie bring you up to speed?" he asked the three agents that typically worked night shift.

"She did," Mark Calloway said as Grace Womack and Herb Davis nodded. "It's horrible."

"It is," Nathan agreed. "And here's what we need to do to find the bastard responsible."

He refocused on the group as a whole.

"How many cases were in El Paso?"

Lizzie flipped through her notes. "Thirty-one in El Paso, another twenty-three in and around Fort Stockton."

"I want you, Mark, Grace, and Herb to leave tonight. Split into pairs. One pair to work the onsite reviews and get file copies gathered up in El Paso while the other pair does the same in Fort Stockton. Make sure you make contact with city officials and get permit data while you're there."

"You got it," Lizzie responded.

"Annie, I want you and Ben to head to New Braunfels and check out the -"

He paused and looked to Lizzie.

"Three," she prompted.

"Thanks," Nathan said then resumed his directive to Annie and Ben.

"Head to New Braunfels to investigate those three cases."

"We'll get on the road within the hour, and we'll ask about permits, as well," Ben confirmed.

***

Forty minutes later, before she and Ben left to start their drive down to work the New Braunfels leads, Annie stuck her head in Nathan's office doorway.

"Nathan, we heard back from a lady with the City of Lubbock. The permit on file there was issued to an All Fun & Games Carnival,

LLC," she said as she walked toward his desk. "She's emailing us a copy of the paperwork. In the meantime, I ran a search for that company name. Here's a preliminary report on them. They're based out of Wichita Falls."

"Great, thanks," he answered as he took the file from her. "And keep pushing to get answers from Midland and San Angelo about *those* permits, please."

"Will do."

He followed her back to the bullpen area where Ben was waiting for her to return.

"Did they already leave?" he asked, pointing to Lizzie's desk.

"Yep, she and Grace headed out about twenty minutes ago. Herb and Mark left right after that."

***

Lizzie touched the hands-free button on her steering wheel.

"Agent Zimmerman."

"It's Nathan. Lubbock answered us. The company who was issued an operations permit for July eleventh through July thirteenth is called All Fun & Games Carnival, LLC. I have a feeling that El Paso and Fort Stockton's permits will be for the same company. If they are, call me immediately."

Grace spoke up.

"I'm texting Mark now to let him and Herb know this, too."

"Thanks. You guys be safe, and I'll talk to you soon."

***

Nathan went home and spent time with his wife and son. Once Charlie was down for the night, he retreated to his home office to expand upon the initial research that Annie had started.

I need information, but I don't want it getting back to the killer that we know about him.

Need to tread very carefully here.

"Well, well," he murmured as he reviewed the spring article that had announced the change in the company's day-to-day management. "I think that's an excellent place to start."

It took him over an hour, but he finally found what he was looking for - the full name and home address of the company's founding - and recently retired - member, Anthony Stallis.

Nathan shut down his computer, added the documents he'd printed out to the folder Annie had given him, and placed the folder in his briefcase.

After that he made his way to bed so that he'd be well-rested for his early morning drive two hours northwest to Wichita Falls.

***

By the time they got to Big Spring it was well after ten p.m.

"No point driving all the way through. We need to be sharp," Grace had answered when Lizzie mentioned that they were coming up on the midpoint of their trek. "I work nights so I wouldn't mind it too much, because I'm wide awake, but you *already* look tired, and we're only halfway there."

Lizzie grimaced even as she admitted, "Yeah, I am. The one thing that's still not right yet after getting hurt in that explosion is my stamina."

"I think you need to cut yourself some slack, girl," Grace retorted. "You bounced back from that a lot better and faster than most people would have."

They pulled into the first hotel parking lot they came to, and as they'd exited the car Lizzie noticed Herb's car had turned in behind them and parked.

"Great minds," Mark Calloway called out to them after he worked his lanky frame up and out of the passenger seat. "I was just telling '*Mister Power-Through-It*' here that even if we keep going and reach Fort Stockton tonight, no one's gonna be open for us to talk to, anyway. *Maybe* the coroner, but definitely not any city offices."

Herb Davis grinned even as he shrugged.

"I don't like stopping. Ever. I wanna get where I'm going. Drives my wife and kids nuts," he deadpanned. "But Mark's right. There's no point in being there before eight a.m."

"After you," Mark said with a flourish as he opened the main lobby door for his female counterparts.

Within fifteen minutes each agent held a magnetic keycard that accessed the single-occupancy room each had booked, and all four were headed toward the elevator.

"She said breakfast is served at what time?" Herb asked.

"Starts at six-thirty," Lizzie confirmed.

"Perfect. I'll see you guys at breakfast, then."

***

Nathan Thomas left his home at six-thirty on the dot. Due to road construction, commuter traffic was already a bit bottlenecked until he got just north of Fort Worth, after which the congested roadways cleared nicely.

He was politely knocking at Anthony Stallis' front door just shy of nine a.m.

***

By the time Nathan reached his destination his four agents in West Texas had already had breakfast and set out again. Herb and Mark turned off the interstate and headed south on their way to Fort Stockton when they reached the city of Monahans, Texas.

Meanwhile, Lizzie and Grace maintained the south/southwest path along I-20 that would lead them straight to I-10, then their target, another five hours away.

***

Ben and Annie arrived at the New Braunfels city hall complex shortly after nine a.m. and were greeted by a friendly receptionist.

"Permits? Oh, sure. Just down this hallway to your right," she indicated.

***

"I appreciate your being willing to talk with me about the company, Mr. Stallis," Nathan began as he took a seat on the older man's living room sofa. "Particularly since I arrived uninvited."

Stallis waved his hand in dismissal.

"You wouldn't be here if it wasn't important, am I right? Although I don't see how an old codger like me can be of any help. My days lately consist of golf when my rheumatoid arthritis isn't flaring up, and treatments when it is."

"You could be much more help than you know," Nathan said earnestly, "and what I'm about to talk to you about is very sensitive. It's imperative that this is kept quiet. But at the same time, I need some information to help me solve what I'm working on."

"And you figure since I built the company from the ground up, I'd be an excellent inside source of information?" Stallis asked with a fierce scowl.

"Actually, yes," Nathan said simply.

The man's scowl disappeared into a sunny smile before he roared with laughter.

"Sounds very cloak-and-dagger," he countered, "and quite possibly the most excitement I've had in years. I love it. What would you like to talk about?"

"Well, sir," Nathan leaned forward, "to put it bluntly, I strongly believe that someone who works at All Fun & Games Carnival, LLC is using the legacy you built to aid them in killing people. I need to find out who, and quickly, so I can put a stop to it."

Stallis' weathered face emptied of all humor in an instant, replaced with a stubbornly set jaw and a furious expression.

"Agent Thomas," he replied solemnly, "anything at all you need, you just let me know. And this conversation won't leave this room."

"I was hoping you would say that," Nathan admitted. "Now, for starters, I need to know the carnival's travel schedule."

"Which one? These days we've got four of 'em out and about at any given time."

"The one I'm interested in was in Lubbock from the eleventh to thirteenth of July."

Stallis stood abruptly and motioned to Nathan.

"Let's move this into the home office," he suggested. "My nephew doesn't know it, but I still log in on occasion and poke around, just to keep tabs on things. I should be able to get you whatever information you need with no one the wiser."

A few minutes later, Stallis was scowling again, this time at his computer screen.

"What an idiot," he growled, unknowingly echoing the late Jake Morgan's sentiments. "Gonna have to have a talk with that boy. He's running my crews into the ground booking stuff this way."

"There," Nathan pointed. "Right there. Any way you can maybe alter that and make those two disappear, or at least delay them?"

"I certainly can," Stallis replied, "but the question becomes what to do with them during that patch of down time, Agent Thomas. A lot of the pieces are huge. They can't just be parked on the side of the road."

The comment sparked an idea.

"What about this?" Nathan began, and shared his concept with the older man.

"I like the way you think. Yeah. I bet we could make that happen, for sure."

Nathan grinned.

"Let me make a quick call."

***

It was just after ten-thirty when Nathan thanked Anthony Stallis and shook his hand, then took his leave. He'd added several printouts to the contents of his briefcase as a result of the very fruitful conversation - and he'd also obtained one vital phone number.

"We can trust him," Stallis said firmly when he'd mentioned altering Nathan's plan just a bit.

Stallis had dialed the number, placed the call on speakerphone, and they'd both spoken at length with the man on the other end.

"I do have one question," Nathan said toward the end of the conversation, "and it doesn't really pertain to what's going on, I'm just curious. When your Dad retired, why didn't *you* take over running the company?"

A short laugh preceded the man's answer.

"And deal with all the paperwork and scheduling and financials and stuff? No way. I'm *much* happier working the circuit. No desire at all to run the whole company."

***

With his resolve doubled Nathan swiftly walked out to his car for the return trip to Dallas. It wasn't until he'd buckled his seat belt that he realized he'd missed a call from Annie.

"Sorry about that," he told her. "What's up?"

"We're done in New Braunfels and heading north. I'm looking at a copy of the New Braunfels permit. Same company, Nathan."

"Good to know. I need you to make stops in Round Rock, Waco and Hillsboro. Get the permit information and make contact with the coroner's office in each place. It's a safe bet that the death toll is actually higher than fifty-four. If there are any like cases, don't wait on them. Ask them to send us copies of the files."

There was a long silence.

"You got the schedule, didn't you? That's great! We can get ahead of this guy now," Annie exclaimed.

"*Precisely*. But our timing will have to be perfect. We're only going to have one chance at this."

***

He'd gotten up at five a.m., his excitement threatening to override his common sense.

One town closer, he'd thought with glee as he'd launched himself, fully awake, from his bunk.

I'm glad, too. These past few days have been so... boring.

He'd showered, dressed, eaten, and had his part of the setup on the transport hauler ready to go well ahead of schedule before he secured his pickup truck on the tow dolly behind his motorhome. A short ninety-minute hop up Interstate 45 lay between him and the last normal setup; it was just a question of exactly when the convoy would leave.

As he watched the clock tick away into afternoon, he fought back a wave of impatience.

Not much longer until the game's on again... the next two days cannot possibly pass soon enough.

At two p.m. the first transport rumbled to life and left the lot.

It's about damn time, he thought to himself as he waited to take up his position toward the back.

***

While Nathan was plotting out how exactly to catch a prolific killer, Joe Wallace arrived for his daily afternoon visit at the rehab facility where Pete Jenkins was slowly coming to grips with his new normal.

"So, I got some news this morning," Pete said suddenly, his tone turning melancholy. "They cut me loose, Joe."

"Cut you loose?"

"I found out I'm being medically retired. Mandatory. No chance to appeal it. And even if there was, I'd be stuck at a desk my whole career and we both know it."

He shrugged as he pointed to the papers on the tiny table beside his bed.

"I'm so sorry," Joe said gently as he skimmed the documents. "I know how big a blow this must have been."

The young man nodded solemnly, and sighed.

"All I've ever wanted to be is a detective, Joe, and it's never gonna happen. What do I do now?"

"I know, son. But this whole thing got me thinking, and I have a proposition for you. You don't have to answer me now, just think about it, and we'll talk more later, if you want."

Pete raised an eyebrow.

"Come work with me when they let you out of here," Joe said simply. "This private investigator stuff of mine is getting way out of hand. I've got a lot more cases than I can work by myself, and you're a wizard with technology. I could sure use the help, Pete."

"I'll think about it," was Pete's reply after a long, thoughtful silence.

"Good. Now then. Have you caught any of the preseason games?" Joe asked in an effort to cheer up his young friend. "I have. Man, that new running back they picked up in the draft is something else."

***

By two-thirty p.m. Nathan's teams had confirmed that the permits issued in Fort Stockton and El Paso were to the same carnival. Each team had checked in with Nathan and were told to make arrangements to have copies of the case files in each jurisdiction shipped up to Dallas.

"Come on back," he told each pair. "We have a trap to set. They can overnight us the files."

***

The convoy had just rolled through Ennis when it was pulled over by Department of Public Safety troopers; every single passenger vehicle and camper in the group was directed to park in the weigh station's adjoining rest area and await further instructions.

Then the Department of Transportation's onsite staff descended to begin the process of painstakingly checking each and every transport hauler, not only for the proper road permits, but driving logs and inspection records.

Clint Asters gathered his crew.

"We're here until they tell us we can leave," he said with a frustrated sigh. "And it looks to be a full-blown inspection, so chances are good we're going to miss our time in Waxahachie completely. But there's nothing I can do about it. Sorry, guys."

His staff grumbled amongst themselves before retreating to their campers.

Once he'd returned to the privacy of his own motorhome, he pulled out his cell phone.

"Agent Thomas? Clint Asters here... Yes sir, they stopped us in Ennis just like you and Dad planned. From the looks of things, we could be tied up here for as long as twenty-four hours... No, sir, I didn't notice any reactions from the guys that seemed strange... Yes, sir. I'll call you when we're cleared to leave. Hopefully all this will give you enough time."

***

Back in his office, Nathan Thomas hung up the phone and smiled a predator's smile.

"And now to confirm phase two," he murmured, and swiveled toward his desk phone to make another series of strategic calls.

***

Both teams dispatched to far West Texas had opted to drive straight through on the return trip once Nathan told them the plan. Herb Davis and Mark Calloway beat their counterparts back to Dallas by a few hours. A tired but determined Lizzie and Grace reached the Metroplex just after midnight.

Lizzie dropped Grace off at her car in the employee garage before she headed to her apartment to get some much-needed sleep.

"If I'm not up by six-thirty, wake me," she told Donny as she crawled into bed beside him and snuggled close.

She was asleep before he could even answer.

CHAPTER TWENTY

At eight a.m. Ben, Annie, Lizzie and Nathan met up with the lab supervisor, a senior officer from the Dallas Police Department, and the three other agents that Nathan had pulled into the active investigation.

"Currently, the whole convoy is stopped here," he said, and pointed to the first position on the map, then slid his finger up to an area of Dallas, "and their destination is *here*. Not a great deal of distance to travel, but when you've got great big transports that need pilot vehicles, things can move really slowly."

"Not to mention restricted routes," the Dallas policeman chimed in. "Certain roadways just weren't built to handle overweight or oversized loads. There are issues with bridge clearances, among other things, so those transports won't have a choice - they'll *have* to take a specific route in, which will also slow it all down."

"Exactly," Nathan confirmed. "Which means we've got a definite window of two hours, at least, once they're cleared to leave."

"Any word yet from your contact, Nathan?" Lizzie asked.

"Not yet," Nathan said with an evil grin. "But I asked both DPS and DOT to be very, very thorough and to not rush. *At all*. Pretty much all that's left to do after this meeting is wait for a phone call, then mobilize."

"So," he said as he retook his seat, "let's do a full run-down of what needs to happen once we get that call - starting with where I want everyone positioned."

***

By the time the convoy obtained the proper oversize and overweight permits to replace the originals - that had mysteriously gone missing, courtesy of one Clint Asters - almost twenty-four hours had passed.

And when they were, at last, cleared to leave the following afternoon, one crew member in particular was beyond ready to get going.

Wasn't going to run my experiment in Waxahachie anyway, he reasoned as a means to console himself at the lengthy disruption.

The site foreman's words to the crew still echoed in his thoughts and made him shiver all over with excitement.

"We're ready to roll, gentlemen," Clint had told them. *"Finally. Waxahachie is a no-go at this point, so it's straight to Dallas for set up. Let's get moving."*

His belly tightened in anticipation as one by one the haulers fired up their engines and prepared to finally get underway again.

A little over one million people live within the Dallas city limits alone, he recalled with a megawatt smile as he turned his motorhome's ignition key. *And over two million county-wide... it's gonna be the biggest batch of test subjects yet.*

***

At three-ten p.m. Nathan walked out to the bullpen to address his team.

"The site foreman just confirmed that they've been released by DPS and DOT," he announced, "and we have a good two hours before they get here. Let's go get into place."

***

The convoy's leading vehicle made the sweeping left turn into the two-hundred-fifty-acre park in Dallas, Texas just before six p.m.

Unbeknownst to everyone in the convoy except the site foreman, federal agents were already tucked strategically throughout the entire venue, including Nathan's perch high above it all in an adjoining building's vacant office space on the tenth floor.

"Recorder ready?" he asked Baxter, the agent manning the high-resolution telescoping camera beside him.

"Yes, sir."

Nathan knew from his conversations with Clint Asters that the operating permit the carnival had been issued wasn't valid until the following day.

"And if someone *is* messing around with stuff, they'd have to be doing it during overnight hours," Clint had explained. "There's way too much activity during the day, and even more while the carnival's running at night, for anyone to be able to tamper with anything without being caught."

"Okay," Nathan said to Baxter on an exhale. "Nothing to do now but wait and watch."

***

Late afternoon gave way to evening, then to nightfall.

"Switch to infrared," Nathan told his cameraman, then raised his own night-vision binoculars to peer through them at the now darkness-shrouded setup below.

***

Finally, he thought to himself, and giggled as he once again dressed all in black, then checked for the third time to make sure his workbag was fully stocked and ready.

He channel-surfed to pass the time, waiting until almost two a.m. before he snuck out of his motorhome and crept stealthily toward the drink station closest to where he'd parked.

***

"We've got movement," Nathan's wingman murmured.

"Yeah, I see him," Nathan acknowledged, and watched as the mysterious figure accessed a small booth at the south end of the horseshoe-shaped configuration.

Nathan slowly reached down and gave his walkie-talkie's microphone button a series of bumps. Single muted chirps in reply let him know that his agents at ground level were watching closely, as well.

When the mystery man got to the halfway point of the layout, Nathan decided it was time to spring the trap. He sent three rapid pulses along the walkie talkie links.

"You keep recording. I'm heading down," Nathan told the agent to his right, and received a single nod from Baxter in acknowledgment.

***

He'd baited six of the twelve drink stations and was making his way to the seventh one when he was suddenly bathed in brilliant white light.

"What's going on, buddy? Can't sleep?" Clint Asters asked softly from behind him.

He spun around, barely succeeding in masking his furious surprise.

"Yeah, I get insomnia a lot," he mumbled, adopting the defeated posture and dimwitted drawl that he'd hidden behind for so long.

"That so? Do you always carry a bag around with you? Let me take a look at that."

The site foreman started walking toward him.

His long-repressed rage began to grow, swelling beyond his capacity to contain it any longer. He snarled, his right hand keeping a tight grasp on his workbag as his left dove swiftly into his front pocket and came back into view holding a switchblade.

He screamed, a horrible, feral, wailing scream that seemed to emanate from his soul, then started to lunge at Clint.

The single thing that stopped him cold was the feel of a Glock nine-millimeter barrel tip pressed against the back of his head.

"I wouldn't do that if I were you," Lizzie growled deep in her throat.

More lights illuminated the scene, and he swallowed hard as he saw he'd been completely surrounded by both plainclothes agents and Dallas police officers - and that more than one weapon was pointing at him. Any chance of escape, however small, had passed.

He dropped the knife and the bag and fell to his knees, raising his hands high above his head even as he glared hatefully at Clint Asters, who he was certain had ruined his grand scheme.

"Smart choice," Lizzie told him, not moving her weapon away from close contact with his cranium until the handcuffs were firmly in place.

Nathan nodded in satisfaction.

"Read him his rights and take him in," he instructed Ben, who moved forward to comply.

Ben recited the Miranda warning to their suspect as he was checked for any other weapons. Officers found two keychains plus one solitary key in the man's pockets, but nothing else. Ben pulled on gloves before he picked up the keys and showed them to Nathan.

"Thanks," Nathan said when a team member offered up an evidence bag to put them in as their suspect was tucked into the back seat of a squad car. "Ben, go with them for processing. I'll be along in a while."

As he watched the suspect being driven away Nathan couldn't shake the nagging feeling that he'd seen him somewhere before. But he couldn't place him, so he dismissed it for the time being and refocused his attention on the next steps.

"Annie, you're on point to get this knife and bag collected and get our lab techs moving on the drink stations that we just watched him access. Those are priority; I want *everything* in those six confiscated for testing immediately. We'll start on the other six plus the full-on site inspection as soon as there's enough daylight. Make damn sure our people know to use biosafety level two handling protocols *at a minimum*, please."

"On it, boss," Annie said, then keyed her radio to organize and launch the evidence collection process as she walked away.

"Can your men help me secure the perimeter? No one in or out?" he asked the senior Dallas officer onsite.

"No problem, whatever you need."

Nathan swiveled his head to look at Clint.

"Which motorhome is his?"

"I'll show you. Right this way."

***

"If you could wait out here, please," Nathan politely said to Clint, and the site foreman nodded.

It only took a few moments to open the motorhome's outer door, and Nathan and the remainder of his team stepped up and into the space. Once inside, Nathan tried key after key on the two keychains to open the locked door leading to what they fully expected to be a normal bedroom space.

"Wait a minute," a frustrated Nathan said under his breath. "This one's got to be by itself for a reason."

He retrieved the lone key from the bag and slid it into the lock, pleased when it turned easily.

But what he saw when the door swung open left him breathless, and he hurriedly shut the door again.

"Everybody out, right now. No one goes any further, " Nathan barked, and all five of them quickly retreated.

When they were outside again, he rapidly rattled off commands, starting with Lizzie.

"I want a physical barrier all the way around that thing - at *least* six feet out, but preferably eight to ten feet. Get with the Dallas officers onsite to get that done. Our lab techs need to process every square inch of this motorhome, but I want them in full hazmat gear before they touch a single thing in there. Coordinate that part with Annie."

"Sure thing," Lizzie replied.

"You guys sure bailed out of there quickly. What the hell does he have in there, exactly?" Clint asked.

Nathan turned his attention to the visibly concerned site foreman.

"Looks like he built himself a full-blown laboratory. Mr. Asters, your crew will not only need to remain sequestered until we're done talking to and clearing them all, but they may also need to be tested for exposure to whatever it is he's been making. And whoever owns the campers parked on either side of this one will need to move them out of our way once I'm satisfied that they weren't involved in this."

"You got it, Agent Thomas," Clint replied. "Just tell me what you want, and I'll make it happen. And you're welcome to use my office trailer for anything you need. It's parked at the far end, so it's not in the way of anything that needs to happen with his camper."

"Thanks, I appreciate it. How many employees are onsite again? Sixty-two?"

"Including the truck drivers and me, we have sixty-eight... well, sixty-seven now."

Nathan turned to his agents and said, "We need to interview every employee here, but there's no way to know if this guy was working alone or not, so I want you doubled up for safety. Grace, you and Herb team up. Calloway, you're with me until Lizzie's finished with the barricade setup. Once that's done, she's your interview partner. Any questions?"

Hearing none, Nathan nodded. "Let's get started, then. Round everybody up and get them over by the office trailer. Mr. Asters-"

"Please, call me Clint."

"Clint, once your crew is assembled, I'll make an announcement that we need to speak with each of them individually as part of an active investigation. I may need your involvement to address any signs of trouble."

"Happy to," Clint replied, "but I honestly don't think that there will *be* any trouble. I've known most of these guys for over twenty years now and they're an honest, decent, hard-working bunch. They'll be surprised, naturally, maybe even concerned, but they'll cooperate."

"Good to know. I want to start our interviews with whoever lives in *those*," Nathan told him as he pointed to the two campers adjacent to the killer's.

***

Screening the carnival's employees began in earnest a little before three a.m., and it was a long but vital process. By the time dawn broke, Nathan's team had fully vetted fourteen members of the crew, including receiving the 'all clear' via walkie-talkie as each employee's living quarters was searched and cleared of suspicion.

By seven-forty the sun had risen completely, and the entire site was swarmed by law enforcement and laboratory personnel collecting evidence. Food and drink items were seized in their entirety from the other six stations for analysis, while every surface of the rest of the carnival's setup was swabbed for further testing.

The first group of fourteen employees was escorted by police back to their now-released campers and supervised as those campers were relocated to the far end of the spacious lot. It was an activity that would be repeated throughout the day.

By early afternoon only the killer's motorhome would remain untouched in its original spot, kept company only by the barricade circling it that Nathan had requested, and an oversized FBI van especially designed to transport hazardous materials.

Once all other vehicles had been moved out of the immediate area, three agents who'd been highly trained in handling biohazardous scenes donned full hazmat suits complete with self-contained respirators, then gingerly made their way into the killer's home on wheels.

***

Nathan Thomas left the scene just before ten a.m.

"Anything else pops, let me know. I'm going to go talk to him," he told his team, then headed to his car.

As he walked, he called Ben to confirm that their suspect had been booked into the Dallas County jail pending further instructions.

"And Nathan, the system lit up like a Christmas tree when they ran his prints."

"Really? Why?"

Ben told him.

"Bring him to the office," Nathan said immediately as he got into his car, "and put him in interview room one. I'm on my way."

"Be there shortly, boss."

A rap on Nathan's window caused him to jump.

"Sorry," Lizzie grinned when he rolled it down. "Can I catch a ride back with you? The lab supervisor just called me. We've already got some preliminary results back."

"Sure. Hop in."

***

Thirty minutes later, Nathan had reviewed the preliminary report on the man that had sarcastically professed his name to be John Doe during his booking.

"The driver's license in his wallet is a forgery," Ben added. "A very good one, but a forgery, nonetheless. If not for fingerprints, we might never have gotten to the truth about that guy."

"What about him?" Lizzie asked as she joined them in the observation room connected to interview room one.

"His real name, and that he fled Minnesota to avoid prosecution over twenty years ago," Ben revealed.

Lizzie's eyebrows raised.

"Before I get in there," Nathan pointed at the glass wall, "what did the lab say?"

"That so far, all the samples tested from those first six stations and his workbag are coming back as one hundred percent matches to Timmy Steward's bloodwork results," Lizzie summarized. "They went into deeper detail, but that's the gist of it. They're still processing the other drink and food station items, and they've started in on some of the swabs that were collected."

Their conversation was paused as the door swung open to reveal the director of the Dallas office.

"Mind if I watch you in action? I'm interested to see how this interview goes," the director said as he stepped inside the observation room.

"Not at all, sir. Be my guest," Nathan answered, then took a deep breath and headed out into the hall then one door down to sit across from the man whose final casualty count had been confirmed at fifty-nine.

***

Nathan's pulse quickened the moment he entered the room and found himself being stared at.

He returned the man's intense gaze, taking in the thin, gaunt face with slight stubble across his cheeks, the stooped posture, and confused blue eyes.

"I was wondering when you'd show up," the man mumbled, sounding feeble.

Gonna duck behind that old disguise, huh? We'll see about that.

"Did you now," Nathan responded in a neutral, all-business tone as he took the chair across from his quarry.

"You're gonna ask me questions now, right, mister? Isn't that how it works?"

"I suppose so, Mr. *Doe*," Nathan drawled as he leaned forward, a dangerous smile playing at his lips. "Or should I call you Dr. Philip Edmund Jamesin, formerly of Nova Scotia, who founded a pain management clinic in Minneapolis, and who was arrested in connection with seventeen mysterious deaths in 1994?"

He watched, intrigued, as Jamesin immediately dropped the affectations, sitting straight and proud in his chair, his blue eyes now sharp and cold, and speaking in a deep, clear baritone.

"Finally. Someone who *might* be worth my time to share ideas with," Jamesin snarled, jutting out his chin in defiance. "I just hope you can keep up with me."

Game on, buddy, Nathan thought to himself, but coolly responded, "I sincerely doubt I'll have any issue with that. Now, shall we begin?"

***

Ben, Lizzie, and the director watched and listened as Nathan and Jamesin verbally sparred.

"That guy's good - but Nathan's better," Ben whispered as Nathan tripped Jamesin up in a contradiction that had the older man backtracking in his statements.

Lizzie and the director grinned at Ben's remark.

"So then why do it at all?" they heard Nathan ask. "Why risk exposure? You escaped custody, and you've successfully hidden all these years-"

"Because being *intentionally* 'lesser than' had gotten old, Agent Thomas," they heard Jamesin explain in a tone that weary adults use to answer the tiresome questions of children. "And because I could, quite frankly. Why else?"

A few moments later Jamesin's offhand comments turned the tide of the conversation, and it caught all three observers completely off guard.

***

"Beg pardon. What did you say?" Nathan asked.

"I said, you don't remember me, do you? But *I* remember *you*. I have an eidetic memory, Agent Thomas. I never forget a face. Didn't my file mention that?"

When Nathan didn't immediately answer, Jamesin waved his hand.

"No matter. I can tell by your expression that you think you know me from somewhere, but you can't place me. I'll indulge you, just this once."

He leaned forward, resting his elbows on the table and his chin in his hands.

"It was last fall, you see. At the festival, not far at all from here. You and that gorgeous wife of yours, and your sweet, loving little boy. You both really should have watched him better, Agent Thomas. It didn't take him long at all to slip away from you both and wander straight over to me, a complete stranger, and hold his little arms out for me to pick him up, like he'd known me all his life."

Nathan's composure began to fracture, and Jamesin's next words broke it apart completely.

"So, tell me, Agent Thomas," Jamesin continued in a smarmy, goading tone, "how is that *adorable* little boy of yours these days? Charlie, isn't it? You know, it's an absolute shame that I didn't get to spend more... *time* with him."

White-hot rage surged throughout Nathan's body and his control snapped as he lunged over the table to wrap his hands around the psychopath's throat.

The next thing he knew, he was being dragged upward and backward by Lizzie and Ben, and Nathan noticed that Jamesin's back lay against the floor. The killer was still seated in his chair, having been tipped over backward with the force of Nathan's attack, and Jamesin was coughing and laughing all at once.

***

His teammates got Nathan up and out into the hallway in a hurry as the director and another agent stepped into the interview room to check on the suspect's condition.

Nathan started to yell, to struggle against them, but Lizzie calmly murmured, "Not here, Nathan. Not here. Let's take a walk, okay? Come on. Come with us."

They got him in the elevator without much resistance and rode it all the way down to the underground parking garage. Once the doors opened and they stepped out, Ben and Lizzie let go of his arms - and found themselves directly in Nathan's crosshairs.

"Exactly whose side are you two on?" Nathan roared at them in unadulterated fury. "You shouldn't have stopped me. You should have let me kill that bastard when I had the chance and saved us all a lot of trouble!"

"I'm sorry that you think that, but what we did was right. And if we had it to do over, we'd have made the same choice," Lizzie snapped back at him, and a visibly miserable Ben nodded in silent agreement.

Nathan whirled and got right in Lizzie's face, yelling so loudly that the veins bulged in his neck.

"Why? Do you know what he could have done to my *son*??? Why in God's name are you *defending him*?"

Lizzie didn't bat an eye or back down one inch. She maintained eye contact with the man that she greatly respected and who, she knew, was hurting to his core at that moment.

"I'm not defending him," she answered softly as she gazed at him. "Jamesin is slime. A pure psychopath. We all know it. But I also know that killing him would have cost you not only your freedom but your *soul*, Nathan. And he's not worth that. Not by a long shot."

A soft 'ding' behind them signaled a new arrival in the garage.

"Agent Thomas," the director said as he walked over to join them, his expression a strange, swirling mixture of anger and empathy.

"Sir," Nathan managed in what Lizzie could tell was a barely controlled growl.

"I want you to know that it hurts me to have to do this, son, but given what just happened, I have no choice. You are suspended until further notice. I need your badge and your gun, please. Now."

"But sir-" Lizzie started to say but was cut off with a single wave of the director's hand.

"Enough, Agent Zimmerman. Stay out of this."

She swallowed hard and took a step back.

"You want them? Fine by me," Nathan snarled as he snatched his badge and gun up and slapped them both in the director's hands. "I have no desire to stay here surrounded by a bunch of traitors anyway."

In her periphery Lizzie saw Ben flinch at Nathan's venomous words as if he'd been struck, but he remained stone-faced and silent.

"And *you*," Nathan sneered at Lizzie, "you've been to my *house*. You've had dinner at my table, and you've held my *child,* whom you professed to love. But now I see you for who and what you really are. Stay the hell away from me *and* my family, you back-stabbing bitch."

And with that, Nathan Thomas turned his back on all of them and stormed away. The trio heard him slam his car's door, followed by a harsh, angry squeal of tires as he left the garage.

A stunned and wounded Lizzie, with big, shocked tears already beginning to fall, looked at Ben and the director and whispered, "I *do* love that little boy - and that's the reason I stopped him. I didn't want Charlie growing up without his father."

Ben clumsily patted her shoulder.

"He's angry right now, is all, so he's not thinking straight. I'm sure he didn't mean any of that, Liz. Give it time. You'll see," he said wistfully in an attempt to comfort her.

But Ben's own bewildered hurt plainly showed in his eyes when she glanced his direction.

Maybe so, but that doesn't make what Nathan just said to me hurt any less, she cried out in her mind.

Her heart broken, Lizzie Zimmerman pivoted slowly and wiped her face with her sleeve as she returned to the elevator.

CHAPTER TWENTY-ONE

Nathan's blind fury had barely subsided by the time he pulled into the driveway at his home. He slammed the car door, then marched into the house and slammed his front door as well.

"What the hell?" Bella yelped from the kitchen, appearing moments later in the doorway separating their cooking space from their living room.

One look at his face made hers drain completely of color.

"Honey... what's wrong?"

He didn't answer, simply brushed past her wheelchair and headed for their bedroom. She watched him go, then pivoted her chair around to look at Jandy.

"Keep Charlie occupied, all right?"

Jandy nodded, and Bella wheeled herself down the hall to go check on her husband.

***

She found him sitting on the edge of the bed, hands clenched into tight fists by his sides as he stared into space.

"Nathan," she murmured as she closed the distance between them and gently laid her hands over his. "Talk to me."

"I've been suspended," he finally managed, the rage on his face and in his voice slowly giving way to a shocked grief. "I lost control and I attacked a suspect and I got suspended, Bella."

She frowned. "That's not like you, at all. What happened?"

"That guy we've been chasing. We caught him early this morning. I was interviewing him, and he brought up Charlie."

Bella's concerned look turned to one of complete confusion. "What?"

"Remember last fall when we took Charlie to the festival and he wandered off?"

"Yes, I do. Scared me to death."

"Bella, the man we found holding him is the same man that's killed all those kids."

"Oh, God," she gasped, eyes wide, her right hand flying to her mouth in horror.

"And he taunted me with that, Bella. He sat across the table from me with that... that *smirk* on his face, and he told me that it was *him* that Charlie had gone up to and hugged. He made it a *point* to tell me. And I just... saw red. I saw red and I lunged at him. I was completely out of control, but I didn't care. All I could think of was that he's a murderer, and he needs to die so that Charlie will be safe."

Neither spoke for a few minutes.

"But that's not the worst thing about it all," Nathan continued, and finally looked at her with brimming eyes. "Ben and Lizzie rushed in and pulled me off of him. They stopped me from killing him and throwing my life away. And you know what I did to repay them for looking out for me? I called them traitors. Said they didn't have my back."

"But they *did*, honey," Bella told him. "You know they did. You know what would have happened to you - to *us* - had you hurt or killed him."

"I know they did. I knew it even as I said it. But I was just *so* angry... and then..."

His voice broke, and he closed his eyes and let the tears fall as his shame crept to the forefront.

"And then, I turned on Lizzie. I was in her face and she stayed calm and that pissed me off even more. It felt like she didn't care. I blew up. All my rage, all my hate, she got all of it. I took it out on her. She didn't deserve it, but that's what I did. I know she loves Charlie and I used that against her, just to hurt her."

"Oh, honey," Bella murmured, and he leaned forward, touched his forehead to her shoulder, and wept.

She wrapped her arms around him as best she could and held him.

"Nathan," she whispered, "you have to make that right."

"I know," he whispered brokenly between shaky breaths. "I just don't know if I'll be able to. The things I said... I may have done too much damage to ever fix it."

***

When the remainder of Nathan's team returned to the Dallas office later that afternoon, the branch director called them together for an unscheduled briefing.

"There was an incident earlier today that resulted in Agent Thomas' suspension," he told them without preamble.

After a stunned silence, several of them started to speak at once, but the director held up his hand to stop any questions.

"I'm not going to get into the details at this time. Suffice to say that he's off this case. Ben, you're the most senior agent on the team, so you're taking point on making sure that our evidence collected is solid, and that the collection methods employed were above reproach."

"Yes, sir," Ben said solemnly.

***

Donny's jaw dropped wide open with surprise, then clenched in anger when Lizzie arrived home and told him everything that had happened.

"Nathan *actually said* all that? To *you*?"

She nodded, swallowing back more tears.

"*Wow*. I'm just.... I'm...."

"Stunned? I was too. Completely blindsided. I knew he was up-set, Donny, but..."

"I'm so sorry, baby," Donny soothed as he took her in his arms. "You didn't deserve that."

"You're right. I didn't. The question is, what do I do now?" she asked as she sniffled, her cheek against his chest.

"What do you mean?"

He felt her move her shoulders upward in a small shrug.

"I don't know if I should stay with the team here in Dallas and ride this out, or try to transfer out to another location... I don't know what to do. I just know that if my team members don't think they can trust me, then it's a problem," Lizzie said, her voice hollowed by pain. "A big one. I *have* to be able to know that the people I'm surrounded by will keep me safe - and trust me to keep *them* safe."

"I don't think it's a decision to make right this minute. Your emo-tions are pretty raw right now. Think about it a while. Give yourself some time," Donny suggested. "But know this. If you decide to move on at some point, I'll go anywhere you want to go, honey."

***

The next two weeks passed by quickly as the team, led by Ben, worked to tie up any loose ends.

The carnival crew was allowed to resume operations once no contamination beyond the six stations Jamesin had tampered with was confirmed.

Identifying the specific components of Jamesin's lethal cocktail had proved to be a more difficult challenge since he had thrown away the labeled containers long before being caught, but the FBI's labs fi-nally solved the puzzle.

***

Nathan found himself reaching for the phone to call and talk to Ben and Lizzie several times but couldn't find the courage to actually dial either number.

They hate me. I know they do. And they should, after what happened.

***

By mid-morning Friday, exactly three weeks after the carnival had arrived in Dallas, Lizzie, Ben, and Annie finished compiling the evidence they'd gathered and turned it all over to the U.S. District Attorney's office.

Around four p.m., Dr. Philip Edmund Jamesin, who'd been denied bail, was formally charged with fifty-nine counts of first-degree murder.

***

Once their part in the case was done, Ben, Annie and Lizzie all opted to take advantage of the branch director's offer - taking the rest of the day off.

Lizzie took a deep breath before she pressed the button to send her final email of the day. She shut down her desk computer and gathered her purse and keys, then made her way down to her SUV. As she put on her seatbelt, Lizzie turned her attention to a very different but very important event looming on her horizon - standing with Faith as her maid of honor at Faith and Rick's wedding on Sunday afternoon.

"I'm still not sure about this," she confided to Donny when she got home. "Nathan will be there. I don't think it's a good idea for me to go. That's his sister, after all."

"And your best friend," Donny reminded her. "And it will upset her if you're not there - she's already said so. Surely he'll be able to at least be civil long enough for his sister to get married."

"I hope so," Lizzie murmured.

***

"Good afternoon, Joe Wallace's office," the receptionist said briskly.

"Good afternoon. My name is Pete Jenkins, and I'm returning Joe's call."

"Certainly, sir. One moment, please."

"Hey kiddo!" Joe said when he picked up the call. "How have you been?"

"I'm good. When did you get a receptionist?"

"Couple of days ago. Like I said, it's gotten so busy I can't do it all myself."

"I've been thinking about your offer, Joe. A lot. And I'm thinking you've got yourself a deal. I'm getting out of here sometime in the next few weeks. When would you like me to start?"

"Can I bring you a laptop? No reason you can't start now, right?"

Pete laughed.

"No sir, I don't suppose there is."

***

He arrived on schedule for his four o'clock meeting, and Nathan Thomas took a seat in the right-hand visitor chair of the branch director's office, nervously waiting to hear his fate.

At long last the man looked up from the folder and made eye contact.

"Agent Thomas, your record up until this incident has been nothing short of exemplary. That, coupled with the emotional intensity of the case you were involved in and the suspect's aggressive and antagonizing manner, have weighed in your favor. I'm pleased to let you know your suspension period is over."

The director reached into his desk drawer and retrieved Nathan's badge and service weapon, sliding both across the desk toward him.

"Thank you, sir," he managed to say as he picked them up.

"But there's one more thing I want to say to you," the director continued, pinning him with a direct stare. "You came down extremely hard on two of your people - and you were way out of line, son. I hope that you intend to make that right, if you haven't already."

"I do, sir."

"Then I suggest you move very quickly to do just that, Agent Thomas. I can only sit on Agent Zimmerman's transfer request until Monday before I'll have to take some sort of action on it."

Nathan was stunned.

"Transfer request?"

"Yes. She submitted it this morning."

***

"Two more days," Faith observed as she and Rick washed and put away dishes. "I can't believe the time went by so quickly. You nervous?"

"Nope. I'm getting married to the most wonderful woman on the planet. I'm not nervous at all. I'm excited."

She blushed.

"I actually think Jandy's even more jazzed than we are, to be honest."

"Aw. That's sweet," he answered. "What does Tony think about it all?"

"You know Tony. He's quiet and rolls with the punches. He hasn't said a lot one way or the other about our wedding invading their house."

"Yep," Rick grinned. "He's definitely quiet. But when he does speak up, he's hilarious."

He flung his dishtowel over his shoulder and looked at her. "Are *you* nervous at all?"

"Maybe just a little. I don't have doubts or anything, but yeah, seeing as how I swore that I'd never get involved with anyone ever again, much less get married, this is a little surreal."

"But," he said, an eyebrow raised.

"But what?"

"Don't try to fool me, I know that look. You're thinking about it again, aren't you?"

"She's my best friend, and he's my brother. And it's been hell."

"You think our insisting they both show up will help Nathan and Lizzie patch things up between them? I know they haven't spoken since... well... you know," Rick mentioned.

Faith sighed. "I sure hope they do."

Their conversation lapsed into a brief silence, and Faith cleared her throat.

"Sounds like halftime is over," she acknowledged when she heard the football announcer's voice coming from the surround sound system in their living room. "I guess we timed dinner out pretty well. Come on, let's go see if they can pull out a win."

"They're twenty-four points down," Rick pointed out.

"I know. That just makes it more exciting - *if* they can rally back, that is."

"Here's hoping - even if it *is* just a preseason game."

***

As Annie switched out discs in the DVD player, Ben read her the highlights of the long message that Deputy Greisen had emailed over.

"Check this out. Those Wise County cases we worked up the profile for? We were pretty much spot on. The lady pled guilty, too."

"Really? Were we right about her having an accomplice, too?"

"Yep, a longtime boyfriend who's worked for the county's road maintenance department for over twenty years. And get this - the boyfriend is the one who made the anonymous calls about the bodies. According to Greisen, the guy knew that she had a serious problem, but he loved her and didn't want to turn her in, and he figured if the bodies were found quickly enough, she'd get caught."

"Go figure. Takes all kinds, I guess."

Ben's phone rang, and he walked over to his kitchen where he'd set it down to charge.

"It's Nathan," he blurted out, and Annie shrugged.

"So? Answer it."

"Hello?" Ben said nervously.

"Hi," Nathan began, "you might remember me. I was the one being a complete ass a few weeks ago."

Ben chuckled. "You could say that, boss. Sounds pretty accurate, actually."

"I deserve that," Nathan said quietly. "And I'm truly sorry, Ben. Really."

Ben exhaled.

"We all have times we get mad and say stuff we don't mean. I know that's all it was. We're good, okay? I mean it."

"Thanks. How's Lizzie? Is she okay?"

Ben paused, then opted to call it as he saw it.

"Honestly? No, boss, she's not. You cut Lizzie pretty deep."

***

Lizzie and Donny arrived at Jandy's at noon on Sunday.

"Hi there!" Jandy exclaimed as she greeted each one with a hug. "Great to see you both. Lizzie, Faith's in the first bedroom to the right; she was just asking if you were here yet. You want some iced tea? I was just going to get Faith some."

"Yes, I'd love some, thanks."

"Perfect. I'll be right back with two glasses, then."

"Is Rick here yet?" Donny asked.

Jandy pointed through the living room.

"Got here about ten minutes ago. He's on the back patio with Tony. You want some tea?"

"Sure," he said, and winked at Lizzie before he followed their hostess into the kitchen.

Lizzie crept forward and knocked on the bedroom door.

"Hey, bestie," she called out. "I'm coming in."

She stepped inside and gazed at Faith, who looked radiant in her dress, her long brown hair swept up into a loosely braided chignon with small tendrils left loose to frame her face.

"You look absolutely stunning," Lizzie told her best friend, and meant it with all her heart.

***

"Are you nervous about today?" Bella asked her husband as he started the car.

"Why would I be?"

Bella shrugged, opting to ease into the discussion. "Well, for starters, I thought Faith asking you to walk her down the aisle might be nerve-wracking."

"Not in the least," Nathan told her. "I feel proud more than anything. And my part is easy. I don't even have to speak at all, so, as long as I don't trip either one of us or step on her dress, I think I'll be fine."

"I don't think her dress will be an issue," she reassured him. "It's a column dress. Jandy sent me pictures. It's gorgeous, and Faith looks stunning in it."

He laughed. "I have no idea what 'column dress' even *means*. Does that mean no big, long poufy thing?"

"Exactly. There's no big, long poufy thing."

"Good. Nothing for me to trip over!" Nathan announced with a chuckle.

Bella paused for just a moment, then pressed on.

"You *do* realize that was part one of a two-part question, right?"

He sighed. "I don't even know if Lizzie will talk to me, Bella. But I'll try and make it right. I owe her that much, at least."

She reached over and squeezed his hand as Charlie excitedly chimed in from the back seat.

"Izzy? Where?"

***

"Okay, it's about twenty minutes to showtime," Lizzie announced as she glanced at her watch. "Anything you need before I step out?"

"Nope, I'm good as far as wedding stuff goes," Faith replied, a soft smile on her lips. "But I do want to ask you a favor."

"Name it."

"If Nathan approaches you, promise me you'll give him a chance to speak."

Lizzie ducked her head, her eyes downcast as she fidgeted under the strain of her best friend's request. "I'm sure he won't even bother. I haven't heard from him at all."

"Just - promise me. Please."

"I promise."

"Fair enough," Faith said, and flung her arms around Lizzie. "See you out there. Love you, girl."

"I love you too, you big goofball," Lizzie answered, but hugged her back before she stepped out of the room.

***

Nathan helped Bella into her wheelchair, then got Charlie out of his car seat and set him down, chuckling as their son immediately ran toward the house.

"Really wish I could be walking around for this," Bella grumbled as she rolled herself toward the front door. "I don't even get to dance during the reception."

"I know," Nathan commiserated. "But once you're all healed up, we'll get a sitter and I'll take you out dancing. How about that?"

"Don't tease me unless you intend to follow through," she said with a smirk.

Charlie entered the house first and immediately noticed Lizzie in the hallway.

"IZZY!" he yelled at the top of his lungs, then barreled her direction.

***

Lizzie froze, unsure what to do. Nathan's words had never left her mind, but they suddenly were front and center as she watched the little boy that she adored running full tilt toward her with his arms open wide.

She noticed movement behind Charlie and lifted her gaze to find Bella and Nathan watching the scene.

Bella smiled warmly and nodded, then turned her chair to continue into the kitchen as Nathan started down the hallway after Charlie.

Lizzie staggered back a bit as Charlie flung himself full force against her legs and wrapped his arms around them.

"Hi, Izzy! Hi!" he squealed, but she was too busy watching nervously as Nathan approached her to respond.

When he got close enough, Lizzie could see his expression, and was shocked. Where she expected to see contempt, she saw remorse.

"Up! Izzy, up!" a small, petulant voice demanded, and she raised an eyebrow as she looked at Nathan, who cleared his throat and said softly, "Go ahead."

She reached down and picked Charlie up. He immediately put his arms around her neck and laid his cheek on her chest.

"I missed you," he said very clearly, and made her cry.

"I missed you too, buddy," she barely managed to reply as she held him tightly, and he lifted his head and touched her face.

"No cry, Izzy. Happy!" he commanded, then kissed her on the cheek.

"Hey, little man. How about you go see if Aunt Jandy has any cookies in the kitchen, okay?" Nathan told his son.

"Cookies? Okay," Charlie answered with a grin, and Lizzie set him down and smiled as he ran with abandon to go find them.

"I know I don't have any right to expect you to listen after what I did, but I really hope you and I can talk for just a moment," Nathan began. "Lizzie, I am so, so sorry. It doesn't matter what was going on at the time, the things I said to you were inexcusable. You've *always* had my back. I know that, and there's no other agent I trust more. And I know that you'd do anything for my family, as well. I hope you know that I didn't mean what I said, and that I'd give anything, *anything*, to be able to take it all back."

He took a step forward.

"I heard about the transfer request. Please don't leave, Lizzie. Please. The team would never be the same without you. My *family* would never be the same without you."

Donny appeared in the hallway behind Nathan, and when he saw his fiancée's tear-stained face, he started stalking toward them.

Lizzie held up her right hand to stop him as she wiped her face with her left.

"It's all good, babe. I'll be there in just a minute."

"You *sure* you're all right?" Donny asked, the growl in his voice making it very clear that he was uncomfortable leaving her alone with Nathan.

"Yes, I'm okay. Really."

When Donny retreated, she turned her focus back to Nathan.

"For the record, I felt the exact same rage toward Jamesin that you did. But I didn't stop you that day just for *your* sake," she said quietly. "I stopped you because I knew that you were about to cross a line that there would have been no coming back from. And it would have ripped you out of Charlie's life. I love that little boy like he's my own, and I wasn't going to just stand by and watch you screw up *both* your lives like that."

Nathan hung his head. "I know, Liz. And I'm truly grateful."

A poignant silence lingered between them for a moment.

"Is there any chance at all that you'll stay, or have I done too much damage?" he asked quietly.

"I need to know that you truly trust me, and that I can truly trust you. That got dinged pretty damn badly, to be honest. And it will take time to repair that."

"I'm just happy the two of you are talking," Faith interjected, poking her head through the open doorway to gaze at them. "Speaking of which. I love you both, and I'm so, *so* glad that you guys are working on this, but can we maybe table it long enough to get me married? The wedding's supposed to start in like, three minutes."

"All right, Bridezilla," Nathan said good-naturedly, and Lizzie and Faith both grinned.

"Nice one, Nathan," Lizzie commented.

"I have my moments."

EPILOGUE

Almost four months later, the holiday season was in full swing.

Lizzie had a long day of typing up reports. Once she was finally finished, she printed them out, stacked them neatly, and carried them into her boss's office.

"Here you go," she told Nathan. "And I saved them out on the server, as well."

"Thanks. You and Donny going to the party at Faith and Rick's?"

"Yep, we'll be there around seven-thirty."

Nathan smiled.

"Good. See you there."

She nodded, then turned and went back to her desk to log out and grab her purse and keys. As she headed for the elevator, the receptionist called out to her.

"Lizzie, this came for you in the mail. I just haven't had a chance to bring it to you."

"Thanks. Have a great weekend."

"You too."

Lizzie looked at the envelope as she rode the elevator down to the parking garage.

"No return address," she mused out loud, "and a postmark from Pocatello, Idaho?"

Pretty sure I'd remember if I knew someone up in Idaho.

She puzzled over it all the way to her SUV. Once she got in and put her seatbelt on, she ran her finger under the flap to open the envelope, then pulled the single page of paper out and unfolded it.

A swift glance at the bottom of the handwritten passage brought a smile to her face, and she began to read the letter.

Dear Zim,

I hope this letter makes it to you. I asked my great-uncle to drop it in the mail for me on one of his trips - can't be too careful, you know - and

I didn't know if your house was put back together yet or not, so I didn't want to try to send it there.

Sorry again about your house, by the way...

Anyway, I've done a lot of thinking, mostly about what you said. You know, the whole 'stop, look around, breathe, and evaluate' deal. And you were right. Being here, I've had lots of time on my hands to really think about everything that's happened and what comes next for me once all this is over.

While I don't have it all completely figured out yet, I did realize one pretty big thing, and that is, being a law enforcement officer just isn't for me.

I know it was a fluke, being caught up in two situations like that. But I see their faces every single night when I dream, Zim. I don't think that will ever go away. And I just can't make myself get back out there and risk having to take another life again - not even to save my own. It's better if I move on and try to plot out a different future for myself.

I want you to know how much I appreciate everything you've ever done for me - even when I was being a complete jerk. I'm grateful to you, and I hope someday we'll get to see each other again. We'll meet up and have a couple of beers or something, my treat.

Maybe someday. Who knows?

Jones

Lizzie carefully folded the letter and tucked it back into its envelope before she put it in her purse.

"Here's hoping, Jones," she whispered sincerely. "Here's hoping."

House of Secrets, Book Six of the Vital Secrets Series, comes out in December 2021

Pre-Order your copy HERE[1]

***

Follow me on Bookbub[2]

Visit my author site at www.2ofharts.com

Join my newsletter and receive 'Cast of Characters', a supplement to the series, Free!

One of the best things an author can receive is honest feedback about their work.

If you could take just a moment or two and leave a review on my book on BookBub, Goodreads, and other similar places, it would mean the world to me.

Follow me on Goodreads[3]

I appreciate your support!

---

1. https://books2read.com/DHHouseofSecrets

2. https://www.bookbub.com/authors/d-f-hart

3. https://www.goodreads.com/author/show/18999540.D_F_Hart

CPSIA information can be obtained
at www.ICGtesting.com
Printed in the USA
BVHW071837030521
606337BV00006B/966